I0706311

STAGE SMART

WORK FOR IT
BOOK EIGHT

ALY STILES

WWW.SMARTYPANTSROMANCE.COM

PROLOGUE—ONE YEAR EARLIER (LARINDA'S STUDIO)

LARINDA

"Babe, ya can't wear blue if I'm wearing blue. That's rule number one in power couples' couture. Ask Alonzo."

No. Because for the seven millionth time, I don't know Alonzo and have no interest in tracking down a stranger just to ask him a question like, "what's rule number one in power couples' couture?"

Also, pretty sure the answer isn't, "you can't both wear blue."

I adjust the phone while gazing longingly at my computer monitor several feet away. Instead of arguing with Jarvis about—*I'm not even sure*—I could be at my desk reviewing the killer tracks I received from some producer friend of Nash's.

Val Andrews.

Apparently, this guy is twenty-two and completely unknown, which is also all *I* know about him. Well, and he's ridiculously talented. He seemed nice enough the few times we spoke on the phone, but he could be an ogre and I'd still be as excited as I am to meet him in about five minutes. The tracks he sent were incredible—way beyond what I expected, even beyond what I thought my music could become, if I'm honest. How he made this happen with limited direction and resources, I have no idea, but I'm giddy at the thought of what we'd accomplish together in an official capacity.

Well, I *was,* until my boyfriend called to inform me that the dress I bought seven months ago for the wedding of a movie-star friend was no longer an option since it would clash with his tux. Actually, no. It would clash with the *pocket square* of his tux, which is also blue, but not a coordinating blue. I begged Jarvis to swap out his pocket square for something that *would* go with my tailored eight-thousand-dollar gown I've had ready for weeks but... a lapel pin? I don't know. As usual with him, I got lost in the confusing web of Jarvis McKinnley's ego. For some reason he's right and I'm wrong, like always.

My phone buzzes against my ear, and I pull it away to see a text from my assistant, Steve.

They're here.

Eek!!

"Okay. We'll have to pick this up later, Jar. I have an important meeting."

"But, Linda—"

"I'm sorry, hon. I have to go."

"The wedding is only a month away!"

And that wouldn't be an issue if I could wear my dress and he wore a—I don't know—*black/white/green/violet/pretty much any other color* pocket square.

"We'll figure it out. Maybe Alonzo can find a coordinating blue pocket square."

I'm not sure if his silence is due to the horror of considering a different pocket square or the suggestion that "Alonzo" would be the one in charge of securing it. I probably should find out who Alonzo is and what he does.

"I'm not arguing with you about this right now, Larinda!" he huffs out.

"Okay, perfect. Same. Have a great ni—"

"Hold on! This *meeting* isn't with that nobody producer, is it?"

Ugh.

"Yes. And he's not a nobody."

"No? Who's heard of him? *Nobody.* So he's a nobody."

"Fine. Right now this second, he is, but he won't be soon. You'll see."

"What I *see* is my girlfriend's future being flushed down the toilet by some loser. I still don't get why you'd pass on Rufus Ricard for a snot-nosed kid."

"He's not a loser, and I'm passing because *Rufus Ricard* makes my music sound like everyone else's."

"Hate to break it to you, sweet cheeks, that's the formula that sells. You want to make money, you make the music that makes money."

"Okay, well, maybe I'm tired of only worrying about the money if it means making the same thing as everyone else. Maybe there's more to this. Maybe there's more to *me.*"

His horrified gasp isn't even a joke. He really gasps like that when someone offends him with words his own brain has never strung together.

"Well! I don't—"

"Oh no! What was that? You're cutting out... Jarvis? Babe, you there? Huh. Guess I lost him."

I hang up.

Whew. Interacting with that man is exhausting to say the least. It's good our schedules don't allow for much of that.

When I sense a presence hovering in the entrance to my studio, I glance back and bolt up from the couch.

"Nash!"

I rush in for a hug, but my friend directs me toward his companion instead.

My heart lurches in my chest. No introduction necessary.

"Oh my goodness! Val!" I throw my arms around the stranger who doesn't seem like a stranger.

The guy tenses for a second, and I'm worried I've scared him until a beautiful grin lights up his face.

Wow.

Sea green eyes shine back at me, deep and mesmerizing in the studio lights. His hair is shoved under a ball cap, and a simple t-shirt contrasts beautifully with the intricate tattoos scattered over his arms and peeking through the collar of his shirt. He's a lot taller than I expected. And... attractive.

You have a boyfriend, Larinda.

Sort of. But it doesn't mean I can't make an empirical observation. For example, I also notice his t-shirt has an ironic *"I'm with the band"* emblazoned on the soft gray fabric and there's a small X tattoo beside his right eye. In addition, his irises are a hypnotic shade of gr... Wait, I already noticed that. See? I notice things. That's me. The woman who notices stuff.

"Hi, Larinda. Nice to meet you," he says. Even the tone of his voice is an enigmatic mix of boy-next-door sweet and rough-rocker sexy. Who is this person? What's his story? Six words in and he's already more interesting than Jarvis.

That's not nice.

No, it's not. True, though.

"You didn't tell me he was so cute," I joke. "Look at you. You're freaking adorable. Geez."

Understatement, but it seems like a safe compromise between how I'm supposed to be feeling and what's really happening in my belly right now. When he blushes—*blushes!*—I'm forcing away all kinds of fizzy bubbles inside. Who the heck is sweet and genuine enough to be embarrassed anymore? No one in my world, that's for sure.

Val's shy smile is something I know I'm going to want to see again. And again.

Maybe this is a bad idea. You cannot afford a crush on your producer. For. So. Many. Reasons.

I force away thoughts of DJ Master Klau$ and how much I'm already going to have to fight my label to let me work with this young unknown.

Work. Yes. Let's get those green eyes staring at a screen and not at me like I'm a puzzle they want to solve. It's not a reaction I'm accustomed to—but one I like way too much, apparently.

Waving toward the desk, I force my brain back to business mode.

"I know you converted the midi tracks to .wav files so I could listen," I begin, "but I told my people to grab all the plugins you use so you don't have to do that anymore. We'll also stick with SoundStage 4 as our DAW to make things easy."

I'm not sure how to interpret Val's surprise. Did he assume I'm a ditzy popstar like everyone else? Why does that thought bother me more than it usually does?

"Is that why you asked what software I was using?" he asks.

"Yes. I figured it'll be a lot easier to collaborate if we're all using the same stuff now that we're working together full-time."

His eyes go wide. Shocked him again, I guess. Nash too, based on my friend's uncertain glance between me and Val. I'm just full of surprises tonight.

"So you listened to what he sent?" Nash asks.

Is he serious?

I grab another chair to join them in front of the monitors. "Of course. Why do you think we're here?"

"To show you what he sent," Nash says.

Now *I'm* the one gaping in disbelief.

"You actually think I wouldn't listen the second you sent the link?" I say through a laugh. Heck, I didn't even read the entire text before opening the folder to see what they'd done with my music.

"So you... liked it?" Val asks.

Hang on. Do they really not know what this meeting is? What exactly did Steve tell them when he set it up?

"*Liked* it?" I nudge the chair beside me in a subtle invitation to my (hopefully) soon-to-be producer.

After scooping my composition book off the desk, I turn to the first page where I scribbled my thoughts on "Too Many Reasons."

"These are my notes," I say. "You're here to review them and start making final decisions so we can get these tracks mastered and released."

The next page in my notebook has me even more excited. "Oh, and I *loved* your idea of adding a rock element to 'Crimson Crush.' We are totally doing that. The label freaked when I told them we're using a new producer and mixing some things up for this album, but screw them."

I laugh at the memory of Rena's and the team's faces when I informed them Rufus Ricard would be free to work with another artist since I'd be going in a different direction.

"You told your *label* about him?" Nash asks.

Why is that so newsworthy? Nash knows how this game works.

"Um. Duh. They kind of have to know I'm using someone else from now on. Contracts and rights and all that?"

What's with all the hesitation, anyway? To be honest, my excitement is starting to slip. I was so sure about this partnership that I stood up to my label for maybe the first time in my career. It was one of the hardest things I've done, and now these two are acting like they're not sure they want this? I force away a twinge at the blow to my enthusiasm—and hope.

"Okay, so let's start with what you did for... you know what? Let's *start* with 'Crimson Crush.' Let me just pull that up."

Maybe if we jump right into my favorite of the tracks, we can pump life back into this potential collaboration.

The silence is loud as I open a window to find the song, my pulse pounding with nerves. I just don't get it. Everything in Val's demeanor and what he's done with my music made it seem like we were on the same page. Without even meeting him, I felt like he understood me better than I understand myself because of the way he was able to pull genius out of my ideas. And now he's just standing there like...

Like we never talked about officially working together. Of course!

"Oh, shoot!" I say, relieved and kicking myself as I turn to Val. "We didn't talk about the money part! No wonder you're confused. So I'm not sure what you usually get, but I was *hoping* you'd be okay with ten per track."

"Ten?" he asks. "Per track?"

Is he disappointed? His work definitely deserves more, but I already have an uphill battle convincing the powers that be to take a chance on this guy—especially after what happened a couple years ago.

"I know that's not ideal," I rush out. "But I think we have the best chance of convincing the label to get on board if we go in low to start. After this album, they should be fine bumping it up to fifteen or twenty, especially if it does well, which I know it will. *Please* say you're okay with that. *Pleeeease.*"

Still no response. Crap, crap, crap.

A bead of panic pulses in my stomach. What if he walks? How could I be so naïve not to have considered that possibility? I just assumed… gah! If he goes, so does the incredible future of my music I've already been fantasizing about.

This is what happens when you go rogue and try to make your own choices!

"Can he get any of that up front?" Nash asks. "Say, thirty-five?"

Wait, there's still a chance?!

"I'm sure we can do that," I say as evenly as possible. "If we can get you an advance, you'll accept ten per song?" I ask Val. That's not a huge payout, but if we do the entire album, that's… I quickly run through the list of tracks in my head. "Okay, well, if there are twelve songs, that's one-twenty, right? So maybe we can do half up front? What about sixty?"

"You… you want to pay me *sixty*?" he says, still looking uncertain.

"Sixty thousand dollars, yes. Then the rest after we complete the project."

I hold my breath while he and Nash exchange a long look. I can't be sure, but it seems like their expressions are moving in my favor.

Please, please, please say that's okay.

I hadn't even realized how much I wanted this—*needed it*—until this moment. My career has always been more about the business than the music, even though that's not what I wanted. I just never thought it could be the other way around, and neither had anyone else.

Until now.

Until this stranger heard something no one else could.

Please, Val. Give me a chance.

"I… um… think that would be okay," he says.

"Really? Eek!" I clasp my hands together—mostly to keep from tackling him and scaring him away. "Perfect. Then let's get started. I had this idea for the intro. You know how you had that cello? What if we make it more of a full orchestra sound so it will really be dramatic when the guitars come in?"

Val's smile erases any lingering doubts. He sees my vision immediately, and suddenly, *I* see more than a new direction for my music. These ideas came from somewhere inside me, plucked from a newly discovered treasure trove of creativity buried beneath years of being forced into a mold. Maybe there's a whole other piece of myself waiting to be freed and explored.

"Yes, and I know exactly which one to use," he says, taking control of the mouse to pull up the plugin libraries. "Wait until you hear this."

* * *

Val

"Whoa. Stop."

I freeze at my sister's weird greeting. The fact that she's even awake at two in the morning is concerning. I thought she evaporated into antimatter after 9:30.

When Nash pokes his head up from our couch, I have my answer. Guess he came over for a booty call after he left me at Larinda's studio.

Ew.

"Hello to you too," I mumble, dropping my laptop bag on the kitchen table.

Her gaze sifts over my face. "What's wrong with you? What's wrong with him?" she directs at her boyfriend. I also notice he now wears a similar expression to the one he had the entire time he observed Larinda and me tonight. As much as I loved being alone with her after he left halfway through our session, I loved not having that smug look hovering inches away from me even more.

"He's in love," Nash says.

"What? No, I'm not."

"Oh shit," Paige says through a gasp. "He is! Guess it went well with Larinda?"

I roll my eyes. "I'm not in love. And even if I was, it's not like it could ever happen. She's basically my boss, not to mention an A-list superstar with an A-list superstar boyfriend."

"She and Jarvis will be broken up in a week. Don't worry."

"Not worried." I grab a soda from the fridge and pop the lid.

"Well, hate to break it to you, little bro, but you're legit glowing," Paige says.

"Glowing? No way."

"Uh, yeah, you are. I've watched you drift around in your dark cloud for twenty-two years. Trust me. I'm very familiar with your angsty default setting, and I have *never* seen you like this. Never."

"She's right, dude. Your melancholy is about twelve shades brighter right now."

"Whatever," I mutter. "I'm tired. If you're doing your weird orgasm competition tonight, don't be too loud."

I ignore their irritating amusement as I escape down the hall to the bathroom. They're being ridiculous. I get that I'm not exactly a bundle of joy—or even on the joy spectrum—but in love? How does a person even *look* in love? That makes no sense.

I lock myself in the bathroom to regain my cool—and stop cold.

Staring back at me from the vanity mirror is a total stranger. Paige was right. There's something in that guy's face I don't recognize. It's a… fine, it's a glow. A ray of light.

It's… hope.

I take a deep breath and study the rare tug of a smile I can't seem to shut down no matter how hard I try to tilt it back where it belongs.

Okay, so maybe I *am* glowing. Maybe a few layers of cynic *have been* burned away to reveal a hint of something brighter.

I guess that's what happens when your dark cloud crashes into the fucking sun.

1—INTERSTATE 80 (LARINDA'S BUS, ONE YEAR LATER)

LARINDA

I made a huge mistake.

"Come on, Larry. What do we always say?"

Steve claps his hands with each syllable, but that's not the problem. He's wearing his "wild" pajamas, which is the bigger issue. "Wild" pajamas equals "wild" night which is not a thing I feel like having right now. On my tour bus. On the way to the first stop of our North American River of Heartbreaks Tour. His official bunk is on the crew bus, but he was worried about my nerves and begged me to let him take this leg of the journey on mine. I said yes, which means…

I made a huge mistake.

"There's no boring in touring," I sigh out in answer to his question. Although my tone says touring is *only* boring. Ugh. I'm such a gloomy gloom-bucket tonight.

The reason? Obviously, it's because I'm exhausted and a little nervous. After all, the first stop on a tour is always nerve-wracking. The expectations are astronomical, the kinks haven't even been found yet, let alone ironed out, and… so many other things that are total lies and not why I'm moping more than my little brother at someone else's birthday party.

The real reason I'm a gloom-bucket is because the person sitting on the couch in my private bus is my assistant, Steve Beltzer, and not my producer, Val Andrews.

You may be wondering why that small fact puts so much boring in touring.

The answer is something I can't admit. Well, not right now. Probably not ever if my label has anything to say about it. And they do. Literally. That directive was explicitly communicated in a two-hour phone call with my manager where top execs whined in incredible detail about a tiny incident forever ago when I *might* have dated a previous producer, then broken up with said producer a week before the album was supposed to drop, thus triggering a messy PR situation and messier legal battle.

Three years later, they're still upset about this. Talk about holding a grudge. Geez. What is it they say about bygones? (No, really. I can't remember. Something about more bygones, I think? Also, what exactly is a bygone?)

Anyway, when the label agreed (*very* reluctantly) to let me work with a new producer for this album, it was made abundantly clear that the no-producer-in-your-pants directive was still very much in play—more so, actually, when they found out my new producer was twenty-two and completely unknown. At that point, the directive become more of a, shall we say, royal decree on pain of death? Apparently, they were already taking a huge risk on "this kid," and had no interest in additional risks like, as a random example, what might have happened that other time three years ago.

A year later, it seems this is still their opinion, based on last week's passive-aggressive message from the label's COO wishing me luck on the tour and affirming how much easier album releases are when they don't involve ill-fated romances with producers.

Seriously, though. The whole thing is totally ridiculous because it's not like there's any chance I'd fall for a guy who's super talented, incredibly sweet, always adorable and sometimes straight-up hot. Hilarious, deep, kind, and most of all, totally genuine in a world that utterly lacks integrity. Yep, Val is the polar opposite of Jarvis McKinnley, my *ex-boyfriend/country music star/person I'm supposed to be pretend-dating right now.*

So instead of spending this evening with the guy who makes my body hum and lungs explode whenever we're together (which is a lot), I get a night of Steve and his "wild" pajamas. To be fair, they *are* really cute. The shorts are short enough to make my Grammie Jane blush, and there's a leopard-print bear paw print on each butt cheek. (And yes, as I'm saying that I realize there are inherent zoological challenges with "leopard-print bear paws.")

"Seriously, sweetie. You're stressing me out. How about an almond? What flavor do you want?"

He sifts through the packets of flavored nuts like he's running his fingers through bath water in a sexy perfume ad.

"Ooh! Blueberry! You want a blueberry almond, Larry?"

My sour mood immediately places blueberry almonds in the same logic prison as leopard bears.

"I don't like when almonds try to be fruit," I mumble.

Steve frowns. "You like hazelnut coffee and that's a nut trying to be…" His point fizzles out as he gets lost in that botanical mystery.

Back to *my* problems.

With a heavy sigh, I lean against the backrest of the couch and stare at the ceiling. I really want to be reviewing music stuff right now, not discussing snack food abominations. We have three new tracks we're working on, and I'm incredibly excited about two of them. I can't stop thinking about what Val did with the build in that bridge on "Third Last Kiss." I've never been so excited to get into a studio and play around with backing vocals. *So* much ear-candy potential in that transition.

"A bean!"

I divert my attention back to my assistant's eager face.

"A bean?"

This is what happens when your pajamas are too wild for the event.

"Yes! Hazelnut coffee is a nut trying to be a bean."

"Or a bean trying to be a nut?"

He frowns again. Gosh, I'm being so mean.

"Sorry. You're right. You drink beans, not nuts, so nuts can be beans but not the other way around."

Except in the case of almond milk. I resist the urge to point this out.

I feel his attention as my gloom returns. Maybe my rare sour mood is because I'm a hypocrite to believe nuts can be beans but fruit can't be nuts. Or maybe I'm just tired. It's probably that.

"I should get some rest for tomorrow."

Steve looks concerned as I push up from the cushion, and I force the most sincere smile I can muster. It's not his fault he's not Val.

"You sure you're okay, Larry?"

"I'm fine. Thanks for being here."

I lean in for a quick hug and squeeze hard. He's a good friend. Sure, he's hurt me in the past, but it wasn't on purpose. He means well, including the time Jarvis tricked him into giving him my unreleased songs while my ex was in a questionable state of morals. Thankfully, Jarvis decided not to do anything nefarious like steal months of my blood, sweat, and tears to pass off as his own. Just over a year (and countless apologies) later, the songs have been released, charts have been hit, awards have been discussed, and bygones can officially be… crap. *Is* it more bygones? That doesn't make sense, though, right?

Whatever. The point is Jarvis and I patched things up for this sold-out blockbuster tour featuring two country music superstars. In fact, he's made it clear he wants our pretend relationship to be real again. Yep, pretty sure, like mega-label Lakebend Records, he also wouldn't be happy if he found out I had feelings for someone else—someone like my talented, up-and-coming producer who's currently asleep on the crew bus.

2—INTERSTATE 80 (TWO VEHICLES AHEAD)

VAL

I can't sleep. At all.

And not because of the extra rumbling caused by getting the bunk right over the wheel well of the bus. This insomnia is caused by the guy across from me who unilaterally decided we're going to be best friends for this tour. At least he's been a good distraction from a brain that keeps telling me I shouldn't even be here. (That's a whole other insomnia-inducing thought spiral.)

All I know about this guy is that his name is Chad Smith and he's some corporate agent representing the tour's meddling sponsor, Sandeke Telecom. He called himself the *Administrative Talent Liaison for Reedweather Media vis a vis Sandeke Telecom*, whatever the hell that is. His business card confirmed it, but why he thought I needed an entire stack of them is beyond me. I kept one and used the rest to plug the crack between the cushion of my bunk and the wall of the bus.

He knows way too much about *me*, though, apparently.

"So what's it like having a birthday in early September?" he whisper-shouts across the aisle.

I cringe as this conversation that doesn't need to happen continues for the forty-third minute. Unfortunately, I'm genetically wired to be polite and it's way too early in the tour to make an enemy—especially someone with the clout of a Sandeke Telecom representative. Or is it Reedweather Media? Or Jarvis McKinnley? I'm not entirely clear on who this guy works for. He also claims to be a "super-secret spy," so I guess that tracks.

"It's… fine?"

He nods with a grave expression. "Probably had issues with birthday parties and such during the school years. What happened when your birthday fell on Labor Day?"

I squint around the dark bus, searching for any excuse to end this weird interrogation. "We celebrated it on Labor Day."

"You probably just made the cutoff, right? So you're young?"

"I'm the same age as anyone born on that day."

He chuckles and points at me. "Hilarious. You know what I mean."

I don't, actually.

"The youngest in your class," he explains. "You just made the cutoff for school?"

"I guess?"

"Were you seventeen when you started college?"

"Technically. I only did one semester, though. Hey, aren't you tired?"

"Are you kidding? This is my first ever music tour! I doubt I'll sleep this entire month!"

Well, that's not good.

With a silent groan, I drop back to my pillow to stare up at the top of my bunk.

"Are *you* tired?" he asks.

"Yeah. Plus, the others are sleeping, so we should probably be quiet."

"Oh! Good point. I'll text you instead."

He pulls out his phone, and I pull my curtain. Sure enough, my phone buzzes a second later. I glance at the display to see,

Which university did you attend?

Yorkshire, I type back.

No way! My best friend Marcos went there! You might know him!

Me: There were twenty thousand students at Yorkshire. I knew maybe twelve of them.

Chad: One time I found out my masseuse knew my ophthalmologist.

Huh. Okay. Mostly, I'm impressed he knew how to spell ophthalmologist. I wouldn't have gotten close enough for autocorrect to intervene.

Me: Was he in the music business program?

Chad: Probably masseuse school.

Me: I meant your friend.

Chad: Oh. No.

Me: Was he a first-year student six years ago?

Chad: No.

Me: Does he have any connection to music in any way?

Chad: His roommate is a musician. You wouldn't like him though. He's a terrible spy.

Me: *thumbs up emoji* (All I got, sorry.)

Chad again: He has brown hair and blue eyes?

Me: The roommate?

Chad: No! Marcos. Well, not blue, more green? Blue-green. Cyan, if you will.

I will not and shut off my phone.

But when I close my eyes to sleep, I don't see glorious nothingness. I see wavy multicolored hair and crystal blue eyes. I see a radiant smile that makes my stomach do an annoying foxtrot every time it rests on me. Basically, what I'm seeing is the most off-limits woman on the face of the planet, AKA my associate and sort-of boss, Larinda Scott.

The truth is I've been crushing on the A-lister since our first phone call to discuss her songs over a year ago. Spending countless hours with her since then has only made my secret feelings unbearable. She brightens my dark world, and somewhere along the way I've slipped into a deep craving for her light. I've never felt this way about anyone, but I'd have a better chance switching bodies sci-fi-movie-style with her on-again-off-again ex who's also on this tour than actually dating her myself. (Weird analogy but accurate.)

Sure we have a blast together and she's friendly—borderline flirty—with me. But the woman is walking sunshine, so "overly friendly" is her default mode. Not a single person can talk to her for more than five minutes without falling in love. I see it every time we join a meeting, do an interview, or attend an event. When the entire world is enamored, what chance does a small-time producer with limited connections and no real status have?

Movie stars and athletes line up to date her. Iconic musicians unapologetically chase her. Pretty sure Perceval Andrews, a nobody who still shares a tiny apartment with his sister, isn't going to make the cut. She's on the Elite List. The only list I'm on is the robocall spam list to refinance a mortgage I don't have.

And now I'll be spending hours upon hours with her, practically living together due to the intimate nature of touring. I was only invited because she wanted to work while we're on the road, which means I'm literally here for her.

I've spent my entire life chasing a bunk on a tour bus like this. It only took an hour to regret it.

3—OKLAHOMA CITY (CATERING)

LARINDA

The room stills when I enter for breakfast. A dozen sets of eyes lock on me, but there's only one pair I'm looking for. Sea green with specks of brown, probably crinkled in irony.

"Larinda, hi. I'm so sorry. Did they not deliver your breakfast this morning?" our tour manager says as he jumps up from his table.

"They did. I just… felt like joining everyone else today."

Bruce stares at me like I've never eaten with the crew in our four tours together. Probably because I haven't.

"Oh, biscuits. My favorite." I grab a paper plate from the stack and pluck one from the buffet tray.

I sense the flabbergasted attention of everyone in the room as I work my way down the table of continental breakfast options. No one has said a word by the time I reach the end with a cup of water and my plate of… a biscuit. Now, to find a seat.

Turning toward the group, I scan the room for a, um, random opening at one of the folding tables.

Just a girl looking for a chair. No big deal. Any seat will do. So many chairs to choose from.

Except only one is across from sea green eyes that make my stomach glad it will only have to digest a single biscuit. The sudden rush of heat makes it hard to do anything, let alone eat. When did this happen? When did our friendship become a crush which became… me eating breakfast with the crew for the first time ever?

"Morning," Val says as I lower myself across from him. "You sleep okay?"

I pretend not to notice the gawking going on around us.

"So well," I lie. "You?"

He nods and lifts his coffee cup to his lips. As usual the pink curve of his mouth is turned up in a slight smirk that makes it clear complex thoughts are going on behind that adorable half-smile. His dark hair is covered with the customary ball cap, while several tattoos peek out from the V-neck and sleeves of his graphic tee. Even the faint woody scent of the shower products he uses reaches across the table to torment me. All that's missing are the studio head-phones around his neck and he'd look the same as every other time I've seen him over this past year.

But today is different. Today the edgy, enigmatic boy-next-door contrast that defines him is particularly alluring. He's a majestic human leopard-bear.

"I'm surprised to see you. I figured you'd get some royal five-star spread delivered to your private bus, not be forced to mingle with us common folk."

His teasing tone immediately calms my nerves. I may be out of place, but when I'm with Val, I always feel comfortable and safe.

"Yes, well, I prefer my biscuits cold and slightly stale, so…"

He snorts a laugh, and I can't help but grin. His rare smiles always send a burst of triumph through me. Pulling them from his melancholy soul has become one of my favorite activities.

"So glad catering could accommodate you," he says, holding my gaze for a second too long. Was there a flicker of attraction in his eyes? It disappears too soon when he lowers his gaze to the table.

You're playing with fire. You can't have him.

Would he even want me? I know he cares about me, probably even likes me as a person, but he doesn't have much patience or respect for everything else about my world. He despises Jarvis. He's never said it, but I can tell by the way he tenses every time we cross paths that he has no interest in pretending otherwise. Jarvis would probably despise him as well if he stepped outside his own orbit long enough to learn other people existed.

A twinge goes through me as I recall the text on my phone this morning.

Jarvis: Hey baby luvin life luvin u see u @ 2 boo got a surprise 4 u

Not sure what that means, but it can't be good.

I responded with an ice cream cone emoji.

"So, um, I wanted to talk to you about 'Gray Rainbows,'" I say as casually as possible.

When his gaze lifts to me again, I lose all hope of ingesting my stale biscuit.

Gosh, he's beautiful.

What is wrong with you?! Why are you acting so weird? You will never survive this tour if you can't get this crush under control. It's Val. It's just Val. Your colleague. Your producer. One of your closest friends...

I clear my throat. Then, take a sip of water to soothe it. "The, uh, turn. After the second chorus."

His dark brow lifts as he waits.

I swallow hard.

"I think we should maybe add some backing vocals on the second line. Pushed way far back, you know? A ton of reverb. Either a harmony or a run. Ear-candy stuff."

"Sure. We can try it."

How does he manage to sound so casual and in control? My entire body is bubbling beneath my skin. Everything in me wants to reach over and brush his warm fingers resting on the table. Trace the intricate tattoos. I love watching those hands skim over the trackpad on his laptop or the keys of a midi controller. So confident and capable like the rest of him. Watching his brilliant mind work is one of the hottest things I've ever seen.

This isn't helping!

"We could even play with a telephone effect or something," he says. "That song has an EDM vibe, so we might be able to pull off a vocal chop as well."

Oh, yes. I like that too.

"That could work. Um, also the strings on 'Too Much.' I like the melody of the riff, but the sound isn't quite right."

His folding chair creaks as he leans back. "Agreed. I already swapped out the symphony orchestra for something darker that has more of a Mellotron feel."

"Ooh, yes. Perfect. See? This is why I love you."

Love?! No no no.

He knows I didn't mean *love*, right? Because I didn't—even if my tone was way softer and more serious than it should have been.

His return smile seems pretty standard and safe, so hopefully he didn't hear my forbidden feelings creeping in.

"That's my job," he says in the playful tone I *should* have used.

"Yup."

My teeth sink into my lip as the silence returns. Conversation has resumed around us now that the others have accepted my presence. It's kind of nice being part of the group. Maybe I *should* spend more time with the crew. They give so much to me. What do I give them besides a job?

I'll see if we can get everyone a hoodie.

I shift in my chair, still trying to think of safe topics when my foot presses against something beneath the table. Val's gaze darts to me, and I realize it must be his shoe.

What should happen next is that we pull back with a surprised chuckle. Maybe make a joke about "playing footsies." We've had plenty of incidental brushes while working together, even playful shoves and arm smacks. This would be easy to correct and laugh off.

But I don't want that. He must not either, because six seconds later, we're still touching. Never has contact with a sneaker generated the kind of electricity I'm feeling in my leg.

His pretty eyes broadcast so many questions and illicit messages as they search mine from too far away. I can't tear my gaze away. It's everything I can do to keep my foot from sliding further up his leg in a sexy, dinner-party ankle caress. (Which is totally a thing people do according to every movie ever.)

Gosh, if this one touch is making me explode, what would happen if I held his hand? Kissed him? Pulled his shirt over his head and finally, *finally* explored the hard flesh of his—

"OMG!"

Val stiffens as his attention locks on something behind me. I turn to face a young blond man with a giant Cheshire cat grin and eyeballs about to pop from their sockets.

"Ms. Scott, I am exceedingly honored to make your acquaintance!"

The man bows, and I swear Val mumbles something about Labor Day. His expression isn't nearly as excited as this person's.

"It's nice to meet you," I say with a smile. "Are you a member of the crew?"

Aghast would be a good word to describe his response.

"No, madam. I am Chad Smith, *Administrative Talent Liaison for Reed-weather Media vis a vis Sandeke Telecom.*"

Oh. Okay. I don't know what that means.

I return a nod, which is the human-reaction equivalent of an ice cream cone emoji.

"Excellent. Welcome to the tour. We're happy to have you."

Probably?

"I hear congratulations are in order." His smarmy tone has me crossing a look to Val, who shrugs.

"Congratulations?" I ask.

"On the engagement!"

Val chokes on his coffee as I stare in stunned silence. I don't have a human emoji for this one.

"Yes! Jarvis told us the good news this morning. Wait, was I not supposed to say anything?" he whispers, as if *that's* the part of this conversation that could be a secret.

"Um… I don't…"

Hang on.

Jarvis' text!

Is he planning to propose today?! No no no no no no no.

I'm still "no-ing" when Val lands a pained look on me.

It's not what you think! I silently scream back.

He lowers his gaze, making my stomach ache. What is happening right now?

"Ah! It *was* supposed to be on the down-low, huh," Chad sighs out. "Don't worry. Your secret's safe with me."

Nope. It's definitely not.

He makes a zipping motion over his lips, then takes off whistling a tune that would absolutely alert everyone within audio range that he's hiding a secret. By the shocked attention of everyone in the room, the "secret" is very much out. Before I can even respond, applause and half-hearted cheers lift from the other occupants.

All except one.

"We should go," our tour manager, Bruce, says in an urgent tone behind me.

I jump when another person grips my arm to guide me up. Steve? When did he get here?

"What… I don't…"

"Not here," Bruce whispers at my ear. "Just smile and follow me."

"But—"

"Now, Larinda. Please," Steve says.

I'm not sure what else to do except push up from the table and follow the leader like I always do. My entire life is dictated by other people, so it takes nothing to fall in step with the human sandwich escorting me from the room. Except, something doesn't feel right this time. I'm missing something. Forgetting… Val!

Bruce has my arm in a polite but firm grip. Steve is on my other side, subtly blocking me in. They're taking me in the wrong direction! I twist back and wish I hadn't when I catch Val's tortured gaze locked on me as they lead me away.

"Wait," I say, tugging against their hold. "I have to—"

"Seriously, Larry. We have to go. We just got news from the McKinnley camp," Steve hisses.

Pretty sure I know what the news is.

I'm engaged? I don't want to be engaged. At least, not to Jarvis.

When I try another look, Val is out of sight. I'll explain it all later. I will, just…

* * *

Val

She's engaged? Well, that explains the odd breakfast appearance if she came to tell me in person. But that doesn't explain what happened beneath the table a minute ago.

My foot still tingles from its collision with hers. For those few seconds, I actually thought…

I'm such an idiot.

Anger mixes with the hurt twisting through my chest. Not at her—at myself for thinking for even a fraction of a second someone like Larinda could be interested in someone like me.

What were you thinking? You are on the cusp of reaching your dream and you were about to blow it with an unrequited crush on your boss.

People wait decades for the break I've been given at age twenty-three. I really need to lock this shit down because I've suffered way too much to lose everything over a pointless crush. Larinda's label is already looking for any excuse to get rid of me.

"Pretty wild, right? Do you think they'll get married on tour? Oh! What if it's at our stop in Duluth?"

I force my attention to Chad and use every remaining ounce of strength to pretend I'm not gutted.

"What's in Duluth?" I ask. It's the only one of his questions I can handle right now.

"Um, an aquarium, for one," he huffs, clearly offended by my lack of Duluth trivia.

Right.

"Have you really never been?" he asks.

"Have you?"

"That's beside the point," he mumbles.

I'm not even sure what he's offended about now.

I lean forward and rest my pounding head on my fists. Larinda is engaged to Jarvis? Just two days ago she made it seem like she'd be fine if they never spoke again. Was she trying to throw me off? Why? Shit, is it because she suspects I have feelings for her?

A fresh wave of anxiety pools in my stomach. Would she fire me for that? It wouldn't be vindictive, but professionally I can see how it would be hard to work with someone who was in love with you.

In love? Am I?

Shit, shit, shit.

"There's a bridge too."

"I'm sorry?" I say, forcing my suddenly very heavy head up.

"A bridge. Duluth has a bridge."

I stare at him. "Are there cities that don't have bridges?"

"Probably," he says with a shrug.

He might be right about that.

"We should get her a gift basket," he adds. To me. The person who can't breathe at the moment. "Is she allergic to nuts?"

"I… don't think so."

"Perfect. My pre-girlfriend can hook us up. Probably even get us the rare unicorns, if you know what I mean. Brooke knows people, but you didn't hear that from me."

I have no clue what he's talking about or what I'm agreeing to as I nod numbly. Scoring some rare Duluth unicorns sounds wonderful relative to everything else in my life right now.

"It's freshwater too," Chad says. "The aquarium, not the nuts."

"Great," I mutter.

4—OKLAHOMA CITY (LARINDA'S BUS)

LARINDA

"How could this happen?!" I shriek for the third time.

I still haven't received an answer I can accept and have no problem shrieking until I do.

"Larry, please, it's gonna be fine. Here, have a cucumber almond," Steve says, holding out the container of pouches.

"I don't want a cucumber almond! I want to know why the heck the entire world knows I'm engaged except for me."

"Larinda, please calm down," Rena says through the screen. The backdrop of her fancy office at the Lakebend Records headquarters in LA looks like it was designed solely for video conferences. Only a person on the other side of her screen could appreciate the artistic skyline of succulents on the shelf behind her. The one with the pink flower on top is the only thing I'm enjoying about this conversation.

"The whole world doesn't know. Just a few members of Jarvis' camp," she says.

"And everyone at Lakebend, apparently!"

"And everyone at Lakebend."

"And my own freaking manager!" I scowl at Mae's square on my screen.

"And Mae. It's going to be wonderful. You'll see. We have it all arranged," Rena assures me. "Jarvis will propose at the end of your set tonight. Try to cry, if possible. We already have the press release and your first appearance as an engaged couple lined up. We'll make sure the media team is prepped so we can capture the rapturous moment from multiple angles. All you have to do is cry and say yes. Every detail has been worked out."

"Except for the fact that I don't want to marry him!"

Silence settles over the group, and I have hope that my position is finally sinking in. That hope fades when Rena's expression hardens.

"Larinda, we talked about this. You wanted to go in a different direction with your music, and we agreed on the condition that you leave the marketing to us. Critics love your new work, but sales and streams are nowhere near what we wanted. We have to do something to spark interest."

"By forcing me to marry someone?"

"No one is saying you're actually going to marry him," Mae cuts in, ever the peacekeeper. "Just say yes for now and we'll figure out how to break you up after the tour. No big deal."

Easy for her to say. She didn't just learn she was the center of an evil faux wedding plot. Also, thanks for rubbing my low numbers in my face. Funny how I finally get taken seriously as an artist and lose the interest of the masses.

"We're sorry you found out this way, but we thought you'd be happy," Rena says.

"*Happy?* Why would I be happy?"

Steve squeezes my arm, and I tug it away.

So help me if he suggests one more dang almond.

"You've always wanted a fairy-tale wedding, right? You talk about it all the time in the interviews."

"Because you tell me to!"

"Oh! What about staging some photos at a bridal shop at one of your stops on tour? Maybe even try on a few dresses?" Mae's giant smile means she clearly didn't hear what she just said.

"His numbers are through the roof right now," Rena adds. "It's the perfect time to hitch your horse to his wagon."

"I think it's the other way around," Mae says.

"What is?" Rena asks.

"The hitching. The wagon goes to the horse. Not the horse to the wagon."

"What? That doesn't make sense."

"It does in the context of nineteenth-century pioneer logistics."

"Wait, isn't the horse supposed to be drinking something?" Steve asks.

"Drinking what?" Rena says.

"Water, I think," Steve replies.

"No. The horse *doesn't* drink the water," Mae cuts in. "You lead it to the water but it *doesn't* drink. That's the whole point of the analogy."

"Idiom," Rena corrects.

"Same thing."

"It's not."

"What even is a horse, though, when you think about it?" Steve muses.

Ah! How is this helping anything?!

I clench my fists, having no idea what to do. This is absurd. This is…

Exactly what we've been doing for the last five years since Jarvis and I started playing this media game to enhance our careers.

I sensed their confusion even before the horse debate. Of course they don't understand why I'm putting up a fight about this engagement stunt when several of our biggest ploys over the years were *my* idea. They especially don't understand why I'd resist when I need to boost my profile more than ever.

But things are different now. I don't know why, but what felt necessary for my career all these years, now feels icky. I can't imagine looking Jarvis in the eye and saying I'm going to marry him, even as a charade.

"Where's this sudden opposition coming from?" Rena asks. Guess they resolved the horse-wagon issue. I'm not entirely clear what that argument was about. "Are you romantically involved with someone else?"

A cold trickle moves through me as soulful green eyes flash through my brain.

A smile that makes my heart burst.

Creative genius that gives me chills.

Is that what my reluctance is about? Can't be. My crush on Val wouldn't interfere with my career. Nothing has ever come between me and my success. Since day one I was willing to do whatever it took as long as no one else was hurt.

But suddenly, I'm not okay with it. Suddenly, the prospect of pretending to love someone leaves a sick feeling in my stomach even worse than the prospect of cucumber-flavored almonds.

"Larinda. Are you involved with someone?" Rena repeats.

"What? No. Of course not."

"Good. Because that's a horse we can all agree on. We need to be very careful how we manage the narrative of your love life, especially now. It's central to your music and image. We don't want another DJ Master Klau$ situation."

Is my ex-producer ex on the agenda for every single meeting?

"Rena is right," Mae says. "And after the Brighthouse gaming disaster, we can't afford another PR mess."

Oh great. Let's throw that corporate sponsorship fiasco in the dumpster fire as well.

Yes. It *was* a disaster, and also the most bittersweet publicity event in the history of publicity events. Nothing went right that day. Everything blew up. But last year's huge mess also gave me one of my closest friends in Nash Ellis, who in turn brought Val into my life. I can't imagine this past year without my producer. I can't even imagine this past breakfast without him.

And we've gone full circle.

"So, just to confirm, you are not involved with anyone?" Rena asks in a firm tone, making it clear there's only one right answer.

"I'm not."

I mean, it's not really a lie. Wanting what you can't have doesn't count in the game of love.

Ooh, nice. Gotta remember that line for later.

"Great. So, it's settled? Because I have to run," Rena says.

"What? No. I—"

"It's going to be a beautiful moment. Historic, even. You'll see," Mae assures me. "Thanks, Rena. We'll be in touch."

"Hold on. I never said—"

"Remember to cry," Rena says as her screen goes dark.

If this actually happens, that won't be a problem. I already feel the heaviness of tears building in my chest.

"I don't want to do this. Please pull the plug," I tell Mae, my voice trembling.

Her smile sags into a frown. "I don't understand. What's going on? This isn't like you. You know we're in a precarious position right now. If you want to keep creative control of your music, you're going to have to give a little somewhere else."

"I get that, but what they're asking is too much. This joint tour is stressful enough. I don't want to deal with an engagement as well."

That was a good coverup, right?

"Okay, but—"

"Mae, I'm telling you. You need to stop this. I'm not doing it."

Mae's eyes grow wide through the screen. Even Steve tenses at my stern command. Have I ever stood up for myself before? Probably not. At least, not when it mattered, but it's my life, my career, and if I don't want to be engaged, I shouldn't have to be engaged. I'm tired of obeying orders. I've been doing what I was told for as long as I can remember. I didn't even know I was capable of thinking for myself until Val came into my life and challenged me creatively. I've loved every second of exploring my art with him this past year, so maybe it's time to explore my *person* as well.

Leave it to Val to make me brave even when he's not here.

"Okay, well, I'll reach out to the McKinnley camp and see what I can do," Mae says in a cool voice. She's mad but so what? She works for me, not the other way around. I have to remember that. I'm a person, not a commodity no matter how much they try to reduce me to charts and graphs.

"But, Larinda," she continues in a grave tone. "Even if I express your resistance to the plan, I can't guarantee Jarvis won't go through with it. You know how he is."

An unapologetic narcissist? Yeah, I know. The whole world does.

"Then I'll talk to him directly. He wanted to meet this afternoon, probably about this. It's the perfect opportunity to tell him *not* to do it."

"Larry… I'm not sure that's a good idea," Steve says. "Telling him not to do something is basically asking him to do it."

"Steve's right," Bruce says. He's still here? "Jarvis hates the word 'no.' Confronting him could backfire."

I cross my arms and glare at the three traitors who are supposed to be on my side. "I guarantee it won't *backfire* as much as if I turn down his pretend proposal in front of the entire world."

"You wouldn't," Mae gasps.

"Watch me," I say. "Now, if you'll excuse me, I have a lot of work to do and a show to prepare for."

Plus, I'm hungry and will scream if I have to eat almonds for another meal.

"Fine. Then, I'll be in touch," Mae grumbles.

"Fantastic. Have a lovely day."

I close my laptop and pull in a shaky breath.

"Larinda—"

"Thank you for your concern, gentlemen, but would you please give me some privacy? I have a lot to process before tonight's show and not much time to do it."

Bruce returns a stiff nod. "Of course. I have to check on the set construction and merch table, anyway. Oh, plus there's a catering mix-up related to that brunch at our Dallas stop and the issue of where to put the four extra crewmembers in Pittsburgh."

"And I have… walking," Steve says.

I return a tight smile. "Sounds good."

They peek back several times on their way to the door, but I busy myself with looking busy so they don't stop and make me actually busy.

Once I'm alone, I release a long exhale, drop to the couch, and text Val.

* * *

Val

Larinda: We need to talk.

No shit.

I stare at the text for several seconds, not sure how to respond. On the one hand, her engagement to her longtime revolving-door boyfriend is none of my business. On the other hand, it's none of my business.

On no hands is Larinda Scott's romantic life my business. If anything, as someone who has a financial and career stake in her success, I should be supportive of any development that will contribute to that end. There's no question an explosive headline to kick off an explosive tour will be, well, explosive.

I'm just hurt that I had to hear it from the Duluth Aquarium's biggest fan instead of her. Yep, that's definitely the only reason for the pain in my chest.

Sure. Where do you want to meet? I type back.

Larinda: Can you come to my bus? Everyone's gone now.

Everyone. I'm not even part of "everyone," apparently.

Of course not. You're just a coworker. She owes you nothing.

I'm probably being extra sensitive because Larinda's engagement wasn't the first bomb to drop on me before 9AM today. Prior to breakfast wedding drama, I woke up to an even bigger blow: an apology and dinner invitation from my parents. After recovering from the initial shock, I immediately messaged my sister, Paige, for a debriefing session. Since she hasn't responded yet, zero debriefing has been done.

One might be forgiven for wondering why a dinner invitation from one's parents would be in the same gut-punch category as finding out the woman you have feelings for is going to marry someone you thought she didn't even like. It makes more sense when you know that the last time I saw my parents was when they extorted me for thirty thousand dollars after legally disowning me.

They've been awful my whole life, and nothing but despicable since I dropped out of college more than five years ago. Every one of our rare encounters has been hostile and hurtful. As the official disappointment of the family, I haven't received a single shred of support from them for as long as I can remember. They've made it no secret that I'm a failure in every sense of the word. In fact, stuffed somewhere in a box in my closet is a packet of notarized papers served by courier that declare me not their son in the eyes of the government. The whole thing was so ludicrous, I've never formally reacted to that soap-worthy gesture.

And then out of nowhere…

Dearest Perceval,

How to begin. You will no doubt find this particular electronical mail delivery letter perplexing as we have not corresponded in quite some time. Our history has been strenuous, to say the least, and we would understand if you chose not to peruse this correspondence in its entirety. It would be especially comprehensible if you chose not to respond to this belated attempt at reconciliation. We hold a sliver of hope, however, that you might find it in your magnanimous heart to take pity on we, your parents, and deign to join us for a meal in the municipality of Pittsburgh, in the state of Pennsylvania. We have reason to believe you will be in that region of the United States of America in less than a week's time. Should you be so inclined to allow us this honor, please respond to this message and provide us with an ounce of supreme relief.

Yours,

Mummy and Papa

Now, let's pretend for a second that this email was written in actual words people use and not an inexplicable attempt to revive nineteenth-century allegorical prose—it still wouldn't make any sense.

My parents are apologizing? (Sort of.) I've never heard them apologize to anyone for anything, least of all me. (I've also never heard them refer to themselves as "Mummy and Papa" but I suppose that fits our new narrative that we now live in a time before the abbreviation "U.S.A." made the rounds in popular linguistics.)

The point is, today has been a hard day. The last thing I want to do right now is visit Larinda on her bus to discuss her eternal love for a guy who thinks cauliflower is broccoli that's gone bad.

So, of course I type back, **Sure. Be there in 5.**

Yeah, who am I kidding? I will always want to see her and listen to whatever she wants to discuss, even if it's her love for another man. I just enjoy being around her, and this past year, I've realized it's even more important than that. I *need* to be around her. She makes me laugh and brightens my world in a way that will make it impossible to go back to the morose existence I inhabited before she burst into my life. So yes, even if she comes with an irritating accessory in the form of a pretentious country singer who has a standing weekly hair-frosting appointment, I will still want to work with her and remain friends. This is also why I need to convince her that's possible because I'm not in love with her.

After making some excuse about an emergency BPM change on one of our new tracks, I cross the parking lot to her bus just a few minutes later.

"Hey," she says with a weak smile.

"Hey," I reply as the door closes behind me.

"Thanks for coming."

"Of course."

I climb the stairs and follow her past the driver's empty seat to the main lounge area of the bus. She drops to the plush pink couch lining the right wall. More seating juts out toward the center to create almost an L-shape. Her bedroom in the back is barely visible through an open door straight ahead, and the granite countertops on the kitchenette to the left sparkle like they've never been used. Every time I'm here, I can't help but think this place is nicer than any hotel room I've ever been in—probably bigger too.

"Almonds?" she asks, holding out a bowl of assorted packets.

The first one I see says "Fruit Punch," and I swear the one below it says "Peanut."

Peanut-flavored almonds?

"No, thanks."

She sits nearby and pulls her leg beneath her to face me. "Sorry about this morning. That must have been…"

She shudders, which is a pretty accurate description of my morning, actually.

"Yeah. It was… a lot. Um, congratulations on your engagement, I guess. I'm sure you'll be happy. Jarvis is… Jarvis."

Okay, so I'm a terrible liar.

Her eyes go wide, then narrow. "Perceval Andrews, are you seriously trying to placate me right now?"

Really terrible, apparently.

"Fine," I sigh out. "I don't get it, Larinda. I mean, I do, but I don't. The guy has hurt you so many times. Betrayed you personally and professionally. He's so far beneath you as a human being, it would be an insult to put you on the same scale. Plus, how could you not tell me?"

She crosses her arms. Her eyes are doing this weird squinty thing that I *think* is supposed to be a glare? She sucks at being mean. Her "terrifying death stare" is most people's stuck-in-traffic look.

"Tell you what, exactly?" she huffs. "That Jarvis and our label came up with some diabolical PR stunt and didn't bother informing me?"

My heart stutters in my chest.

"Wait. So you're not actually engaged to Jarvis?"

She still looks like she's stuck at a red light as she parks a fist on her hip. "After all our time together, do you not know me at all? How could you think I would marry him after everything that's happened? And not even tell one of my closest friends?"

"I'm one of your closest friends?"

"Duh."

I'm one of her closest friends.

"Closest" is good. "Friends" is… not. Still, she isn't marrying that asshole, which beats getting friend-zoned any day.

"Thank god," I mumble, sinking back against the couch.

She puffs out a breath and mirrors my position, which leaves us slouching against the cushion and staring at the roof of the bus. By the feel of her heat and smell of her expensive perfume, we must be close but I'm afraid to look. If I move, I might break the spell, and this brief respite from hell is quite refreshing.

"Fudge on a stick, Val," she says after a long pause.

"Is that an almond flavor too?"

"No. It's a verbal smack on the arm. I can't believe you actually thought I'd marry him. Why did you think I called you here?"

"To smooth things over."

"*No*," she draws out. "I messaged you because you're one of the smartest, most strategic people I know and I need you to talk this through with me and help figure it out. Plus, you're one of the few people I trust."

Wow.

I finally turn my head and immediately regret it. She's even closer than I thought. Crystal blue eyes lock on mine, screaming something in the tense silence, but it can't be what I want it to be. How could it? Every muscle in my body tightens. Blood pounds in my veins.

"How?" she whispers, searching my eyes. "How could you think for even a second that I'd choose him when…"

"When what?" I return hoarsely, my heart thudding in my chest.

Her gaze is pleading as she reaches up and brushes the small X tattoo near my eye.

"When you're right in front of me."

Words evaporate from my brain. Everything… just… gone.

"Larinda…"

She pulls her hand away, leaving that spot burning from her touch. "Sorry. I know you don't see me like that, but…" Her eyes seek mine again. "I'm falling hard for you, Val. I have been for a while. I promise it won't affect our—"

I cut her off with a kiss.

Her gasp becomes a moan as she grips my shirt and drags me closer. Her soft lips surrender to mine, igniting a fire that's been simmering inside me for months. My fingers thread into her hair. Hers clutch my shirt like she can't get enough. Our hesitant kiss becomes urgent, and she climbs onto my lap to straddle me.

She sinks down hard, sliding glorious friction over my zipper before settling achingly deep in a tempting invitation. We resume the kiss, her hips grinding in small, targeted movements I feel everywhere. Pent-up longing fuels each probing kiss and greedy caress. The way she claws at my shirt and sinks her fingertips into my shoulders exposes how long she's been craving this as well.

She yanks off my hat and grasps my hair in a firm hold. The slight burn of her grip fuels the fire as my palms slide down her back and cup her ass in a long-held fantasy come to life.

Damn, this is… I can't even think straight, but I never want it to end. She tastes like ecstasy, feels like a dream.

Our kisses grow fierce. Months of suppressed hunger surge out in an animalistic need to touch and consume every part of the other. She uses her grasp on my hair to wrench us together, again and again, her hips grazing mine and firing hot streaks with each collision. She seems just as insatiable, clutching and writhing to the rhythm of our violent lips and tongues until…

"Wait!" she gasps, pulling back.

Our heavy breathing fills the charged air around us. My heart still pounds scorching blood through my entire body. Her grip anchors us together.

"I… I'm sorry," I say, not sure what I did wrong.

She frowns, and my fear dissolves when she brushes a soft kiss on my lips.

"No apologizing," she says before straightening again, still on my lap.

Her fingers glide over my cheek as she searches my gaze.

"You have the prettiest eyes," she whispers. "I've thought that since the first time I saw you that day Nash brought you to the studio."

"Thanks?" I mumble, not sure where this is going. What just happened? What's *about* to happen?

Her dejected sigh can't be a good sign. Neither is the way she seems to fight herself before dropping her hand.

"I've been wanting to do that for a long time," she says quietly. "So long. I, uh, kind of fantasize about you… a lot."

A pink tint spreads over her skin as her teeth sink into her lip.

Well, damn.

"I've been wanting to do that for a long time, too," I say. "And also fantasizing," I add with a smile. Plenty of that.

She returns it, looking shy as she drags her fingertips along my jaw. Over my lips. Back into my hair for a light tug. It's like she can't stop touching me. She wants to stop, she just can't. I know exactly how she feels. It's why my palms are still running up and down her thighs in slow, steady strokes.

Is this really happening? Or am I actually asleep on the bus and Chad is about to wake me up with his weird morning mantra that's supposed to… well, I don't know, exactly.

"Today is the first day of today. Today is the first day of today."

"I wondered if you did," she says softly. "I *hoped* you felt the same way, but…"

But. No one likes "but" except after the phrase, *we thought they were dead.*

"I really like you, Val. Obviously," she says with a nervous laugh.

But…

"But this can't happen."

I brace through the blow. Apparently, expecting it did nothing to soothe the sting.

"Right. Yeah, of course," I say. Somehow I even manage a weak smile. "You're a huge celebrity, and I'm—"

"An amazing human being anyone would be honored to date. Stop that," she says with a hard look.

Now I'm really confused.

"You're so special, Val. If anything, it's me who doesn't deserve you. I like you so much, it's just …"

Did she take a class on how to shred a guy's heart?

"Be sure to make it slow and painful. Drag it out as long as possible and include just enough false hope to make it especially soul-crushing."

This woman is acing it.

"It's because of DJ Master Klau$!" she blurts out.

Huh. Okay. Didn't see that coming.

I have no idea how to respond to that.

"It was this tiny little thing forever ago where he produced my album, then we broke up, then he sued, then the label had to settle, then the album sort of… didn't happen. Anyway, the details aren't important. What's important is that I'm not allowed to date my producers anymore."

I stare at her.

Still staring.

"Say something," she says, biting her lip. Blue-glass eyes blink back at me with a hint of apprehension.

Say something? I don't even understand what's happening.

"You're not *allowed*? What does that mean? Whose rule is that?"

"The label."

"Any producer?"

"No. Just the ones I'm working with."

"So… me. I'm the only person on this planet you're 'not allowed' to date."

"Yes. Pretty much."

"Great," I mumble.

She sighs and pushes off my lap to take the seat beside me again.

"And this is in writing? Is that even legal?"

"Not in writing, but you know how it is."

I don't, apparently.

"The point is, I *really* like you. Like, a *lot*, but we can't be together for a bunch of reasons."

"I see."

I don't really. I just don't know what else to say. What *can* I say? I suspected from the beginning I didn't have a chance with her, I just couldn't have guessed the reason why.

"I'm sorry," she whispers. "Do you hate me now?"

"Hate you?" I ask, squinting over at her. "Why would I hate you?"

"Because I'm a femme fatale."

I snort a laugh. Can't help it. She glares at me.

"What, you don't think I could be one?"

"No."

She crosses her arms. "I could!"

"Really," I say, making no attempt to hide my skepticism.

Her eyes narrow further. "Yes. I absolutely could."

Does she even know what that is?

"So you go around seducing people in order to put them in dangerous situations and immanent peril?"

"What? No! Ew."

I grin, and she smacks my chest.

"Don't be sassy," she quips. "The point is, I want you, but I can't have you, so that's what it is. If we're caught in any kind of relationship, the label won't let us work together anymore—or worse—and I need you. My music needs you, so, I guess…"

She waves over her hips.

I don't know what that means.

"We need to wear belts?"

"We need to keep it in our pants."

Ah. Right.

Another smile flickers over my lips.

Femme fatale, my ass. She's every literary archetype *except* that one. Actually no. She's just a straight-up mythical goddess. How else would she get me to smile even while she's crushing my heart?

"So that's it, then?" I ask after a long silence.

She looks how I feel as she deflates against the couch, back to where we started.

"I guess so," she sighs out.

"Do you feel like shit right now?" I ask. She snaps a look to me, and I soften the comment with a weak smile. "Because I do. Wanting what you can't have sucks."

"Yeah, it really does." Her frown lifts as something works through her head. "Actually, I would go as far as to say *'wanting what you can't have doesn't count in the game of love,'*" she sings.

"Damn. How long have you been sitting on that melody?"

"Since the meeting this morning. You want to play with it?"

"Hell yeah. I'll grab my laptop. Meet you back here in ten?"

She nods and grabs my fingers as I push to my feet.

"Val?"

"Yeah?"

"If I could, I would."

I clench my jaw and force a nod as she lets go.

5—OKLAHOMA CITY (STILL LARINDA'S BUS)

LARINDA

Wow. Now *that* was a kiss. Five minutes after Val leaves, I'm still collapsed on the couch, tingling and quivering everywhere. Kissing him made me feel… authentic. Safe and free. Val takes the performance out of my existence and lets me be *me* when we're alone. I wasn't even sure who that was until we started exploring the possibilities together. There's nothing hotter than someone who truly sees you.

I know he'll be right back but I'm already regretting sending him away. I miss his smile, his kind eyes. I *really* miss touching him—not that I can afford any more touches if we're going to obey the rules. It was nearly impossible to stop once we started. He felt as good as I expected, so good that my fantasies are going to be brutal from here on out.

My fingers itch to clutch his shirt and drag it over his head. His body is so beautiful with the art he's inscribed on it. I've only seen it a couple of times, always from a distance, and only by accident when he was changing his shirt or tugging off a hoodie. He's a walking museum exhibit, and I'm growing increasingly desperate to explore that human work of art.

When I hear the knock on the door, I'm on my feet so fast my trainer would think I actually like doing cardio.

Since my driver is resting in his hotel room, I have the honor of opening the door myself which means… crap.

My tingles become prickles at the opposite person I was hoping to see.

"Hi, baby," Jarvis says with a sticky smile on his face.

"Hey. What are you doing here?"

"Got the memo, sugar doll. Let's hashtag this out, m'kay?"

Somehow I manage to keep my eyes from rolling as I return to the lounge. If I don't move, there will be a collision, and there's only one person I want to be rubbing against at the moment. Spoiler alert: It's not the one with a two-story wall in his house called *"The Me Wall."*

"What memo?" I ask, dropping to the seat adjacent to the main couch. There's no chance he can sit beside me now. Not that he'll be doing much sitting in those jeans. Did his stylist sew them on?

He skims his hand over the tips of his gelled hair so as not to adjust a single strand, then attempts to lower himself to the cushion closest to me. Except… called it.

I watch with mild intrigue as he contorts his body so his legs don't have to bend when his butt hits the cushion. I guess this would be considered sitting? It's not standing. Or lying down. Definitely not squatting so…

"The memo that you're having second thoughts about us."

"There's a memo?"

"Not an actual memo. It's an emblem of speech."

Is it?

He goes for casual arrogance by lacing his fingers behind his head and leaning back. But since he also can't lean, he just looks like he was about to do an ab crunch and forgot how.

(For the record, ab crunches are one of the few things that man *does* know how to do well. He even wrote a song about it: "Abs and Abby." It's as bad as it sounds.)

"I can't have second thoughts because there were no first thoughts," I say. "There is no 'us,' Jarvis. We talked about this."

His manicured brows knit together. "No, you said you didn't want to be in a relationship."

My manicured brows also knit together. "Yes… exactly."

"So let's not be in a *relationship.*"

I squint back. Are his inside words becoming outside words again? It's really hard to talk to him when that happens.

"Great," I say with some hesitation. "Then are we finished here? I was about to work on something."

"I guess so. Just make sure you cry when you accept my proposal."

He wriggles in an attempted extraction from the couch.

"What? We just agreed we're not in a relationship."

"We're not." He adds a wink. That can't be good.

"So why would I accept your fake marriage proposal?"

"It's an emblem, remember?"

Yes, I remember, and no, it's not.

"Oh! Almonds. You mind?"

He fishes through the bowl and pulls out a pack of blueberry. Of course he does. I knew there was a reason I hated blueberry.

"Jarvis. I have no idea what you're saying. It's not making any sense."

"Really? Is it because you want to see the ring first?"

I don't. I have no clue how he'd access it even if I did.

"You mean, the ring you're *not* going to give me because we're *not* getting engaged?"

"Tsk, tsk, my *linda* Linda."

"Don't call me that."

"What, *linda* or Linda?"

"Both. That's not my name and you don't speak Portuguese."

"No? *Café con leche.*" He waves at the cappuccino machine on the wet bar in the kitchenette across from us.

I don't even know what to do with that.

"Right… Jarvis, I'm serious. Don't propose because I'm going to turn you down."

He sighs and rips open the packet of almonds. "I don't want to do this with you, baby."

"Good. Neither do I. And don't call me that either."

"What?"

"Baby."

"Seriously?" He throws up his hands. "Then what should I call you?"

"Larinda works great. How about that?"

His eyes narrow as he processes this strange request. "I don't know what's been going on with you this past year, but you've stopped being you. It's like ever since that small misunderstanding with the songs, you've been a negative noodle."

"Definitely don't call me that."

"See? That's what I'm talking about!"

"No one wants to be compared to pessimistic pasta."

His mouth opens to respond but I know I've outsmarted him when he returns his attention to the nuts.

"And I wouldn't call trying to steal my songs a 'small misunderstanding,'" I add.

"Okay, well, I came to smooth things over, but clearly you want to keep things awkward A.F. while we're engaged. Those press dates are gonna be… hashtag super fun."

"We're not engaged."

"Well, after tonight, I mean."

"We won't be after tonight, either."

"We will, though. It's not my call. It's what the label wants. If it's about the ring, we can pick a different one. You want one of those ones with just the twig bundles or whatever?"

Huh? I shake off the question.

"No, because I don't want any ring. I told the label and now I'm telling you. We'll have to find a different PR stunt, because I'm not doing this."

He crosses his arms. "Why not? You want to be pregnant or something? We haven't done that one yet."

"What?! No!"

I cross my arms too.

His eyes narrow.

So do mine. I even lean forward with a menacing scowl in an athletic feat I know he can't match.

He still tries, and I bite back a laugh as he slips off the couch, sending his almonds flying. Several ping off the "*café con leche*" machine.

"A little help?" he grunts, holding out his hand.

His exposed wrist displays a new bandana, which means he must have a new "cause" to support. Guess the previous fundraiser for his Teacup Poodle's doggie ropes course is complete?

As much as I don't want to, twenty-six years of being a nice person force me to take his hand and use all my strength to jerk him to his feet. Besides, he can't leave if he's stuck in a bedazzled denim cocoon on my floor.

"Thanks," he says, but he doesn't release my hand.

I tug it away, and he returns a pout any three-year-old would admire.

"Wow, Linda. Hashtag 'sourpuss.' I don't know what your problem is but your choices lately are *ew*. Why are you throwing everything away? Ever since you started working with that loser—what's his name, *Valerie?*—you've been making a lot of *ew* mistakes. Your music was so good and now it's weird. Is that what you want? To make weird music?"

"He's not a loser. He's brilliant. And my music isn't weird. It's also brilliant."

"If you say so," he mumbles. "Tell that to the charts."

There must be one nut left in the package and he does everything he can to get it. Giving up, he flips the bag and dumps it into his hand, along with an avalanche of crumbs. Those get brushed on my floor.

"That imposter is ruining your career. That's all I'm saying." At least he's moving down the aisle now. "You were the Queen of Country and now you're barely an Earl-ess or whatever is under that. Duke-ess? Not princess. That's for sure."

I glare after him, but he's finally leaving and I don't want to distract him from that.

Also, he's wrong… right?

I mean, sure my music is different. Sure I've lost some of my popularity but there's more to a career than numbers. Well, maybe not according to the label. Or the promotors. Or the press. Or the streaming platforms…

I watch in silence as he makes his way to the stairs, but his icy glare at something below him makes me stiffer than his pants.

"Get the frick out of my way," he hisses.

Oh no. Val.

"Excuse me?" my producer says.

"You heard me. You don't belong here. Why are you even on this tour?"

"Why are you on Larinda's bus?"

"She's my girlfriend, loser. Now get out of my way before you ruin my career too."

My heart hurts as Val goes silent. He must be seething, but what's he supposed to say? He can't defend himself. He can't even defend me against the lie about my relationship with Jarvis. No one is supposed to know Jarvis and I aren't actually together.

Jarvis stomps down the steps, and I wince at the *thump* of a body colliding with the door. Did Jarvis shove him?!

I know the answer when Val trudges up the stairs a second later.

His expression… gosh.

My chest aches as he pushes the button to close the door with trembling fingers. His other arm clutches the laptop he went to retrieve.

"Hey," I say softly, rising. "You okay?"

He returns a weak smile. "It's fine."

"It's not fine. Nothing about that was fine. Did he push you?"

"It's not a big deal," he mumbles, moving toward the couch.

I intercept him before he can sit and pull the computer from his hand. After placing it on the cushion, I slide my arms around his waist and settle against him. He releases a heavy sigh and hugs me back.

"It's not true," I murmur.

He doesn't respond and somehow I know what he's thinking. We always seem to read each other's mind.

It *is* true. Not the relationship part, but the rest?

My music is amazing. Plenty of critics and fans agree. Industry power-house *The Tattletale Review* even called me "a pioneer." (Then devoted a thousand words to reflecting on how apocalyptic it was that they could say that about an "insipid" artist like me.) I grinned through the entire article and printed out an excerpt for the wall of my studio.

"Calling Larinda Scott a pioneer is as bewildering as calling a milkshake a culinary marvel, but here we are. The best decision mega-label Lakebend Records made in years was bringing in fresh blood in the form of unknown producer Val Andrews. Dare we say we're actually excited to see what comes next from the formerly insipid and painfully predictable pop-country star."

So *maybe* I had to look up the word "insipid," but whatever.

Working with Val has given me confidence and drive, while opening up creative wormholes I never could have imagined. I don't regret a single thing we've done, I just wish I'd done a better job preparing him for the fallout. People don't like change. They say they do, but they don't really. They want the same thing with a thin façade of *different*. They want comfortable and safe, formulas and predictability. I knew going into this partnership what could happen, probably *would* happen when we challenged the mold, but I didn't know it would hurt so much to see Val get hurt. He's spent most of his life being pummeled for who he is and what he loves, and now it's happening on my behalf.

He's kept his head up through most of the unfair criticism, but I see how it wears on him. Even worse, I suspect the self-doubt runs deeper than he lets on. How could it not when his own parents taught him he's worthless? I've never hated anyone until I met them.

I lean back to study his face. As usual deep green eyes take my breath away. His beautiful soul is right there, on full display, and I have no clue how to resist it. I know we said we wouldn't—*I* said we wouldn't—but I can't stop myself from leaning in for a soft kiss. He looks startled when I pull away with a shy smile.

"Screw it. No one has to know," I say.

"Know what?"

"That we're together."

"We are?"

My heart beats rapidly as I try to read his expression. "Do you want to be?"

Because I've wanted this for so long. Please say yes…

He frowns as he searches my eyes. "Are you sure? If the label finds out, we're done. You lose everything."

"They won't. We'll keep it a secret."

His silence is brutal as he turns my proposal over in his mind. I know it's not himself he's worried about, and he's right to be concerned. But I've spent my life playing a part to help my career. Maybe it's time to use those skills to help my heart.

When his lips tip up in a smile, my world goes bright again.

"Then I guess we're together," he says.

Squealing, I throw my arms around him, and he laughs as he pulls me tight.

"Secretly, of course," he adds with a smirk.

"So secret," I whisper before sealing our pact with another kiss.

6—OKLAHOMA CITY (MERCH STAND)

VAL

"We're together." What the hell am I supposed to do with that?

That tiny phrase has been blaring through my head in a constant loop since what happened on Larinda's bus a few hours ago. She followed it up with a whole list of ground rules for our secret relationship, mostly related to the "no one has to know" aspect of the scenario. Apparently, "no one has to know" means "never on pain of death and every good thing in this universe can someone know." What I *do* know? Within minutes I went from a lonely single guy with a hopeless crush to the forbidden lover of an A-list celebrity.

Operative word being *forbidden*.

The obstacles standing in our way are colossal and insurmountable. We'd lose everything if the label found out she broke their number one rule, and I wish I could say that fact helped temper our attraction. But it appears adding the word "forbidden" to something makes it instantly irresistible. Every second we're apart feels excruciating. She's all I think about. Is she also counting the seconds until we can sneak away and do whatever it is "forbidden" partners do? I still taste her, *feel* her as I lounge beside Chad at the merch table an hour before doors open. (How I got on merch duty with Chad is a whole other story.)

"What do you think?" he asks, stepping back to admire his work with a victorious grin.

I scan the piles of assorted fan apparel. Other than the consistent lack of order, I can't make out a single pattern explaining his thought process.

"Um, well, typically, the same items are grouped *together*."

"Yes, which is why I grouped them by possible purchase combinations."

Hmm.

"I meant, by type. So all the blue tees would go in one pile, the gray hoodies in another, the hats in another, et cetera."

"And perhaps it's time to rewrite the rules on categoric merchandise sales, don't you think? *Innovative Transmutation*, as they say. For example, if someone wants a bumper sticker and a hat, right here. Large hoodie and signed poster? Here. Extra-large hoodie and signed poster? Here."

He's not going to list every one of the twelve billion combinations, is he?

"Besides, I needed room for the Sandeke Telecom proprietary Mer-Nut goodies."

I don't even try to interpret that sentence.

"Okay."

He nods, pleased at my agreement and shoves a giant box toward me. "Do you mind?"

"Mind what?"

"I'll handle the concert-y stuff if you'd be kind enough to take care of the Mer-Nuts? *Good* care, if you know what I mean."

When he winks, I know I don't, but he returns to his incomprehensible sorting of "concert-y" stuff, so I yank open the box. I'm no less confused when I see what's inside.

The first item is a packaged—I don't know, actually. It's plastic and has a shiny tail fin. It's also wearing a monocle. The text on the packaging reads, "Lord Brighthut." Also, "Collect all six!"

There are six of these things? Why is there even one?

"Neat, huh?" Chad says with a knowing grin.

"I guess?" The definition of that word is broad enough.

"Can I tell you a secret?"

"Sure," I mumble.

I pull a handful of the weird plastic fish out of the box.

"I helped design every single item in that carton. Even sat on the test panel."

Interesting. Isn't the point of a test panel to *prevent* things like this from making it to market?

"Wow," I say, holding up another… thing. This one has a crown. A scepter is glued to its hip-fin, presumably because it has no arms to hold a scepter.

"Can I tell you another secret?"

Can I say no?

"Sure."

He leans close. "Don't tell anyone, but I'm not actually a music tour person."

No shit.

"Right. You're the *Talent Liaison* for Sandeke Telecom."

He snorts a laugh and shakes his head at my ignorance. "No, no, my friend. I'm not that either. Well, I *am* but in the same way Antarctica is a country. That's just my cover."

"Your cover?"

I'll leave the Antarctica thing alone for now.

"I'm here undercover," he whispers.

Oh right. The spy thing.

"Wow. So you're spying for Team Jarvis?" I joke.

When his expression grows suspicious, so does mine.

"How did you know?" he hisses.

"Know what?"

"That I'm undercover for Jarvis."

"You just told me."

"No, I said… Wait! Who do you work for?!"

Pretty sure the entire planet knows the answer to that.

"Larinda," I say.

He huffs as he straightens and returns to his pointless anti-sorting.

"Obviously, which is why I can't tell you more."

"You just told me, though."

"No, I said… never mind. Put the merkins behind the collectible figurines."

I choke a little. Did he just say *merkins*? He knows the primary audience for these concerts are preteen kids and their parents, right?

I scoop a pile of fabric squares from the box and stare at… yeah, still don't know what I'm looking at. Whatever it is would make a terrible merkin, but I don't really have a theory for anything else. Apparently, they think they can get ten bucks for it, though.

"These are… merkins?" I ask, glancing back at Chad who is now *scowling* while placing things in random piles. My own sleuthing abilities must have upset him. Not sure why since all I did was repeat back exactly what he told me but, admittedly, I don't have a ton of tactical spy knowledge. Maybe the latest spy trend is to tell everyone you're a spy and confuse the hell out of them.

"Yes. Merkins. You know, like napkins but with Mer? Mer-Kins."

Oh.

His impatient tone makes me positive none of this ever saw a serious vetting process.

"Right. Um…"

"It's a double entendre," he huffs, clearly annoyed at my ignorance.

Yep. Got that much.

"I see." I clear my throat and do my best to arrange the "Mer-Kins" in nice piles. No way in hell I'm selling these to a bunch of twelve-year-olds tonight. He'll be running this table on his own. I'll see if Bruce needs anyone at the main stand.

"You know what that is, right?" Chad asks.

"A merkin?"

"An entendre."

"Yes, I know what an entendre is."

"It's a metaphor, Val."

"Well, no—"

"Take for example, an egg. It's a key phase in a chicken's reproductive cycle but also a breakfast food. A metaphor, right?"

Pretty sure that's just the food chain, but okay.

Chad scoops up one of the fabric squares and flattens it tenderly between his palms.

"In this case, we have this cloth here that's part Mer, part Kin. Mer-Kin. *But wait!* See the designs?"

"More Mer… things."

"Yes, but not just random ones. They're a family. See where I'm going with this?"

"Not really."

"Try to keep up, Val."

"Sorry."

"Anywho, this one is the grandma. The uncle. The little sister. A cousin. Another cousin. Also a cousin… The point is, they're all related. Yes, this is a napkin, but these little ones are also *kin*. So Mer-Kin *and* Mer-*Kin*. Get it?"

Right.

"Okay," I say with a tight smile. "Cool."

I have zero intention of explaining what an actual merkin is. May I never have to have that conversation, or anything close to it, with this person.

As Chad goes back to work, my thoughts return to the less amusing aspect of his info dump. I can't begin to guess what any of the Jarvis spy stuff means, but the fact that there even is a Team Jarvis is concerning. I've never trusted the guy, and now I have evidence that I shouldn't. Why would he need a "spy" in the first place? And why would it involve Sandeke Telecom and their weird-ass fish dolls?

I have no idea, but whatever the reason, it can't be good for Larinda. My instinctive need to protect her triggers all kinds of alarming scenarios in my head. From now on, I'll have to stay close to her and even closer to Jarvis, who hates me. I'll also have to work my new bestie Chad to find out what the hell Jarvis is up to, all without anyone being aware of what I'm doing. Which means...

Fantastic.

Now I'm a spy too.

* * *

As soon as I finish pulling all the fish crap from the box, I sneak away to call Nash. I can count on one hand the number of times I've called him without warning, but it's highly unlikely I'll have another chance to talk privately anytime soon. Once doors open, I'll be too busy working, and after that I'll be shadowed by Chad until I'm able to pull the curtain on my bunk. I swear the guy would hover outside the bathroom door when I take a piss if there was enough room on the bus to hover.

My heart rate picks up while the phone rings. What if he doesn't answer? What if he thinks I've lost my mind? What if—

"Hey, dude. Everything okay?"

Whew.

"Hey, Nash. Thanks for picking up. You have a sec? Sorry for the call but it's kind of urgent and I don't know when I'll get another chance. You know how it is on tour."

"One hundred percent. I have to restring my guitar, though. Mind if I put you on speaker. It's just Abram here."

Abram? Great. *That* won't help my pounding pulse. I've chatted with Redburn's iconic lead singer a few times since my dream-date hang with him last year (thanks to Nash), but I'm not sure you ever get used to interacting with your idols.

"Hi, Abram," I say.

"Hey, man. I've been loving what you and Larinda are putting out. Her stuff's actually good now. You're one helluva producer, dude."

And there go the rest of my words. Why am I on the phone again?

"Th-thanks. It's been fun working with her."

"We can tell. You two have great chemistry. You've got a good thing going."

"Which is why you won't screw it up with something silly like a relationship, right?" Nash says.

I swallow hard. Right.

"Oh. Yeah. No, of course not. That's actually why I'm calling."

Silence.

"Wait, no! Not because we're in a relationship. Just... I'm calling about her. Well, about a possible threat to her and I wanted to get your thoughts."

"Threat? Let me guess... Jarvis?" Nash grunts. "There's no chance that tour ends without someone losing an eye. I don't know what Lakebend was thinking putting them together."

That losing eyes make great headlines.

I hear the distinctive whine of a guitar string getting stretched and tuned.

"Sort of. Maybe? I don't know. That's what I'm trying to figure out. There's this guy on the tour named Chad."

And *that's* the distinctive *thunk* of a guitar string getting smacked.

"Hang on. You don't mean Chad Smith, right? Please tell me it's not Chad Smith."

"I think so. His business card says he's the *Talent Liaison* for Sandeke Telecom—along with a bunch of other shit I don't remember."

"Well, that's not good," Nash says.

"Is he the Mer-Berry dude?" Abram asks.

"Mer-Nut," Nash corrects. "Pretty sure they're nuts. Unless... Did this guy say anything about weird mermaids?" he asks me.

Ah. Those fish blobs were *Mer-Nuts*. That makes sense. Well, as much as that *can* make sense.

"Afraid so. I just dumped a bunch on the merch table."

And *that's* distinctive snort-laughing.

"Sandeke is sponsoring the tour," I mutter. "*Anyway*, that's not why I called. This Chad dude was saying some strange stuff about being a spy? I don't know. He made it sound like he's working for Jarvis, and with all the shit that went down last year between Larinda and Jarvis, I don't like it."

"Uh-oh. I was afraid of this. Have you talked to Steve, yet?" Nash asks, all humor gone from his voice.

"Her PA?"

"Yeah. He's a lot, but he's also loyal and knows everyone. You're right to be concerned. If your gut is telling you something's up, it probably is."

"Okay. I'll bring Steve into the loop when it feels right. So you don't think I'm overreacting?"

"There's no such thing as overreacting when it involves the diabolical partnership of Jarvis McKinnley and Sandeke Telecom. Neither have a shred of conscience or regard for anyone except themselves. I wouldn't discount any possible threat if it furthers their interests. You just have to figure out what that is. Once you know the endgame, you can decipher their plan and stop it."

Well, I already know what Jarvis wants: to be the only human in the universe.

"Hey. We got your back," Abram says. "You need any help, give us a ring."

"Thanks."

Because what help could I possibly need to singlehandedly take on the world's biggest country music star and telecom conglomerate in order to protect the woman I'm not allowed to love?

7—DALLAS (LARINDA'S DRESSING ROOM)

LARINDA

So, here's the thing…

I said yes.

I also didn't sleep a wink. In fact, even breathing has been a challenge since everything blew up at 7:57 last night. That was the moment Jarvis stalked onto the stage in the middle of my last song with a giant bouquet of roses, a flock of backup dancers, and a hot mic to sing two minutes of drivel asking me *"to be my o-o-only wife, for my lo-lo-lonely life."*

And I panicked.

Which means I forgot how to function.

Which means ten thousand people watched me slip into default mode and do what I was told to do:

Say yes.

I even cried like they wanted when I realized what I did and how much I regretted doing it.

Val hasn't said a word since. No visit to my bus demanding answers. No phone call. Not even a text. He wasn't backstage when I walked off with my new "fiancé." He wasn't at the "celebration party" or in attendance at the strategic video call with the label. He also wasn't on his bus when I pretended to look for Steve before returning to mine for the night. In fact, he wasn't anywhere I could find and I'm worried he didn't even follow us to Dallas.

I chew on my nail as I stare at my phone. My ***"Can we please talk?"*** still sits unanswered in our text stream. There are three more before that, also unanswered. Would he hate me enough to abandon the tour completely?

A cold rush spreads through me. What about our music? Did I also ruin the best thing that ever happened to my art? Did I really lose Val and my inspiration as a result of a single word?

Man, I hate the word "yes." I've spent my entire life saying yes, so maybe it's time to say no.

No to almonds.

No to itchy costumes they have to stitch and tape on me.

And definitely *no* to getting engaged to people you don't like.

The breathing thing is starting to become a real problem, and I scroll to my conversation with Steve.

Me: How's your bus this morning? Everyone sleep okay?

Steve would tell me if there was drama. You know, like if someone pooped in the shared bathroom (big no-no). Or if the air-conditioning broke down. Or… I don't know… if a certain producer never showed for roll-out and they left without him.

My phone buzzes, and I glance down, heart racing.

Steve: Fine. And no clue. Not everyone snores. Let's say sure? Everything okay?

Crap. What does "fine" mean? Is it fine as in *fine,* or fine as in *there's nothing worth discussing because I'm not the biggest fan of Val Andrews, so the fact that he quit the tour isn't on my radar?*

For the record, Steve's dislike for Val isn't personal. He doesn't like anyone who distracts my attention from him, and Val is incredibly distracting. My assistant was even jealous of Nash until my new friend helped me survive the world's worst video game festival last year—not to mention the whole Jarvis-trying-to-steal-my-songs scandal.

Jarvis.

My text stream with him is the mirror image of the one with Val. A whole bunch of gray messages litter the left side and almost no blue ones occupy the right. It's not that I don't want to respond to his gushy proclamations about our fake future together… actually, no. It is that.

Jarvis: Let's grab breakfast. We can hashtag this out.

No. My new favorite word dances through my head.

No, no, no.

I don't want to grab breakfast or *hashtag* anything with him. I have nothing to say. After years of sort-of sometimes dating, he knows I panic under pressure.

He knows how hard it is for me to fight a lifetime of being conditioned to follow orders. He also knew going ahead with the proposal after I explicitly told him not to would trigger both of those reactions and give him the "yes" he (and everyone else) wanted. He used me against myself, which only infuriates me more.

And now I may have lost Val.

I'm tempted to head over to the crew bus for a totally random hello to whichever crewmembers happen to be on that vehicle, but the reaction to that gesture would be even more dramatic than yesterday's breakfast appearance. Some days it sucks being a diva.

My phone buzzes again, and air rushes from my lungs at Val's name. He responded! But wait... what if it's bad?

Potential Val Text: I hate you and decided to relocate to Oklahoma City permanently. Don't call me. Also, your music sucks.

Well, probably not the last thing. He's too nice to say something like that. Plus, it's his music too, so that would be awkward.

With a shaky hand, I open the message.

Actual Val Text: **I'm not mad. Hurt, but not mad. We can talk. When's good?**

Potential Me Text: RIGHT THE HECK NOW!!!

Actual Me Text: **Whenever. I'm alone in my dressing room if you want to pop in now.**

My teeth sink into my lip as I watch my screen for a response.

Bubbles!

No bubbles.

More bubbles!

No bubbles.

Bubbles again and... ah! Is he trying to torture me as payback? Maybe. I guess in the grand scheme of things, agreeing to marry someone hours after telling another person you're secretly dating them is worse than being indecisive about what to say in a text message.

Val: Okay. Be there in 5.

Thank the heavens!

Me: Great. Bring your laptop so people think it's a work thing.

Val: Of course.

Me: I'm so sorry, baby. It was an accident, I swear. You're the only one I want. You're all I've thought about since. Please forgive me. Please don't give up on us. Please please please try to understand. I need you now more than ever. I'm not just upset, I'm scared. I didn't want this. I

DON'T want this. I'd do anything to be in your arms right now. I care about you so much, maybe even love—

DELETE!!!

I stare at the empty text box.

Actual Me Text: **Great. See you soon.**

* * *

Val looks tired when he peeks into the room, laptop in hand. Cute, because he always looks cute, but tired. Guess the night wasn't good for him, either.

His ball cap is off today, so his messy dark hair looks particularly tempting. I never told him this because our crushing was still a secret back then, but his new haircut from a few weeks ago is sexy as heck. The longer layers on top are the perfect length for gripping in the heat of passion, while the buzzed fade on the sides allows for the fun of tickling your fingers over the soft stubble. Having the chance to finally indulge in the fantasy yesterday makes this whole fiasco so much worse. All I want to do is climb in his lap and play with his hair (and other things). Instead, I'll be lucky if he ever lets me touch him again. Plus, the sweatpants. I don't know what it is with hot men in sweatpants, but he really shouldn't wear them if he doesn't want me lusting.

"Hey. Thanks for coming," I say.

"Of course. Thanks for inviting me."

So formal.

I feel a rare frown settle over my face.

You're in love with this man and engaged to another you can't stand.

That would make anyone frown, I guess.

I rub my palms on my yoga pants. "Would you, uh, like some alm…?"

I stop at the expression on his face. He probably doesn't want almonds.

"I don't love Jarvis," I blurt out.

"I know."

"Oh."

I bite my lip and watch his fingers tighten around the laptop. They should be touching me instead. I should be enjoying the heat of his body, the taste of his lips that got to be mine for five whole minutes. Funny how I did everything I could to prevent Jarvis from sitting beside me in this same scenario, and now I'm doing everything I can to encourage Val.

But he doesn't budge, so I'm stuck in the middle of a couch, staring up at him as he waits for me to explain why I'm engaged to someone else.

"I panicked."

He stays quiet as his gaze sifts over my face.

"I told him not to do it, but then there were the dancers and the feathers and the horrific A-A rhyme scheme and I just… I don't know what happened."

"You said yes. That's what happened."

I wince. "Yeah, but I didn't mean *yes*."

"Right. So by yes you meant no?"

His jaw clenches, and I chew on my nail again. When his attention shifts to the jewelry case on the table, I cringe at the obnoxious ring glaring from the top pouch. I don't know how many carats that diamond is but it would feed a family of rabbits for a week. Pretty sure Jarvis told the jeweler to take their five most ridiculous rings and smoosh them together. Then had them add a gold twig for some reason.

"I told him yesterday we're not a couple," I say in a pleading tone. "I will tell him again today. I'll tell him every day. The whole world, even! I don't care about my career anymore. It's not worth these games and lies. I just want you, Val. You and the music are the only real things in my life. I'm so sorry."

I hold my breath as his eyes follow the path of his finger along a seam of the couch.

"Say something. Please."

He sighs and looks up. "What do you want me to say, Larinda?"

"Anything!"

"The pumpkin flies at midnight."

I can't help a snort. "*What?*"

"I don't know. I heard my sister say it once and it's been haunting me ever since."

"What does it mean?"

"No idea." His weak smile hurts as he lowers his gaze again. "I should probably go."

"Val… please."

"It's okay. I get it."

"You don't! Clearly you don't."

His eyes land on mine again, soft and open with everything I love about him. He's always so beautiful and kind, despite the pain he wrestles with inside. I hate that I'm the reason he's hurting right now.

"I do. We live in different worlds with different rules," he says. "I'm not mad. I will always support you and be here for you no matter who you choose or what—"

I jump up and capture his face in my hands. He tenses, but I don't let go. I can't. The only time I truly feel like myself is when we're together.

"It's you," I whisper. "It's just you."

When I kiss him, it only takes a second for the fire between us to burn away the obstacles. After shoving the laptop on the table, he tangles his fingers in my hair and tilts my head to deepen the connection. I can't stop the slight moan at how good it feels to have him again. I wasn't lying. I would give up everything for this man, and the fact that he would never ask that of me is just more of a testament to the treasure I'm holding.

I slide one hand up his neck as the other grasps the messy locks I've been craving since the last time he was mine. Our mouths melt together, our bodies sliding and locking in all the right places. I'm desperate to drag him back to the couch and show him how much I want him.

He runs his palms down my back, guiding my front into an aching collision with his. Our kiss becomes ravenous as my insides buzz with pent-up electricity. I need to feel his bare skin on mine, to explore more of him—*all* of him—and I grip the hem of his shirt to strip it off. But he stops me with a gentle hold on my wrist.

My disappointment fades at the tender expression on his face.

"Talk to Jarvis," he says, framing my cheek with his other hand. "Take time to figure out what you really want. The stakes are too high to rush into anything."

I know what I want. I literally have it in my hands, but he's right. This is too important to mess up, and it's not fair of me to ask him to ignore the fact that I'm formally engaged to someone else.

After one last kiss, I rest my cheek on his shoulder and burrow into his warmth. He locks his arms around me and presses his lips to my head. If I could stay here forever, I would.

"I'll talk to Jarvis again and make sure he understands," I murmur. "I promise I'm going to fix this. I want *you*, just you. Will you please forgive me and still be my secret boyfriend?"

I feel his sharp inhale at my words. The long silence has my heart pounding. After way too many seconds, he sighs and drops another soft kiss on my hair.

"Talk to Jarvis, then we'll discuss the rest."

8—DALLAS (JARVIS' DRESSING ROOM)

VAL

These are the factors that led to me being alone with Chad in Jarvis' dressing room:

1. I left Larinda's dressing room reeling and completely lacking presence of mind.
2. Chad decided he forgave me for possibly being a spy and needed my help with an *exceedingly* important project.
3. I might actually be a spy and this seemed like a great opportunity to do spy shit.
4. Rena from Lakebend Records said I have to.

"Should we put the cutout against the wall or beside the mirror? Beside the mirror, right?"

I don't respond because Chad is talking to some older man on a video call, not me. He's talked to this person at least twice a day since the start of the tour. Last night it seemed like the call was for the sole purpose of saying good night. It was weird even before he referred to the man as "Mr. Reedweather."

Despite the dramatic pretense, as far as I can tell this "exceedingly important project" doesn't seem to involve me at all, however. I thought it might get me facetime with Jarvis to further my goal of unearthing any scheming plots against Larinda, but mostly it's entailed listening to these two speak in a made-up code that's incredibly easy to decipher. Jarvis isn't even here.

Correction. Technically, I *am* getting facetime with that scheming jerk, it just happens to be a life-sized cardboard face at the top of a life-sized cardboard cutout of the man. Interestingly, the only distinguishable difference between the real man and the cardboard version is the *"It's a streamin' thang!"* slogan plastered across the middle of the cardboard version. For the record, the three-minute ode to Sandeke Telecom's internet service that spawned this now-famous catchphrase somehow hit two charts.

"Is there a radiator?" the man named Reedweather asks.

"Not that I can see," Chad replies.

"That's too bad. They say it's always best to place things in front of radiators whenever possible." His sage tone almost makes that seem like irrefutable advice.

Put things in front of radiators. Got it.

"How about by the mirror, then?" Reedweather says.

"Excellent suggestion, sir!" Chad agrees, forgetting that was his idea twelve seconds ago.

He moves fake Jarvis, who's already stationed in front of the wall-length mirrors, three inches to the left.

"Any word on Project Hummingbird?" Reedweather asks.

My brain immediately switches to "actual information" mode when Chad's gaze flickers to me.

"Nothing of note to report. All is going according to plan."

He winks at me.

"Excellent. So you've developed a plan?"

"So many plans! Prepare to be astounded when you read the report. I've added twenty-three crystals and even recruited a valuable asset."

Another wink for me. The crystal thing—no clue—but am I the asset? It's either me or cutout Jarvis, so I guess it's me. I suppose beating out a piece of paper for a job I don't want is better than losing to it.

"That's my boy. *Dogmatic Positioning* as they say. Well, I must go. Important things, you know."

"Of course! I keep forgetting it's Friday. I'll call you later."

"No need. I'll still be doing important things then."

"It's totally fine! I don't mind. Have a great day, sir. Tell Mary Lou I said hello. Oh, and check your email because I may have sent a teensy-weensy surprise. Hint: *it's the table of contents for the report!*"

I'm pretty sure the man hung up a while ago, but Chad doesn't seem to notice.

"That's my boss," he tells me after shoving his phone in his pocket. "Well, *our* boss now."

No.

"Thanks for helping with this. I couldn't have done it without you," he continues.

"I mean… I haven't really done anything." Except lean against this wall. If that's why I'm here, I'm nailing it.

"Don't say that! Reedweather thinks you're great!"

"Really? That's… okay. So, the guy you talk to all the time is your boss?"

"Yep."

"Cool."

Wait, is he putting makeup on the cutout?

"To reduce the shine," he explains as he brushes powder over the photo's cheeks.

"Don't you pay to have a glossy finish?"

"Yes, but the gloss is for public displays, not the photoshoot."

"There's a photoshoot?"

"Of course." He steps back to admire his work. "What do you think?"

That it looks like a cardboard cutout of Jarvis that used to have a shiny face but now has a powdered substance on it.

"It's… tall."

"I know, right?! So tall. You ready?" He waves me toward the cutout.

"Ready for what?"

"To be famous, silly!" His expression clearly isn't interpreting mine.

"Huh?"

He pulls a camera from the bag.

Hang on. No. *Hell* no.

"Don't take this the wrong way, but the left is probably your stronger side," he says.

"You want me to pose with this thing?"

"Absolutely. Why do you think I invited you here?"

For literally any reason *other* than posing with a life-sized image of Jarvis in his dressing room.

"I—I'm not sure that's a good idea. I work for Larinda, not Jarvis. I'm not comfortable giving the impression he and I hang out."

"Exactly." Another wink.

Okay, what's up with the winking?

"No. I mean it."

"I know. That's why it's perfect. Plus, you have the look the committee wants."

"What committee?"

"The campaign committee."

"Chad, I'm sorry, but I have no clue what the hell you're talking about."

He sighs as if he's the one being put out by this conversation. "You know. The *look*! Edgy but not aloof. Cool but not too cool. Good-looking but not unattainable. Gen Z-ish but not fully Gen Z, you know?"

He waves over me. His bright smile is the only reason I know those were supposed to be compliments.

"Chad. Dude. I think—"

"As soon as Rena suggested you this morning, we loved the idea."

"Rena *suggested* me?"

"Of course. You're a good-looking guy, my friend. You should give yourself more credit. Versatile too. You ever think about stripping? I have a friend who could get you set up. Remember the guy I was telling you about?"

"The ophthalmologist?"

"No! But that would be amazing. Can you imagine those appointments? I'm talking about Nate."

"The one who went to Yorkshire."

"No, that was Marcos, but he could help too, maybe. I'd have to check. Nate is an amazing instructor, though, so try him first. Taught me everything I know."

"About...?"

"Stripping."

"Hold on. *You're* a stripper?"

"I don't like labels, Val. Some dibble, some dabble. Anyway, you don't have to pretend to kiss him or anything. Just maybe put your arm around him?"

"Huh? Kiss who?"

I'm so lost.

"Jarvis. Obviously."

He throws his arm around the large cardboard figure, and now I'm even more confused about why the ideal place for this activity would be in front of a radiator.

"You can leave your shirt on."

What?

"Okay, look, man. I appreciate the vote of confidence, but I think we need to—"

Saved by the crashing door... until it leads to real Jarvis and several members of his entourage.

Awesome, because *that's* what this scenario was missing. A pompous jackass who hates me.

"Mr. McKinnley!" Chad cries. Then bows.

Jarvis twists a quick smile before landing his cold gaze on me.

"For the record, I'm not a fan of this," he directs at me.

That makes two of us. Whatever "this" is.

"Liquify me," he barks, snapping his fingers.

Within seconds a servant—I mean, assistant—shoves a glass of lemon water into his hand. He takes maybe half a sip before handing it back.

"Let's get this over with," he grunts, stomping toward the slightly faker version of himself. I can't help but notice they're wearing the same outfit.

Chad pretends to adjust settings on his camera, while Jarvis pretends he's not standing beside a replica of himself. The ease with which he does this makes me think that might be a standard part of his day. If anyone would interact with a life-sized reproduction of themself on a regular basis, it would be this person.

"Let's do the cutout image first," Chad says.

Jarvis steps back to make room for something. When five gazes lock on me, I realize I'm the something he made room for.

I still don't know what I'm supposed to do.

"Don't smile in this one," Chad tells me.

That shouldn't be hard.

"You will have to get closer and maybe look at him?"

"Who?" I ask.

"Jarvis."

"Cutout or real?"

"Cutout. I just said that."

"Yes but... never mind," I grumble, then plaster a fake smile on my face.

"I said *don't* smile for this one."

Oh. Right.

"Don't look unhappy, though. You're glad to be in the presence of such musical magnificence, just not smiling about it. You're overwhelmed... but with awe, you know?"

I pull in a deep breath.

"Perfect! Don't move."

Do I look different than I did a second ago? Because I still feel like a guy who would rather be doing anything other than this.

"Okay, I think we got it. Oh wait! No. You need to take off your security badge. You can't look like you're part of the tour."

"I *am* part of the tour. And I'm literally in his dressing room."

"Yeah, but it's about the *aesthetic*."

"The *aesthetic*? I don't—"

"Quit being a whiny wasp and just do what he says," Jarvis snaps.

I shoot him a glare and rip the lanyard over my head.

"Yes! Keep that face but turn it toward Jarvis… other Jarvis. Great! Now, Real Jarvis."

I'm already in a living nightmare when Real Jarvis shifts closer. Too close because his denim jacket brushes my arm, and I'm nearly choked out by the aggressive cologne he's wearing. Does he get daily sandalwood injections?

"You need to look at each other. You're besties now!"

Nope.

Jarvis slings his arm around me and tugs me against him.

"Smile," he growls through a clenched grin.

I force something that can't be worse than what his mouth is doing.

"Perfect!" Chad says.

Jarvis immediately drops his arm and jumps away like he just realized we were touching. No confusion on my end.

"We done?" he snaps. "I need to get to hair and makeup."

Seven hours before the show?

"Yes, sir, Mr. McKinnley, sir!" Chad says.

"Great. This changes nothing," Jarvis fires at me as he stalks toward the door. "Nothing. If anything, it un-changes things that already changed!"

"Absolutely. Not a thing," I say. "Unless it's the unchanging things."

His forehead gets all scrunchy. "You know what they say about people who stick their noses where they don't belong."

"No. What?"

I see the moment he discovers he might not know what people say about that.

"Never mind. Send those to my publicist. Do not post a thing yourself," he directs at Chad, who salutes.

"Aye, aye, Captain. Break a leg tonight! Dallas, am I right? So many horseshoes."

Jarvis grunts and yanks open the door. Then must realize it's his dressing room.

"Out," he growls, waving at those of us who aren't him.

Gladly.

In a perfect world, I will never again find myself in his dressing room (or near a radiator if this is their main purpose).

He spins away from us and immediately gets lost in his own reflection. He probably doesn't even remember we're here once he sees himself.

I'm eagerly following Chad to the exit when I see the open notebook he tossed on a chair by the door earlier. Are those scribbles song lyrics?

Step 1. Get engaged.

Wow. Pure poetry.

Step 2. Get her to dump me.

Whoa. What the hell?

I glance at Jarvis but he's still busy admiring himself while being "liquified" more aggressively now.

I check the notebook again and see an equally concerning message beside the second one:

(Better if she cheats!!)

This is not good.

What else did Jarvis write in this disturbing memo to himself? Pulling out my phone, I check his status one last time. For once his lack of awareness for anyone but himself is a benefit to society.

"You coming?" Chad hisses from down the hall.

"Yeah," I whisper, then snap a photo of the notebook.

9—DALLAS (RESTRICTED AREA)

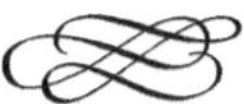

VAL

"You wanna help me write the report?" Chad asks as we retreat from Jarvis' dressing room.

My mind is reeling, my heart racing at what I just found. Those ominous notes could only be referring to one person and one relationship. I'm desperate to review the photo and learn more of Jarvis' bid to hurt Larinda, but not until I'm alone. I can't trust anyone, especially the world's worst spy right here.

"It's for the big boss," Chad adds with a sly smile I'm in no mood to interpret.

What are we even talking about?

"Hey, I'm gonna head back to the bus," I say.

His expression falls. "So you don't want to write the report with me?"

"What report?"

"*The* report. For Mr. Sandeke."

I'm so lost. Who the hell is Mr. Sandeke and why does he need a report?

"Thanks, but I'm good."

Chad looks disappointed, but I don't know how I'd be any help writing a report for someone I don't know about things I also don't know.

"Fine, then I'm not putting your name on it."

"That's fair. I'll see you later."

"Where are you going?"

"Just need to—"

"Hey! You can't be back here!"

We freeze at the hostile shout and twist back to find three large, disgruntled men stalking toward us.

Security. Crap.

"No, it's fine. I'm with Larinda," I say at the same time Chad says "I'm with Jarvis."

Double crap.

The security guards must not be moved by our assurances when they form a human wall and motion us in the opposite direction.

"Seriously, guys. I'm Val Andrews, Larinda's producer," I say, stepping toward them. Frustrated, I reach for my all-access badge, and…

Oh shit. I left my pass in Jarvis' dressing room!

"And I'm with Jarvis!" Chad repeats, adding a salute that doesn't actually help.

"You're with Jarvis," a guard says dryly. Okay, I do *skeptical* but this guy nails it as he scans Chad's pink polo shirt and khakis.

"Yes. I'm Chad Smith, the Administrative Talent Liaison for Reedweather Media vis a vis Sandeke Telecom. I'd give you my card but they're gone."

A hundred percent sure Chad's business card wouldn't get us out of this situation anyway.

"Great, so that means you both have security passes," another guard says. The way he's looking at our chests means he's noticed we don't have those.

"Yes. And we do," I reply as calmly as possible. "It's just, I left mine in Jarvis' dressing room and—"

"I thought you said you're *Larinda's* producer," the man says, crossing his arms.

"I am, but—"

"It was for the Smile Surprise photo campaign," Chad explains. "Well, and for the report, but mostly the campaign. We haven't decided whether to include images in the reports," he whispers to me.

I fire a hard return look and silently beg him to stop "helping." He winks.

"Media aren't allowed back here. No one is without a pass. Let's move."

They grab our arms and drag us in the opposite direction of where I need to go.

"I'm telling the truth!" I say, tugging against their grip. "Call Larinda. Steve, Bruce—anyone! They'll tell you."

"We don't have to. That's why there are passes."

"Yeah, but—"

He jerks me forward, and I try to rip my arm away. All hope of a brazen escape fades when someone grabs my other side.

Shit shit shit!

"Let go of me!"

"We've got a situation in corridor E," the third says into an earpiece.

A *situation?!*

"OMG. We're getting arrested," Chad whisper-shouts.

How is he happy about this?!

"I'm telling the truth!" I say. "We're part of the crew. We have bunks on the—"

"Shut your mouth or we'll shut it for you."

Would he? I can't tell but he definitely stole that line from page two of the training manual for fictional mobsters.

Fear and anger course through me as they lead us to an empty room at the end of the hall. Panic joins the mix when they force us inside. Can they do this? Don't they need a warrant or something? I want to see that manual.

"You'll wait here until we sort this out," one of them barks.

The other one is still talking into his earpiece. "Yeah, we got two for trespassing. Maybe one for assault and attempted kidnapping."

What?!

"Yeah, call them in. The tall one is being difficult. Blond one is cooperating. We've got the suspects in the northeast holding tank."

What is happening right now?

"We'll be back," the guy growls, then slams the door.

I don't even bother checking to see if it's locked.

"This is so friggin' cool! I've always wanted to get arrested!" Chad cries.

I clench my fist and glare at him. "We're not arrested, and this is *not* cool."

"I can be in a documentary now!"

"That's not how that works. Dammit! This wouldn't even have happened if you hadn't made me take off my security badge. Wait, why aren't you wearing *yours*?"

He shrugs. "Same reason. It was getting in the way of the camera. All tangled up, you know?"

He fishes through his pocket.

And pulls out his badge.

"You had your pass this whole time?! Why didn't you show it to them?!"

He gives me a patient look as he loops the lanyard around his neck. "Because you didn't have yours. If you were going to prison, so was I. Leave no man behind."

That's... kind of sweet, actually. Also ludicrous.

Ah!

I lock my hands on my head as I start pacing. We have to figure this out before the real cops come. I pissed off security just enough to give them incentive to make my life difficult. The Mer-Nut king over there will be fine with his "cooperation" label (and badge he magically found), but I'm still screwed unless we come up with a solution.

I pull out my phone to call Larinda but there's no service in this arena dungeon. Of course not. Why would something swing my way?

"Fuck," I mumble, lowering to a squat while I think. Within seconds, I'm fully seated on the cold, concrete floor, leaning against the wall of our "cell."

Chad looks like he's rehearsing for his documentary interview.

"Do you think I should have an accent?" he asks. "I should, right? Possibly from Oregon? They have the best trees if you're into that sorta thing."

I don't even understand the question enough to respond.

"What exactly is it you do for Jarvis?" I ask instead. "Why are you here?"

Maybe it's all an act with this guy. Maybe he's really some genius covert operative who does this crap to trick people into letting down their guard. Then when you least expect it—

"Oh man! I think this ginormous pile of boxes is all paper towels. It can't be, right? What would you even do with that many paper towels?!"

Or not.

When he approaches the mountain of janitorial supplies, I prepare to stop him from whatever bad idea is forming in his head. There's no way I'm restacking those before going to prison for not having the proper badge.

"You said you're a spy," I continue, trying to distract him from getting us in more trouble. "What exactly is your… mission?"

Yep. I just said that, but it's totally worth it when he forgets all about the towel windfall and drops to the floor in front of me.

He leans forward and scans the empty room as if there might be surveillance. If there is, I'm positive they're way more concerned about Chad messing up their piles than whatever he's about to say.

"I could get in a lot of trouble for telling you that. There's a code, you know."

"Yeah… I got that. But if I'm going to be your… *asset*, you'll have to tell me what I'm supposed to do, right?"

"Hmm. Good point." He wraps his arms around his legs and rests his chin on his knees. "Okay, I'll tell you, but you can't freak out and blow our cover."

Pretty sure we're way past that.

"I promise."

He nods and checks once more for the invisible threat. "The powers that be think Larinda is up to something."

I nearly choke and come dangerously close to breaking my promise of *not freaking out* (with laughter).

"Are you serious?"

"Of course. One never makes light of spy subversions. It's in the code. You'd know this if you helped with the report."

"Right. Sorry."

"Anywho, you know how Larinda is the spokesperson for Brighthouse like Jarvis is for Sandeke Telecom?"

"She used to be, but not anymore."

"Or so she *says*."

"No, she really isn't."

He winks. "Exactly. She *isn't*."

"She isn't."

"Okay, well, she might be, and if she is, then she's probably planning her revenge."

Her revenge? Larinda doesn't even hurt insects. Not kidding, she's terrified of them but insists on having them safely removed from a room and reinhabited in their natural environments.

But I've learned arguing with this guy gets you nowhere except a locked storage closet with a crap-ton of paper towels.

"Revenge for what?" I ask.

"Do you remember about a year ago when fellow telecom giant Brighthouse had that ransomware attack during their video game event that almost ruined them but sadly didn't?"

Disturbingly, I do. Very well, since my sister and good friend Nash were a huge part of that whole blowup. But I'm thinking that information might hurt my chances at more intel, so I keep it to myself. Dirty spy move? Probably, but desperate times…

"I remember something about it," I say casually.

"Well, we did that. *I* did that."

Pretty sure Nash and Paige did it, but whatever.

"Okay. So what does this have to do with the tour and Jarvis?"

"That's what I'm here to find out," he says in a low voice. Oddly, he doesn't wink with this one. It felt like a winking moment.

"So you don't actually know why you're here."

Guess that makes two of us.

"Don't be silly! Sandeke Telecom is sponsoring this tour. I'm representing their interests."

"But you don't know what those interests are."

He opens his mouth to argue, then closes it again. Then furrows his brow and huffs. "Well, I also run our merch table."

Oh right. The mutant fish.

He waves me off. "Anywho, the point is, if Larinda and Brighthouse are planning to exact their revenge on Sandeke and Jarvis for the ransomware thing, I'm here to stop it."

I have zero faith he'd be able to do that, but since there's also zero chance of that happening, I guess the math works.

"Okay, well, I can assure you that Larinda does not represent Brighthouse anymore and therefore has no intention of *exacting revenge* on anyone."

"Right."

Now he winks?

My response is cut off by scraping at the door, but any relief fades when it opens to what appears to be an entire *contingent* of security personnel. Fantastic…

Accompanying the three guards who "arrested" us is a woman who could be their boss, two people who look like actual police officers—and Jarvis. It's the last one that scares me the most, especially when he settles a vicious look on me.

Yeah, I'm guessing he's not here to return my badge.

"These guys with you?" the woman who's probably the security boss asks.

"He is, not him."

I don't need to see Jarvis' emphatic finger point to know which of us got which label.

"You, out," the woman says to Chad. Her gaze drifts to the lanyard that's now around his neck, and I see the confusion on her face before she pats herself on the back for resolving this crisis.

"You can go back to work. You, come with us," she says to me.

"But I—"

"Didn't we discuss this already? Do we have to put you in real jail?" one of the guards says. Jarvis' smug look might be worse than the prospect of real jail.

"No, of course not," I rush out when someone grabs my arm. "He's right. I don't work for him. I'm with Larinda. Like I said from the beginning!"

"Right. You're with Larinda but your pass is with Jarvis," another guard says. "You holding on to his pass for him?" he asks Jarvis.

Well, I know what that response will be.

"Not that I know of," Jarvis replies with a sneer. "We done here? I was in the middle of having my belt loops redone."

"Of course, Mr. McKinnley. We apologize for the disruption."

"He hates me!" I cry. "Of course he's going to—"

"*You* need to shut your mouth," the head guard snaps at me. "You're in enough trouble."

I clench my fist in frustration and turn to my last hope. Chad and I were besties a minute ago. "The code" and all that? But his apologetic look doesn't inspire a ton of confidence. Nor does the long string of words he mouths that I can't interpret.

He's still talking silently when the crowd of security personnel drag me down the hall in the other direction. How many resources are being wasted to bust a guy for dropping a lanyard?

"Leave no man behind, right?" I call out, twisting back for a targeted look at Chad.

He nods. Then winks.

10—DALLAS (SIDE LOT)

LARINDA

I spot him immediately. It's not hard when your heart and mind are wired to find someone… or when there's only one person in a parking lot.

Val is slumped against the side of the building, his head resting on his knees. I'm not sure how long he's been there, but his SOS messages had been on my phone for over an hour before I saw them. After telling a few white lies to escape Steve, I rushed here as soon as I could.

Thankfully, it's early enough in the day that there aren't many people around. Any fans would be lining up at the main entrance, and most concert personnel have been confined to the back lot. This small side entrance must not be used for much other than ejecting badge-less trespassers.

"Val?"

He glances up, his eyes flooding with relief and exhaustion.

"Larinda? Hey. Sorry to bother you with this, but I didn't want to involve anyone else in the drama."

He pushes up from the gravel as I approach.

"I totally get it. Good call. Besides…"

After scanning the area to make sure we're alone, I take his hand and thread our fingers. When I bring them to my lips, he closes his eyes with a long exhale.

"What happened?" I ask.

His gaze flickers to me before lowering. "Long story. Short version is I lost my all-access pass and they kicked me out of the venue. Do you think we can get another one?"

There's a waver in his voice I've never heard before. He's always so composed, so strong.

"Hey, what is it? You okay?"

I brush his cheek to force him to look at me. His green eyes are particularly captivating in the sunlight. I hate that they're filled with pain right now.

"Yeah, of course. Just a stupid misunderstanding."

"Val."

He shrugs. "It's nothing. Not worth getting into."

"It's not? Because you look awful."

"Great. Thanks."

I roll my eyes. "You know what I mean. I'm worried about you."

"I know. I'm fine. Really."

He pulls me against him, and I sigh as I slip my arms around him. Everything feels better once I absorb the solid warmth of his body and breathe in his familiar scent. Woody and fresh, with a touch of citrus—it's like a drug for me now. I absently run my fingers along the hem of his sweatpants at his lower back.

"We shouldn't be standing here like this. Someone might see us," he says quietly. But he doesn't seem any more eager to let go than I am.

"We'll just tell them we're role-playing a song for lyric inspiration."

His chuckle sends a soft breeze through me. My world is always lighter when he laughs.

"I think the lyrics for 'Third Last Kiss' could use some work," he says with a glint in his eyes.

"Is that so?" I brush my lips over his. "How much work?"

"So much." He cups my face and drags me in for a real kiss.

The fire is immediate and all-consuming.

I grip his hair as he flips us around and crowds me against the side of the building. His hard body presses into me, rubbing in all the best places. My hips are already writhing for more, and he deepens the kiss to arouse more hot, needy anticipation. I can't get enough as he rocks against me again and again, each thrust swelling into a deep ache of longing. It feels amazing, and I love how easily the sweet boy I love becomes a sexy hunter when I want him to be.

Like now.

In the parking lot.

Where anyone could see us.

He must have the same thought when he breaks the kiss with a frustrated sigh and rests his forehead on mine. Eyes closed, bodies still locked in excruciating alignment, we breathe through the tension for several long seconds.

"What am I going to do with you?" I whisper, my insides still sparking and sizzling. How am I supposed to let him go?

"I'm a big fan of this," he replies with an adorable smile. I'd give up everything for that smile, and it fades way too fast.

"I'm going to find a way," I say softly, running my fingers along his jaw.

He searches my eyes for a moment and I don't like the doubt I see there. In me or himself?

My phone buzzes in my pocket like some kind of alarm clock for fantasies.

Wake up! Your sucky situation is waiting! Also, parking lots are bad places for secret rendezvouses!

"Remaining," I say as I reluctantly straighten from the wall.

"Remaining?"

"The second line of the first verse in 'Third Last Kiss.' It should be remaining instead of waiting."

A slow grin leaks onto his face as he shakes his head in amusement.

"Nice edit," he says.

"Thanks for helping with the research."

His laugh earns one more kiss before I check the message on my phone.

11—DALLAS (RESERVED ROOM)

LARINDA

Yep. Totally forgot about brunch with my family. I wasn't entirely sure there *was* a plan for brunch. They live an hour from the venue, which is just enough time to make a visit required, but not enough for me to travel. My call-time is five tonight, so a brunch date at the venue seemed like the perfect compromise. Well, until getting caught up in the drama with Val and totally forgetting about it.

Thankfully, there's an easy solution.

"Are you sure about this?" Val mumbles as I practically drag him through the building toward the room Bruce and Steve arranged for our reunion. He looks concerned as he scans the halls for some hidden threat, and I can't tell if it's nerves about meeting my family or fear of getting abducted by the Badge Police again. Either way, it's so hard not to take his hand, but we can't risk any PDA on this tour. (Fine, any *more* PDA.)

"So sure," I say, glancing back at him.

Doubt flickers in his eyes, causing a pinch in my chest. How can he so effortlessly flood others with confidence, but not have any in himself? His name is already popping up in conversations about elite producers. People are constantly flirting with him, both professionally and romantically. (Although, since he's always the same level of polite, I can never tell how much he notices or cares.) I've even had a few mega-star friends ask about him for their own work. Despite all of this, he still sees himself as an unknown dreamer playing with beats at his kitchen table. Sometimes the humility is refreshing. Most of the time, it makes me want to strap him to a chair in a million-dollar studio and force him to see how amazing he is.

Also, that might be illegal, but whatever.

"Don't you want time alone with them?" he asks, slowing as we approach the open door. A shrill laugh blares from inside. Guess they're here.

I grab his sleeve and yank him forward.

"Pretty sure they'll want to see you more than me," I say.

"What?" Now he really looks concerned. "They know about me?"

I squint at this highly intelligent, clueless man. "Do they know about the extremely talented producer who revolutionized my music and has become the talk of the industry? Yeah, they've heard of you."

"You know what I mean."

I sigh and press him against the wall beside the door, just out of view.

"They know how important you are to me," I say gently. "Hey…" I tug his sleeve when his worried gaze drifts to the door. "They're going to love you."

Anxious green eyes land back on me, and then it hits me. Of course he's nervous about meeting my family. I've seen what the word "family" means to him. Those are the people who tell you you're worthless. Who drag you down and mock your dreams. They freaking extort money they know you don't have just to hurt you. Gosh.

My heart hurts as I slide my hand down his arm and squeeze his hand.

"They're going to love you," I repeat. "I promise."

He returns a tentative nod, but words won't convince him. I'll just have to show him.

After a final reassuring squeeze, I release his hand and move toward the door.

"Eeeek!" Mama screams, arms flailing as she runs toward me.

Within seconds I'm laughing through a crushing two-person hug. Then three. Then four. Geez, how many are there?

We're a knot of laughter and limbs as we greet each other like it's been years, not three weeks since I was home for Tia's twenty-first birthday party.

"Hey, everyone. I can't believe you all came!" I say, warming at the sight of the entire family. Wait, is that my aunt Lucy and uncle Howard? Unsurprisingly, my mother's sister and brother-in-law are more interested in critiquing the offerings on the refreshment table than greeting me.

"And you must be Val!" Mama cries, turning her gush on him.

Val stiffens when she throws her arms around him and administers the patented Scott Family greeting. I'd intervene but it's kind of adorable. He has no idea what to do as she squeals and squeezes, and when Dad goes in for a hug as well, Val looks totally lost. He doesn't seem upset, though. In fact, I detect the slightest smile peeking out.

"Well, look at you!" Mama says, scanning Val from head to toe. "Look at him, Randall," she directs at my father.

"I'm looking," Dad says.

"Aren't you a cutie pie? Larinda, why didn't you tell us he was so handsome? Isn't he handsome, CeCe?" she shouts to my aunt.

"Stunning," she calls back without looking up from her inventory of the bagels. I see the spreadsheet and rating system already at work in her head. After fifty-some years of data collection, that thing must be massive.

Val does, in fact, look stunned. I'll give her that.

"Ah! I just want to eat him up. Don't you want to eat him up, Randall?"

Dad doesn't look as excited about eating my producer but claps him on the arm just the same.

"It's great to finally meet you, son. You're younger than I thought. You can't be much older than Tiara."

He motions toward my sister, who's already blasting giant heart eyes at my secret boyfriend. Crap. Didn't think about that. To be fair, I didn't know Tia was coming. Or Aunt Lucy. Or Uncle Howard.

I scan the room for more hidden family members, and sure enough, my baby brother, Ian, is stretched out on the couch playing some game on his phone. He probably doesn't even know I arrived.

"You single, Val?" Dad asks.

"Randall!" Mom cries. "But are you?"

"Mom!" I say.

"What? It's a fair question."

"Tiara's single," Dad explains to me. "From what you've described, he'd be a great son-in-law. Best to keep it in the family, right?"

Oh my gosh.

"Don't listen to them," I grunt as I take Val's arm and pull him further into the room. "Anyway, hello, everyone. This is Val Andrews. Val, this is my mother; father; sister, Tiara; brother, Ian; along with my aunt and uncle."

"The 'everything' bagels have fennel seeds," Uncle Howard calls by way of a greeting. "I despise fennel seeds."

"It's fine, Howie," Mama says. "So, Val, tell us all about yourself."

"Um, well—"

"You're from New York City, right?" Dad asks. "A real tough guy, huh?"

"Oh. Uh, not really. I mean—"

"Yes! Look at those muscles," Mama says. "CeCe, did you see his muscles?"

"There's no chive-and-onion cream cheese, either, Ruby," my aunt says. "There's no chive-and-onion cream cheese," she also tells me.

"Not too much muscle, though," Mama continues. "The perfect amount, really. Don't you think, Tiara?"

My sister bites her lip like she has plenty of thoughts about Val's muscles, but thankfully is too shy to share them. I wish my parents had that issue. I knew they'd love him. I didn't prepare for the fact that they'd love him too much.

"Hey, so the new hamster. How's that going?" I cut in before this weird conversation can resume.

For the record, I also think Val has the perfect amount of muscles but that's not something I ever planned on telling him. It's not something anyone should ever tell anyone, really. Which means it would be the first thing my parents say.

"It smells like shit!" Ian calls over from the couch.

"Ian!" Mama cries. "Apologize right now!"

"To what? The hamster that's not even here? Sorry, Muffy!" Ian declares in a dry tone.

Mama crosses her arms and shoots a glare at my brother. Typically, I'd jump in to prevent this from escalating, but Muffy's odor is a vast improvement over the previous topic. I know Val thinks so as he shifts awkwardly, waiting to see what will be thrown at him next. His smile is more amused than offended, though, and the relief is real. This could have been way worse.

"That's quite the interesting tattoo you have beside your eye," Dad says. "Don't see a lot of face tats in our circles. What's it mean?"

Like that, for example.

"Dad," I groan. "Don't answer that," I say to Val.

"We're just curious, sweetheart," Mama says.

"Yes, but—"

"It's fine," Val cuts in with an uncomfortable smile. "It's a long story. Short version is my parents were upset about my life choices and said if I ever got a face tattoo, they'd disown me. So I did."

Oh.

My own parents are silent for maybe the first time ever as they study Val with shocked, sad expressions. My stomach aches when his jaw clenches like he's fighting something heavy and dark. I've often wondered about the tiny X by his eye. It seemed like such a simple and insignificant design to put in arguably the most prominent place on your body. Guess there's nothing "insignificant" about it after all. There's definitely more to this story.

"Wow. And did they disown you?" Tia asks.

I fire a glare at my sister, but she's glued to Val like Jarvis to his own reflection.

"Yeah," he says in a flat tone.

More silence.

"They sound like dicks," Ian adds, looking up from his game.

A smile tugs at Val's lips as he shrugs. Mama doesn't even yell at Ian for that one.

After several long seconds, she claps her hands and turns to me with an overly enthusiastic smile. "So tell us about the engagement! We want every gory detail."

Well, crap.

Val's expression dims again as I swallow air down my very dry throat. I think I need a bagel too. I don't mind fennel.

"It's good," I mumble on my way to the snack table.

A neat pile of fennel seeds now rests beside the tray of bagels. A second pile of onion flakes is amassing beside it as Uncle Howard takes issue with that garnish as well. He knows there are plain ones, right?

"Larinda! We drove all this way to congratulate you in person," Mama chides, tugging me around by the elbow.

"You drove less than an hour, and you didn't even know I was going to be engaged when we discussed this."

I certainly didn't. In fact, now is the perfect time to tell them it's not real. That I'll be breaking it off and—

"Well, I already booked an appointment with Bethann. Remember Bethann from Sunday school? She's so good with preparations. She did Uncle Burt's funeral—may he rest in peace. Remember your great-uncle's funeral? Wasn't it elegant, Randall?"

"Very elegant," Dad says. "She did the 'Block of Blocks Block Party' too, didn't she?"

"With all the blocks! Yes! Remember that, CeCe?" she calls to her sister.

"Too hot, too loud, and nobody likes that many squares in one spot," Aunt Lucy snaps. "The bagel spread was nice, though."

Ouch.

"Well, anyway, Bethann is so excited to help. So is the Neighbors In Need committee and my book club. Oh! And I was able to get us an appointment with Letisha! Remember her from middle school choir? She does dresses now and they're fantastic. Aren't they fantastic, Randall?"

"Very fantastic."

"You're already booking things? Don't book things," I say, anxiety swirling in my stomach.

Tell them.

"Nonsense! I've been waiting my entire life to plan my child's wedding. I brought the box of binders. Did you bring in the binders, Randall?"

A *box* of binders?

"Now's probably not the best time," I say before they can retrieve whatever that is. "Thanks, though."

"Gotta say. We were a little surprised," Dad says. "You've been dancing around with that fellow for so long. We were wondering if you were ever going to hitch your wagons together. Guess it's time to finally make room in the corral."

Ugh! And when did wagons and horses make such a comeback?!

"Thanks, Dad. But—"

"I'll say this, though." He gives me a hard look and points his someone's-getting-in-trouble finger in the air. "If I ever find out that he so much as gives you a look you don't like, he'll need an entire team of stylists when I'm done with him."

Uh-oh. Dad is not going to like the truth about this engagement and what Jarvis did to get it.

"He already has a team of stylists," I mutter.

"Another team, then. He'll need an entire league of teams, you hear me?"

"I hear you."

Great. Now what?

I turn back to the bagels.

How can I tell them the truth when Mama already has her social calendar booked with wedding events and Dad is threatening to mess up Jarvis' hair? Pretty sure "bullying me into being engaged when I explicitly told him I didn't want it" would count as an offense in my father's eyes. The last thing I need in my life right now is a murder trial. Plus, I hate disappointing my family. I love them dearly and they've always been so supportive of me.

Even worse, if I tell *them*, I'm telling everyone. In case it wasn't obvious, they're not exactly vaults of discretion. The entire world would know this whole thing is a sham before I even got to the hallway. As much as I want that, I'm not sure I'm ready for the fallout. There will be an explosion when the engagement is called off, and I've been conditioned not to do anything without considering all possible ramifications. I have no doubt the label already has a detailed, outlined plan vetted and in place for when the time comes.

Even if I do go rogue and break things off on my timing, I need to make sure I have my own PR plan in place to control the narrative before jumping on that landmine. I've barely processed the mess as it stands, let alone who I'd be hurting and what I'd be damaging when I blow it up. I'd have to warn Mae, my manager, Steve, and a host of other people first. I'd definitely have to make sure Val is prepared for the fallout that will undoubtedly land on him. In fact, he'll probably be hit the worst when he becomes the easiest target and scapegoat for all parties involved.

Val. He's been silent this entire time, and when I peek at him, a grinding twists in my stomach. What's he thinking right now? Are his pleading looks begging me to set the record straight or begging me not to? See, that's the problem with selfless men. They're so hard to predict. I had it easy with Jarvis.

Suddenly, I decide I also don't like flakes of stuff on my bagels and start a new pile of poppy seeds. Uncle Howard shoots me an approving look.

"Were you surprised?" Mama asks. "Where's the ring? Why aren't you wearing the ring, sweetie?"

The ring!

Crap, crap, crap!

"Oh. I… uh…"

"She can't perform with it on," Val says.

I cast a surprised glance at him, but his expression is unreadable.

"Gets in the way of the equipment," he explains.

"Ah, yes. Good point," Mama says. "Maybe you can have a smaller one made. You probably should, anyway. It was quite garish from what we saw on the internet."

Garish is a good word. There's not much about this situation that *isn't* garish, actually.

Val's gaze lands on me, and I see the flash of pain before he blinks it away. My chest hurts, my throat… so many things hurt right now. I can't imagine how hard that must have been for him to say. Actually, I can imagine it because it would gut me if our roles were reversed. It also proves he agrees with my decision not to disclose the truth yet.

"I like your hat," Tia says to him.

Somehow he manages a smile. "Thanks. Tiara, right?"

"Yeah, but everyone calls me Tia."

"Cool. Larinda says you're going to culinary school. What's that like?"

I want to cry and scream as he subtly leads my sister away to give me privacy with my parents. Sometimes I hate how well he reads me. How much he cares about me. How he'd do anything for me, including support my attachment to another man if that's what I wanted. But it's not what I want. It's *not,* I just…

My parents' eager grins are hovering dangerously close to my very generous threshold for personal space.

Tia laughs at something Val says, and a stab of jealousy shoots through me when I see her swat his arm. She's clearly enamored. How could she not be? You know what else I hate? That I don't have to wonder for a second if Val will cross a line with her. He won't. I trust him more than I trust myself, even though *he's* the one being wronged in this moment.

But most of all, I hate that I'm in love with the most incredible person I know, and I can't tell anyone.

"The tomatoes are sliced vertically," Aunt Lucy snaps. "Who the heck slices tomatoes vertically?"

12—DALLAS (BACK LOT)

VAL

Here's a fun game:

What's worse? Watching the woman you love pretend to gush to her family about marrying someone else or knowing there's a direct threat against that woman that might require you to continue watching her pretend to gush about marrying someone else?

Oh wait, I know. It's the third option: knowing there's a direct threat that requires you to *participate* in the gushing.

I'm supposed to be helping Chad run the merch table right now. The concert is in full swing, and I already know from Oklahoma City that his questionable merch sorting system doesn't work so great in practice. He'll interrogate me later, but this is also my only chance to call in an ally (literally), and right now my mangled heart and mind need all the support they can get. As soon as I made it to the dark parking lot with our buses, I sent Paige and Nash a video chat request. Typically, this area is the last place for privacy, but everyone else is busy doing what they're supposed to be doing.

I've opted to leave the personal shit out of this conversation and focus on the practical, since I'm not supposed to be feeling anything other than concern for Larinda as a friend and associate. I have no idea how to explain the personal stuff, anyway. I can't talk about the pain of watching her make wedding plans with her family. How it feels to stay silent while the entire world celebrates a man who is straight-up horrible and borderline criminal. No one can ever know I'm cracking apart inside, because I can't do anything that will risk exposing our relationship.

Nope, I get to bear this catastrophic gut punch all on my own.

My sister and her boyfriend are quiet as they study a laptop screen that must show the images I sent.

"This is so messed up," Nash mumbles. "You said you found this notebook in Jarvis' dressing room?"

"Yeah. Please don't ask me why I was there. *I* don't even fully understand why I was there."

"We don't want to know, trust me," my sister says.

Her humor fades as she squints at the laptop. "So that asshole is setting her up again."

"Looks like it," I say.

"Did you tell her yet?" Nash asks.

I shake my head. "I need more information. It's clear his proposal was fake and some kind of setup, but for what? What does 'it's better if she cheats' mean?"

"Oh, see, *cheating* is when one person in a committed relationship engages in a romantic encounter with—"

I fire a glare at my sister, and she returns a sardonic grin. She also still owes me a conversation about the other (parental) crisis in my life, so this is going to be a long video call for her. I recommend she ration her snark wisely.

"I'm aware of what *cheating* means. What I don't know is what it means to Jarvis in this context. Why is it better if she cheats? And why propose in the first place if he wants her to dump him?"

"I don't know," Nash says. "But I'm guessing none of those answers are great."

It's better if she cheats, even had a smiley face beside it. Nothing good ever comes with a hand-drawn smiley face.

"I don't like anything about this," I say. "From the beginning this whole engagement thing felt off. Neither of them wants it, apparently, so why is it happening? It has to be more than the media games they play."

"I agree," Nash says. "Something's up and it feels major. I bet this goes deeper than we think."

"You think Lakebend might be involved?" I ask, my stomach tightening further.

"Jarvis is their biggest artist. They have to be, right?" Nash says.

"And Larinda has been at odds with them lately," I say. "You don't think…"

Shit.

Nash looks how I feel.

"Where's your next stop?" he asks.

"Little Rock."

"Arkansas?"

"Is there another one?"

"Probably," Paige interjects, and I shoot her a look. Is Nash planning to meet up with the tour to help sort this out? He really cares about Larinda and was on the frontline of her last crisis with Jarvis. He'd be a crucial ally to have. Let's hope he doesn't bring my sister.

"Great. We'll be there," she says.

Crap.

Deep down, I'm relieved, though. This is huge, bigger than I thought, and who knows how far it goes? Having actual allies in play will be essential to pulling off a rescue.

"Okay. What do I tell Larinda?" I ask.

Nash furrows his brow. "Nothing. Let's make our visit seem like a surprise, so she doesn't suspect anything. Definitely keep Jarvis' plan quiet for now. You were right not to jump the gun. We don't want to trigger anything before we know what the hell we're triggering."

I take a deep breath.

"The most important thing is to make sure Larinda doesn't call off the engagement," Paige says.

"Definitely," Nash agrees. "Do everything you can to keep them together until we can figure this out."

Oh, is that all? Just convince the woman I love to stay engaged to a man I hate without explaining why?

My sister's apologetic expression doesn't make me feel any better. Worse, actually, because it means she suspects the feelings I don't want anyone suspecting.

"We got you, little bro," she says softly. "We're going to figure this out."

There's that sad puppy look again. Yep, no question she knows I'm in love with Larinda. I have no energy to tackle the parent thing anymore, either. Paige is off the hook for that too.

"We'll see you in Little Rock," she says.

13—LITTLE ROCK (THE GREEN ROOM)

LARINDA

"How did coffee with your parents go?" Steve asks.

It's an hour before the VIP meet and greet, and I've never been so excited to pose for photos with random strangers. I'll take anything that isn't sitting around talking about my messed-up love life or planning a fake wedding.

I give Steve a pointed look and discreetly nod toward the other occupants in the room.

He nods back.

"Coriander, Sage," he calls to the women currently debating the merits of iced coffee versus regular coffee versus… milk? "Would you mind giving us a minute? We have… important… business… stuff."

I shoot him an irritated look, and he mouths an apology. Thankfully, my childhood friends don't seem to notice the obvious lie. They don't notice much, which is helpful in most situations.

"No prob!" Sage chirps. "We just found out there's a hot tub outlet around here. Want anything?"

"Do I want a hot tub?" I ask, staring at her. "No, thanks."

They actually look disappointed. What exactly was their plan?

"Well, let us know if you change your mind," Coriander says on her way to the door.

Sage flutters a wave and follows her out.

"They know a hot tub outlet isn't a room of usable hot tubs, right?" I say.

Steve shrugs. "Maybe? Either way, it'll keep them busy for a while. Remember the candle outlet?"

I cringe. "So many candles."

"So many."

I've known Coriander and Sage (previously Mary and Laura) since I was ten. We had nothing in common except our fifth-grade classroom and mutual appreciation for glitter pens. They just really liked following me around for some reason. More than fifteen years later, they still do and I've never had the heart to ask them not to.

I'm not great with confrontation.

"So the meetup?" Steve asks.

"Right. Yes. I had it."

"*And...?*"

"Not good."

His shoulders sag along with my mood.

"Not good because they didn't like that the engagement wasn't real?"

"Not good because I didn't tell them the engagement wasn't real."

"Larry..." he exhales.

"I know, okay? It's just... ah! Mama was so excited about shopping for dresses, and Dad would have tracked Jarvis down and messed up his hair if I told them the truth. Plus, you know how it is. They would've blabbed and everything would have blown up. We're not ready for things to blow up, right?"

I'm not a huge fan of the way Steve is looking at me. He should really save his ire for the next part.

"I didn't talk to Jarvis yet either," I say, peeking through my fingers.

His death stare does a great job of lasering through the gaps.

"So Jarvis still thinks you meant yes when you said yes?"

"Well..."

"Larry!"

"I was going to tell him at lunch, I swear! But there was this Meyer lemon crisis and then he had to go do some cardboard photoshoot thing? Not sure. And now he's been in hair and makeup since. You know what would've happened if I disturbed him while he's being pampered."

Steve grunts, but his expression softens slightly. "I don't like this for you, Larry. Any of it." He waves his hand and deposits his fist on his hip.

"I know. I don't either."

"Well, we need to get you unengaged as quickly as possible. I get that we're not ready to go public, but there's no way my Larinda is marrying a man who's running a fundraiser to re-landscape his estate."

Oh. Okay. That explains the orange charity bandana Jarvis was wearing. I guess it makes sense since the puppy ropes course construction probably destroyed his lawn.

"I'll schmooze Mallory and see if I can get a read on his schedule," Steve continues. "There has to be a time we can get him alone."

I return a corroborating nod, but my pulse is racing at the thought. My brief brush with standing up for myself and saying "no" the other day seems forever ago. I was so proud of myself, and look where it got me—exactly the same place as if I'd said yes.

Because you did *say yes.*

Not the point.

A knock at the door draws our attention, and my heart thumps for a different reason when Val pokes his head in.

We haven't seen each other except in passing since the meeting with my parents yesterday. I've been desperate to talk to him about what happened, but it's been one thing after another. Even arriving in Little Rock didn't help. An industry brunch followed by an interview and radio appearance mean we haven't had the chance to connect even for a brief chat, let alone the soul-searching purge we need. The second I got to the green room to relax, I sent him a text to come find me.

"Hey. Sorry to barge in. Is now a good time?" he asks me. His gaze crosses to Steve. "You want to, uh, work on that song?"

"The song! Yes. Of course. The song. Do you mind?" I say to Steve. "Maybe go check on Coriander and Sage and make sure they don't buy too many hot tubs?"

Val lifts a brow, and I shake off his question.

"You sure?" Steve says, firing an irritated look at Val. "You don't want to finish discussing… the business stuff?"

"No, I'm good on the business stuff."

Steve grunts and stomps toward the door.

"Do I want to know about the hot tubs… and business stuff?" Val asks once we're alone.

"Nope. I only need you to come here."

He hesitates for just a second before approaching me, and my world transforms into sunshine again as I lean into him. His arms fold around me, washing away the drama of the last few days. The familiar smell of forests and subtle citrus filters into my lungs and sends an electric charge through my veins. Combined with the firm, warm pressure of his body, the feel of his lips on my hair—everything about this wrong moment seems right.

"I've missed you," I murmur.

"I've missed you too." His voice is somehow gravelly and soft at the same time. Sexy and sweet, like everything else about him.

There's no doubt in my mind I'm in love with this person. Fully, irrevocably in love with him and nothing will ever—

"I don't think you should break up with Jarvis."

Stop. The. Track.

"I'm sorry?" I pull back to see his face.

He won't meet my gaze, which can't be a good sign.

"I've been thinking about the whole thing nonstop, and I don't think you should give everything up for me. I don't want you to."

"Val…"

"No, I'm serious." His beautiful eyes carve a hole in my stomach when they drift to mine.

"I am too," I say. "I told you I don't care about the fallout. We'll figure it out. We'll—"

"And what if *I'm* not ready for it? What if *I* don't want to lose everything?"

I flinch and stare at him in disbelief. "Are you serious? Y-you…" Shaking my head, I step back to put more distance between us.

"You're used to having everything, Larinda. I just got something for the first time. Maybe I'm not ready to lose it so soon."

Tears press on the backs of my eyes, and I force them away. I don't cry in front of people (except when instructed, of course). Another talent I've perfected over the years.

He looks like he's in physical pain as he shoves his hands in his back pockets and averts his gaze. Where is this coming from?

"Val, please. What's going on? I know you don't want that. I can see it all over your face."

I reach out and grip his sleeve, tugging when he closes his eyes.

"Talk to me. We've never kept things from each other. Whatever it is, we'll figure it out like we always do."

He shakes his head and opens his eyes again. "When everything blows up —and it will—you have a huge support system and an entire network of backup opportunities. You know what I have? A chair at my sister's kitchen table in our tiny, cluttered apartment. I have nothing without this. Don't you see? As soon as you're done with me, *I'm* done."

When I'm *done* with him?

I drop my hold, paralyzed by conflicting emotions. I want to smack him and hug him at the same time. He thinks so little of me? Of himself?

He pulls his ball cap off to adjust his hair before sliding it back on. It's a gesture I've seen him do a thousand times, one of his many nervous tics. He also taps the desk with his left hand when he has an idea he's struggling to manifest and twists his chair in small arcs whenever he gets overly frustrated. I also know his green eyes are deadly when he wears that hoodie with the phoenix on it, he loves tomatoes but hates ketchup, orders couscous anytime it's on the menu, and has never said an unkind word about another person, even those who have hurt him.

I know everything there is to know about this person, and I know I could never ever be *done* with him.

"Anyway, I should go," he mumbles. "Good luck tonight. You're killing it. Your show is incredible."

He starts away, and I grasp his wrist.

Our eyes meet, my skin burning at the point of contact. I've never wanted to kiss someone so much in my life. How could he think for a second I'd want anyone other than him?

"You have a right to an opinion on this as well, but you're wrong if you think this is a choice between you and Jarvis. This is a choice between you and no one. You can sacrifice yourself, or whatever this is, but it won't change my position on the engagement. I'm not going to pretend forever. I will be breaking it off with Jarvis as soon as I figure out how."

His expression morphs from concern to fear as he steps toward me. Weird.

"Please, Larinda. I totally understand your position, but please don't break it off yet. No one expects you to marry him, just… don't break up with him. I'm begging you."

Wow. Is he seriously that afraid of losing his job? I squint at him, rare anger bubbling inside me. Well, I *thought* I knew him, but I guess not. How dare he ask this of me? Is he really that selfish? His career is more important than my heart and soul?

"Got it. Well, no need to worry. You're a great producer. If you're that concerned about a paycheck, I'm sure we can find you a new artist to keep you employed," I snap. "Who knows? Maybe they'll be an even bigger career boost for you than I am."

He flinches but doesn't retaliate as he looks away. "I'm sorry. The last thing I wanted to do was hurt you."

"Yeah? Well, you did. I thought you loved me, and now I find out you only love my name. You can freaking have it, then!"

I don't know what that means, but it sounds awesome and like a total mic-drop dig as I march away.

The moment would have been perfect too if I hadn't seen him rub the center of his chest before I slammed the door behind me. I know everything about him—including the fact that that gesture means he just did something he didn't want to do.

14—LITTLE ROCK (M&G OR MEET & GREET)

VAL

Well, that went well.

I'm not sure what I was expecting when I decided to lie to Larinda and break both of our hearts, but it wasn't that. In the moment it seemed like the right choice. Now, not a single thing feels right. Worst part, I may have inadvertently made her even more intent on breaking up with Jarvis and playing into his devious, manicured hands. I have no choice anymore. I'll have to tell her about the plot—once she's willing to talk to me again.

As if losing Larinda (and probably everything else) isn't bad enough, my parents just sent a follow-up message looking for a response to their previous email. Since I haven't fully processed the first one, I have no idea what to do with this:

Dearest Perceval,

You keep us in agony with your silence. We beg of you to partake from the fountain of forgiveness and bestow upon us the mercy of your RSVP.

Lovingly yours,

Mummy and Papa

What nineteenth-century ghost is writing this shit for them? Guess this is what happens when you attempt your first ever apology in your fifties.

The day got worse when Chad recruited me for "an initiative" minutes after I returned to the bus to hide and regroup. While I had no interest in any "initiatives" orchestrated by the genius behind ten-dollar fish-themed pubic coverings, I was very interested in learning more about the plot against Larinda, even if she hates me now.

I guarantee it's not more than I hate myself, though. Leave it to me to screw up an entire trope by letting my "grumpy" snuff out the sunshine in our fairy tale.

"You know how famous people do the M and Gs," Chad whispers.

Why is he whispering?

"Meet and greets? Yeah, what about them?"

He shakes his head while referencing something in his zip portfolio. "No, it says M and G. 'Jarvis M and G *Initiative*.' See?"

Yep, "Jarvis M&G Initiative" is typed in nearly unreadable font at the top of a blank page. Also, the way he keeps pronouncing "initiative" has me regretting everything about this.

"Ninety-nine percent sure that's referring to a meet and greet," I say.

"Fine. Whatever. Whether or not it means that—"

"It does."

"—is irrelevant. The point is, we need to find an octopus. A real one, if possible."

Oh.

He continues walking as if there might be an unclaimed octopus on our path to wherever it is we're going.

I'm a *hundred* percent sure there won't be.

"Can I ask why we need an octopus?"

"For the skit."

He checks something off a list, and I scan the empty corridor trying to determine what we just accomplished.

"We're doing a skit?"

"Not us, silly. The fans."

"At the meet and greet?"

"The M and G, yes."

"With an octopus. Possibly a living one."

"I said *real*. Doesn't have to be alive."

"I... okay."

It's not like we'll encounter an octopus in any state of health.

"So have you been working with Jarvis for a while?" I ask.

"Since the beginning."

"Of his career?"

That seems unlikely.

"Since his partnership with Sandeke Telecom."

Way more likely.

"What are your thoughts on the guy?"

"That's a great question, Val," he says.

"Thanks."

"What do you know about killer clowns?"

Not enough, apparently.

"Um… They generally should be avoided?"

He pulls to a stop and spins toward me. "Precisely. How did you know that?"

"I guess, movies? And common sense?"

He pats my arm. "Well said. You'll make a great spy one day, Mr. Andrews."

Hopefully, that day is today. "So… killer clowns?"

"Ah! Right. You know what happens before they bite you?"

"They… grab you?"

"No, Val. They give you a balloon. Sometimes a balloon animal, but most aren't that skilled."

Hang on. Is he suggesting what I think he's suggesting?

"So, you're saying Jarvis—"

"Shh! Never use names. Rule number one. Autumn Blaze. It's *Autumn Blaze*."

"Oh. Sorry."

"Apology accepted. Larinda is Hummingbird in case you didn't know."

"I didn't. Thanks. Do I have a code name?"

"Of course."

"What is it?"

"Labor Day."

I think he's joking? He doesn't look like he's joking. He's not joking.

"Huh. Okay. Good to know. So *Autumn Blaze* gives you a balloon animal, but really he wants to kill you?"

"It's looking like we're on the same page, my friend."

He winks, thus ending the conversation.

Are we? Maybe. At the very least he's validated my stance on accepting balloon animals from strangers.

* * *

"Do you want to run the skit or should I?" Chad asks as we approach the massive line of fans.

"I don't understand what the skit *is*," I reply.

Not that I'd be able to do it even if I did. I can't seem to concentrate on anything other than the giant red backdrop in the distance. Behind it is a photographer, security detail, and two country stars posing with people who paid a fortune for a signed tour poster and grainy snapshot with their idols.

On this side of the curtain are scores of impatient fans waiting for their turn, several irritated employees managing them, and an overzealous talent liaison posing as a spy. (Or is it the other way around? Still haven't figured that out.)

And *this* is the side I'd rather be on. I have no interest in watching Larinda play engaged couple for an endless string of photos that will get plastered all over social media and embedded in people's "Best Of" life moments. I saw the "garish" ring on her hand when security escorted her past a few minutes ago. She saw me too, but pretended not to. Guess she's still pissed. And engaged.

"Excuse me! May I have your attention, please!" Chad shouts. When that doesn't work, he waves his arms above his head. When that doesn't work, he starts jumping. When that doesn't work, he does both until the loud chatter fades into quiet bewilderment.

Say what you want about the guy, but his methods are remarkably effective (with the exception of selling concert merch).

"Before we begin, I have to make an apology," he says in a grave tone. "Unfortunately, I was unable to secure an octopus for this event, so we'll have to proceed sans octopi. Unless... Does anyone happen to have a spare?"

"A spare octopus?" I mumble. "You think one of these people brought an octopus with them?"

He returns an annoyed look. "It's worth asking, right? Little Rock is known for..." He scrunches his brow as he realizes he doesn't know what Little Rock is known for. I don't either, but I know it's not octopuses.

"Okay. Well, we can still make this work. May I have a few volunteers?"

Inexplicably, several people raise their hands. Then I remember:

1. They don't know Chad.
2. They're bored as hell.
3. They probably errantly think their participation will benefit them in some way.

"Lovely! You, you, you, and you."

The four volunteers take one step, then look around uncomfortably.

"It's okay. Come forward," Chad coaches.

They don't move.

"They're worried about losing their place in line," I tell him.

"Oh, right. It's okay. I guarantee you will keep your spot."

I'm not sure he has the authority to do that, but people trust anyone with a clipboard (or zip portfolio, in this case).

"Excellent. Have you ever been in a skit before?" he asks the first fan with an eager grin.

"Yeah," the guy says.

Chad deflates but manages to brush off the setback. "Well, I'm sure you haven't been in a skit at a Jarvis McKinnley and Larinda Scott concert, correct?"

That's a safer bet.

Sure enough, the guy shakes his head.

Chad beams. "Excellent. Then let's begin. What is your name and what's your favorite Jarvis or Larinda song?"

"Uh, well, my name is Bill, and my favorite song is 'Ain't No Day Like Today' by Jarvis McKinnley."

"A true classic! Did you all hear that?" Chad shouts. "This is Bill and his favorite song is 'Ain't No Day Like Today.' Who else likes that song?"

A spattering of applause trickles in, but mostly people aren't sure what's happening… which is fair.

"Excellent. Thank you, Bill. You may return to the line. What about you?" Chad asks the next person.

Bill hesitates for a moment, staring at Chad, then returns to his spot in line. Thankfully, the couple behind him let him in because I already have a bad record with concert security and want no part of enforcing Chad's guarantee.

The next "actor's" name is Jen and her favorite song is "Billboards and Billiards" by Larinda.

She returns to the line.

Kris likes "Treehouse of My Heart" by Jarvis.

Ed likes "Moonlight Musings" by Larinda.

Wait. Is this the skit? And where would the octopus have come into play?

"Well, that was fun, wasn't it?" Chad exclaims with a clap. "Who's ready for a sing-along?"

Hell. No.

Thankfully, I'm rescued from the musical version of this "skit" when Bruce approaches and pulls me aside.

"They need you behind the curtain."

"Me? Why?" But we're already walking.

"Not sure. Jarvis asked for you, specifically."

Any relief at being spared Chad's weird theater production fades. This can't be good. I have no idea why Jarvis would want me with them for any reason other than to rub the engagement in my face and provoke me into trouble.

Okay, yeah. That's why Jarvis asked for me.

Anger mixes with dread as we walk, but I have no idea what to do. I can't exactly refuse the request without causing drama and making *myself* look like the asshole. I'm out of time anyway, and we duck around the curtain to see exactly what I was afraid of: Jarvis with his arm around Larinda, and Larinda wearing her perfected stage smile.

I've seen her use that smile while walking on four-inch heels with painful blisters. I've seen it while she was deathly ill with the flu. I've seen it while having her heart broken from a brutal review, while being told time and again to be what *they* want, not who she is, and while her world crashes down on an international stage. She's the quintessential professional and can plaster that smile on her face through incredible pain, so this smile means nothing other than she's playing her role to perfection.

My fists clench with resentment at Jarvis for what he's doing to her, at Larinda for letting him. At this entire situation that is wrong and complex and completely impossible. At myself for making it worse and not knowing how to get us out of it.

"Next!" the assistant managing the line says as another one ushers the current fan away. The person is still starstruck as they stagger out of view with an expression that's the opposite of what mine must be.

Larinda looks surprised when she sees me, so whatever this is wasn't on her radar. That is *not* surprising.

The next fan is already being wedged between them for the photo op, so Larinda doesn't comment as Bruce leads me behind the photographer.

"Oh, Valerie. Excellent," Jarvis says. "One sec. Babe, maybe come a little closer."

He tucks his arm around Larinda and pulls her against him. That move was solely for me, and my nails dig into my palms.

I fire a glare at him but remain silent. What can I say?

"Do you think we should get a kiss shot?" Jarvis asks. Larinda snaps a look in his direction, but he plays innocent.

No chance in hell that's happening. I don't care about blowing up my career.

"You asked for Val?" Bruce interrupts, already annoyed—and he doesn't even know Jarvis made him a recruiter for a petty pissing match.

"Right, yes," Jarvis says. At least he's distracted from the idea that was about to earn him a fist to the face. "You're so good with technology, being a producer and all."

He holds a cell phone in my direction.

Yep. This is more confusing than Chad's skit.

"Um…" I glance at Bruce, but his shrug doesn't help.

"Photos, Valerie," Jarvis says in an irritated tone. "Hurry up. We need to move this along."

"You want me to… what, exactly? And my name is Val."

"Whatever. No one cares. I need you to take photos for my pages. We've been so busy with being famous and engaged that I haven't had time for fun BTS shots for my millions of fans."

Only I can see Jarvis' targeted sneer before his expression morphs into pleasant supplication.

"You want me to take photos for your social media pages? Don't you have a social media manager?"

Probably a whole team of them.

"Yes, but they're busy, and besides, I've seen your work. You're so good with pushing buttons and pressing on things. Thanks so much!"

Yep. He's taunting me. This entire thing is a pathetic A-list power play, because the fact that he holds every card, the box they came in, and the plant that manufactures them isn't enough, apparently.

"We really need to move this along," the photographer snaps at me. At *me*, as if I'm the reason for any of this. I'm still trying to understand what *this* is.

Either way, with a dozen witnesses and multiple careers in the balance (including my own), I have no choice but to take his phone as he tucks himself beside Larinda again. Her perplexed expression turns apologetic as it lands on me. The rock in my throat lodges in my stomach.

"Oh my goodness. Congratulations!" the new fan says as she's positioned between them. "You two are, like, the perfect couple. You can totally tell you're meant for each other."

"Thanks, sweetie," Jarvis says with an oily smile. Larinda's is more of a stiff lip-twist.

"So nice of you to say," she manages.

"This would be a great shot, Valerie. You mind?" Jarvis says. "Be sure to get her ring. It's so lovely. Did you see the twig?"

I'm burning from the inside out when Larinda's pained gaze brushes mine. Her stage façade is slipping. As much as I want to scream right now, I have to pull it together to keep her from losing it, which could lead to losing a lot more.

I laser a cold stare at Jarvis and force down the ache in my chest.

He wants photos? Fine. He's fucking getting photos.

Jarvis looks damn proud of himself for his clever game as he resumes his role and poses for the real photographer. I snap a picture of his shoe.

Next, I get a close-up of the pole supporting the right side of the backdrop. Actually, the rivet halfway up would be so beautiful juxtaposed against the fabric beside it. Strength and softness, you know? He's right. I'm so friggin' good at this.

I crouch down to get an artistic view of the stunning bolt and take eighteen shots of it from the same angle. Shifting slightly to the right, I get another twenty or so. The lighting is better from here. Bet it would be amazing about six inches higher. I straighten a little to get twelve more. Maybe he'll frame one of these masterpieces.

Jarvis shoots me a silent critique, but since he wouldn't know what I'm photographing, his ire must be from the fact that I'm smiling.

Yes, that's right. Two can play at this game.

And that's when it hits me. It's not the power that fuels him. He already has more of that than he can ever play with. His sadistic game is extracting it. He loves watching people fall into his traps and accept his reign over them.

So what's the best way to strip away that fun? Give it freely.

"Lovely," I say, lining up beside the photographer. "Larinda, can you turn your hand a fraction to the right? Other hand. Yes! Perfect, don't move."

I feel the real photographer's aggravation at my interference, but Jarvis unwittingly gave me a license to do whatever I want right now.

He's pissed as I snap a few more shots with exaggerated "photographer" posturing. On one knee, then the other. Tilting forward, leaning back. I've never conducted a photoshoot in my life, but I've witnessed plenty. I can play the part all day if he wants.

Now *this* is a skit. Where's Chad when you need him? God, I'd love to have an octopus right now.

"Beautiful! I need more from you, Jarvis," I instruct. "Stop asking if you're a rockstar and *tell* me."

Jarvis returns a look that's telling me something very different, and I bite back a grin.

"What's your name?" I ask the new fan that rounds the corner for their turn.

"Me? Um, R-Reece?"

I nod and motion toward Jarvis and Larinda. "Great. Just stand between them. Give us your best smile, Reece. This is going on Jarvis' social media pages."

"Really?" the person asks, eyes wide.

Jarvis fires a furious look at me, but what's he supposed to do? He literally told us that's the reason for this charade.

I pretend to be oblivious as I snap a few more photos, this time careful to stay out of the real photographer's way. I'm only interested in annoying one very specific individual.

"Be sure to check back later to see your picture on his page!" I call to Reece as the guy leaves. "Who knows? He might even make it his profile pic!"

The guy returns a giant grin.

"I'm serious," I say to Jarvis, angling the screen toward him. "It's a good one. You look divine. So, who's next?"

"Actually, I think that's plenty of photos. Thanks," he grumbles, motioning for his phone.

"Oh, you sure? I really don't mind. You were right, as always. I'm so good at this. Wait until you see the magic I captured on the curtain frame behind you."

I'm no expert, but in my opinion his current expression does *not* seem very camera friendly.

He shoots out his hand, and I approach with a sigh.

"Well, let me know if you need my help again. It was fun," I say with the brightest smile I can muster.

Larinda is holding back a laugh, and a burst of warmth shoots through me when our eyes meet. There's no doubt she caught what just went down. She has a reputation for being shallow and clueless, but that's just one of the many ways in which she's misunderstood. This woman is deep and complex, and peeling back her layers this past year to find the intelligent, creative person inside has been an honor and aphrodisiac. There's nothing sexier than brushing the secrets of someone's soul for the first time.

But my efforts to dramatically return Jarvis' phone are thwarted by her sudden squeal.

Alarmed, I follow her excited jog-jump toward... Nash and Paige? Guess they made it. I probably have a message on my phone that I missed since I was so busy with Jarvis'.

"Hey, Larinda," Nash says with a huge grin. "Surprise."

She's still "squeeing" as she throws her arms around him and does an adorable hug-hop thing. Even his girlfriend (AKA my uptight sister) looks on in amusement.

"You're here!" Larinda cries. "How did you get here? Wait, *why* are you here?"

She's still bouncing as she steps back to hold him at arm's length and scan him. Forget protecting her from Jarvis' plot. I'm glad we surprised her for this moment alone. She could use a win.

"We were in town and thought we'd stop by," Nash says. "Steve was able to get us in."

Larinda laughs and shoves him. "Whatever, rockstar. Like you needed to be on a list to get through the door."

He shrugs. "Hey, you're the rockstar. I'm just—"

"A soon-to-be Oscar-nominated artist, blah blah blah. Yeah, we know," Paige mumbles. Nash tosses her a grin that draws an eye roll from my sister.

"Hi, Larinda. It's great to see you," she says. "Sorry for interrupting. Nash insisted on crashing your meet and greet."

"It's fine! I'm just so glad—"

"Actually, we really do need to be getting back to it, baby," Jarvis says, coming up beside Larinda.

Wow. Talk about a superpower. His ability to sour every drop of positivity is remarkable. If Jarvis earned a spot in comic book lore, he'd be The Rancid Wrangler. Wait, no. That's too cool of a name. The Curdler. Yeah, that's it.

Nash's expression is what mine must look like whenever Jarvis is in visual range.

"Of course," Paige says, taking Nash's hand to calm him before there's an epic clash of celebrity forces. *Bike Boy versus The Curdler. Coming to a meet and greet near you!*

(I still don't understand why Nash jokes about being called Bike Boy, but even Paige calls him that when she's feeling particularly annoyed… or frisky. Ew. Back to the present nightmare.)

"We'll catch up with you later," she says to Larinda. "Let us know when you have some downtime. Maybe after the show tonight?"

"That would be great!" Larinda says. "We should have plenty of time to catch up before we roll out."

Her gaze brushes me, and I wilt under the silent message. *My secret girlfriend is available since I won't be taking up her downtime anymore.*

We need to resolve this mess quickly. I'm not sure how much longer I can take this tension between us. It's been two hours and I'm ready to fold.

"Great," Nash says. "Kill it tonight. We'll find a place to crash until then."

"You're welcome to hang out on my bus," Larinda says. "It should be empty."

"Really? You don't mind?" Paige asks.

"Not at all! I'd love that. I'll meet you back there as soon as I finish my set."

"You're not gonna watch me tonight, babe?" Jarvis asks with a pout.

Larinda's brow creases, and once again this man triggers a violent gene I didn't even know I had.

"Oh, do you watch *her* sets?" Nash asks in an innocent tone that is far from innocent. He must know he doesn't.

"Actually, maybe you're right. It would be good for you to rest and spend some time with your friends," he says to Larinda. "You have my blessing."

Nice recovery, asshole.

He moves in to kiss her cheek, but she shrinks back with an awkward smile. Yep. I'm going to be a murder suspect before this tour is over.

Paige grabs my arm so it doesn't happen right now. "Mind if we borrow him for a little?"

"Please," Jarvis says, guiding Larinda back toward the curtain. "We're not even sure why he's here."

Larinda winces, and I return a glare, but a firm hand drags me away before violence can ensue. I don't even have a superhero name but it wouldn't stop me from taking on The Curdler.

Wait. I guess I'm "Labor Day," right? Maybe I could talk Chad into *Captain* Labor Day, at least.

"Everyone's watching," Paige mumbles as her grip tightens around my bicep.

I glance back for one last look at "the happy couple." Only Jarvis looks happy, having won again. Of course he won. He always wins. Even when he loses he wins.

"Seriously. Not worth it, man. We'll figure it out," Nash whispers, joining Team Paige on this one.

I hate that they're right and I have no choice but to let them lead me out of the VIP area. I also can't help but notice that they're wearing their all-access passes. Good for them. The security on this tour is stellar.

15—LITTLE ROCK (LARINDA'S BUS)

VAL

"I'm going to kill him. I will," I hiss as soon as Nash, Paige, and I escape into the hall.

"Figuratively!" Paige clarifies for whichever government agency might be listening. Seriously. Does *everyone* operate under the assumption the universe is run by spies? How did I not know this?

"Jarvis is an ass, and we *will* take him down, but we have to be smart about it," Nash says. "He's too powerful and connected to act rashly."

"I know, but… ah!"

"Hey." Paige grabs my arm and pulls me around. "We're going to solve this, little bro, but we have to do it right."

I release a heavy breath and manage to rein in the rest of my anger… until I see my sister's smile.

"What?" I snap. "What could possibly be funny about this?"

"Nothing," she says, still smiling.

"There's obviously something."

"I've just never seen you like this."

"Like what?"

"Worked up. You're the most chill person I know."

"She's right, actually," Nash says. "What's up with you? I get that Jarvis has a master's degree in aggravating people but that's nothing new."

"Nothing's up. I don't know what you're talking about." I double my pace through the corridor toward the back lot.

"Now he's running. I've *never* seen him run," Paige says from behind me.

I fire an irritated look back at her, and she returns a grin that only sisters seem to have.

Paige and Nash wisely remain silent for the rest of the journey to the parking lot.

"Oh shit," Nash says as we approach Larinda's bus. "It's locked. We'll need the…" He goes quiet as I punch in the code for the door. "Wow, I guess not. She gave you the code, dude? Damn."

Nash slaps my arm, and I do an excellent job of ignoring him as I climb onto the bus and drop to my favorite spot in the lounge.

"Look how he just makes himself at home. How many hours you spend here, baby bro?" Paige teases.

You know what would be awesome? If they stopped talking.

I throw my arm over my face to block them out.

"Dang. This is incredible," Paige says, eyes wide as she scans the space. "It's practically a luxury hotel suite. Is this like the bus you were on when you worked for Abram?" she asks Nash.

He snorts a laugh. "I was on the crew bus, babe. No."

"Fine. Well, maybe now that you're a huge rockstar, you'd get a bus like this."

"I'm not a huge rockstar, and I don't tour."

"When you become one and start touring."

"I may never be and I may never tour."

"Yes you will. Do you want to tour?"

"I don't know. Not really."

I'm just glad they don't need me for any of this.

"Okay, little bro, now spill."

Crap.

I lower my arm to find two expectant stares waiting for the wealth of information I've gathered since the last time we spoke. Other than discovering Arkansas' woeful lack of octopi and the favorite songs of four strangers, I don't have any updates.

"Nothing new to report."

"Seriously? Come on. We know that's not true," Paige says.

"Fine. I guess the fact that I made Larinda hate me like you told me to is an update."

"Hmm. Is that what we said?" Paige asks, tilting her head.

So maybe that was a tad passive-aggressive. Let's hope they don't read too much into it.

"Wait…" Nash says, eyes narrowing on me. "You didn't… Oh shit, you fell for her, didn't you?"

I concentrate on the ceiling again. It *is* a nice ceiling. Paige is right to be impressed.

"Val! What did I tell you?!" Nash groans.

"Not to fall for her."

"Exactly! This…" He runs a hand over his face.

"Relax, babe," Paige says. "It's not like he can help how he feels."

"Yeah, but… this is bad, dude. Real bad. You can't tell her, okay?"

I scrunch the side of my face and shrug.

"You told her," Nash mutters.

"I mean… *technically*, she told me first. We were even a secret couple for a day before I blew everything up this afternoon."

"*What?!*" Paige and Nash screech in unison. Is that a couples thing? Fun. There's so much for Larinda and me to look forward to.

"Yeah, so, the 'crush' is sort of a bit more," I say.

Their shocked, slightly horrified expressions tell me this situation is as bad as I feared. Might be worse, actually.

"She's engaged!" Paige informs me.

"Yeah. I'm aware."

"To someone else!"

"Also aware."

"You're her producer, dude," Nash says.

"Am I? Wait. Knew that too."

So glad they're here to help.

"Shit, shit, shit…" Nash mumbles, locking his fingers on his head.

My sister has been stunned into wordlessness, which in my experience, is a very hard thing to do.

"Who else knows about this?" Nash asks.

"No one. You shouldn't even know, I just have no clue how to fix this situation without your help, and I don't know how you can help if you aren't aware of that tiny hiccup."

"Tiny hiccup?!" Paige cries. "Seriously, Val. What are you thinking? You can't have a secret relationship with an engaged superstar!"

"You already know the engagement isn't real," I say.

"Yes, but she doesn't!"

"Actually, she does, just not for the right reason."

"Fine, then the rest of the world doesn't," Paige snaps.

That part is true.

"This is a disaster waiting to happen, man," Nash says. "Like, it honestly couldn't get much worse for you."

I grunt and stretch out on the couch. "Hey, I have an idea. How about we skip to the part where I called you *because* I already knew this crap?"

Nash throws up his hands but calms down after a few more seconds of aggressive pacing. "Fine. What about Jarvis? What does he know about you and Larinda?"

"Not much," I say.

"From what I saw, that hostility was personal. He must at least suspect you have feelings for her."

"Okay, yeah. So, that."

"Val!" Paige cries.

"What? Fine. He probably more than suspects it. He's done everything he can to make my life miserable since we rolled out."

"Dude, Jarvis is the last person you want to go head-to-head with," Nash says. "He's a huge name with limitless resources."

"He's got Sandeke Telecom backing him, for heaven's sake!" Paige adds.

"Yep."

"He has a million reasons to want to crush you," Nash says. "And a million ways to do it."

Guess we're back to listing things I already know. Definitely not telling them I can recite the capitals of every country in Europe. We'll be here all day.

"I understand all of this, believe me. The question is, what do we do about it?"

They exchange a look.

"No effing clue, dude," Nash says, shaking his head.

"Great. Well, this has been productive." I push up from the couch. "Want anything to drink?"

They're silent as I help myself to a bottle of water from the fridge.

"No, thanks," Paige mumbles in her *capitulation* voice, so yay for that. "You think Larinda would mind if I look around?"

"Not at all. Just don't move anything."

"Of course not."

Paige takes off to explore, which feels like a win until it leaves me alone with Nash. Does he have a capitulation voice? Let's hope so.

"Look, man. I get it. I do. I saw the chemistry you two had since day one, but, dude. This is bigger than some fling. You understand that, right? Even if you find a way out of this Jarvis engagement mess, what's your future? I love Larinda. You know that, but that woman goes through boyfriends like her flavored almonds. I don't doubt she has a crush on you, but that shit means something different to people at her level than people like us."

I lower my gaze, my heart crumbling into my stomach like the world's worst almond flavor.

"Believe me, I know all that as well," I mutter. "I'm nobody and she's…"

"Hey, that's not what I'm saying. You're a great guy. If anyone deserves someone like Larinda it's you. It's just, she lives in a different world. I'm not saying she's lying to you about her feelings. I'm sure she's being sincere. I just don't want to see you hurt."

Way too late for that.

"I know, okay? Honestly, you're probably right. She'll get sick of me and—"

"Um, guys?" Paige calls from another room. "You should see this."

"See what?" I shout back.

"It's in Larinda's room. You told me not to touch anything, so you need to come look."

"In her room? No way. I'm not invading her privacy."

Paige pops her head through the open door. "Normally, I'd totally agree with you, but she gave us permission to be here and this is extenuating circumstances."

I glance at Nash, who shrugs. "You know your sister. If she's willing to break a rule, it must really need to be broken."

That comment earns a glare from his girlfriend, but he's not wrong.

None of that prevents it from *feeling* wrong as I drag my feet toward Larinda's bedroom. There better be a global crisis that needs our league of useless superheroes to justify this invasion. When Paige waves me toward a notebook on her bed, I spin back to the door.

"Nope."

"Just look at it," she says.

"Not a chance. There's no way I'm reading her private thoughts."

"They're to you."

I freeze and turn back slowly. "What? They're about me?"

"Not about you. *To* you. It's a letter. Think about it. She sent us to her bus. She had to know you might see it. Even if she didn't, she clearly intends to give this to you soon."

I'm totally confused, but my feet must not be as they move me toward the sacred object on the bed. My heart pounds as I scan the beautiful handwriting I've come to adore. God, I'd even miss her handwriting if we parted ways.

The entire right page is covered in text, and I can tell it continues on. This note is either really, really good or really, really bad. I'm still not sure if I should read this, but there's no way I can't now.

Val,

I don't know where to begin. I wanted to say this in person but I was afraid it wouldn't come out right and I'd forget something. You're very distracting. Did you know that? It's your eyes or something. They're too pretty. Your smile too. Also your hair. See? It even happens on paper.

Anyway, I've been thinking about what you said today in the green room. It gutted me, but the more I thought about it, the more I realized none of it made sense. You don't care about money or fame or any of that stuff. None of your reasoning was consistent with everything I know and love about you.

That's right. I said it. The things I LOVE about you. So many things, because I am so completely in love with you and I think it's been developing for a very long time. I won't even say you're everything I've always wanted, because I never dreamed there could be someone like you. You're kind and genuine and so incredibly talented. You make me laugh and see me better than I see myself in a lot of ways. I love who I am and who I'm becoming with you. You make me brave enough to be myself instead of who I'm supposed to be. I don't just want you, I need you, and if it ruins my career, so what? You're my muse. You're the piece that was missing in my music, so there's no point in continuing without you. Now that I know what our music can be together, I can't go back to letting it be less. What's more, I can't go back to accepting less for myself and my heart.

I love you, Perceval Andrews. I want to be with you and I will do whatever I have to do to convince you of that. I don't know why you tried to break things off between us, but I know it wasn't for a selfish reason. You don't have a selfish bone in your body. If I had to guess, it's because you're trying to protect me from something. You can tell me what that is, or don't, but it makes no difference. I'm ending things with Jarvis once and for all, regardless of the consequences. If you don't feel the same, I won't tell the world who my heart really belongs to, but that won't stop it from being yours.

I will always love you.

I will always fight for you.

And I'm willing to wait.

Yours always,

Larinda

16—LITTLE ROCK (STAGE LEFT)

LARINDA

"If you give me a reason to stay, I'll give you two to walk away…"
Colored lights streak through the air and pepper the stage surface beneath me as the music blasts through my in-ear monitors. My heart is racing, adrenaline pumping like it always does when I step in front of thousands (sometimes millions) of people. It's a high I'll never get used to. Nor do I want to. There's something magical about transcending reality to the place where the music lives, where performance lifts me from a woman with a gift to a goddess in her paradise. It's not about the adoration, though. It's about that one brief moment of seeing myself for who I really am, the part that only reveals itself when someone is fully connected with what they love.

"I'm not here to have fun
    I'm here to be the one
    That got away
    If you think I can't play your game
    You better be right or you might find
    You've always been playing mine."

I sashay across the stage, my backup dancers following in a tightly choreographed shadow. Sweat beads all over my body, but I barely feel it. For the last hour, it's just been me and the music. Me and twenty thousand strangers who were brought together by something that came out of my head and heart. That's what music is. That's the power it has, and the reason I will never let anyone take it from me.

"I need your help with this last chorus, Little Rock!" I shout while waving over the crowd. The responding eruption is so thunderous it shakes the floor. I pull out an in-ear monitor so I can absorb the magnificent response while the instrumental echoes around us. The audience gets louder and louder with each beat pushing us toward the explosive climax we feel in our blood.

"They say I'm just another pretty girl with a pretty voice!" I roar over the swelling music. "You know what I say to that?"

The cheering explodes.

A grin breaks on my lips.

I tip the mic back toward me with a vicious smile.

"I'm *pretty* dang sure they're wrong!"

* * *

I'm accustomed to the rush at this time of the night. Blood racing through my body, senses on high alert, euphoric, limitless energy—none of it is new as I move through the underbelly of the arena after my set. What's different is the cause of the reaction, which is so much more than the typical performance high I'm used to. This anxiety comes with faces and lingering uncertainty.

Nash is here, yay! I can't wait to catch up with him and give him a real hug after our initial reunion was cut short by Jarvis' ego. But that's not the face haunting me all night. Even on stage, when normally I'm so in the zone nothing can distract me, he did. This thing with Jarvis is annoying, but being out of sync with Val is rocking me to my core.

I remembered too late about the letter I left on my bed. I was going to give it to him tonight anyway, but there was a whole plan that went with it. Part of me has been praying he won't find it. The other part desperately hopes he has. I don't trust myself to actually go through with it and everything in there needs to be said.

I know I have a bad track record with men, but Val isn't just some guy. He's my person on so many levels and the thought of losing him has been... well, it made me write a letter.

On top of that, I've been tormented by my sister's text earlier today. Her question was totally fair and should have been harmless. Of course she developed a crush on Val and wants his number. She has no reason to think he's off-limits or that her interest would gut me. If anything, I should be glad we did such a great job hiding our relationship. But "glad" is not the emotion coursing through me at the moment.

"You good?" J-Dawg asks as we approach my bus. "Need anything else?"

This is my first tour with the newest member of my private security detail. He came highly recommended by Nash's roommate Marcos, and so far has more than lived up to the hype.

"Yes, I'm fine. Thanks, guys."

"We'll wait here until roll-out," Travis says.

"Great, thanks. Hey, uh, one thing maybe." I bite my lip as the shocking request circles through my mind. Am I really going to do this?

"Everything okay?" J-Dawg asks, his eyes softening with concern. His massive size, shaved head, and endless tattoos make him the perfect intimidating force, but underneath is a teddy bear that makes me feel not just safe, but cared for.

"Yeah, of course. It's just, Jarvis and I had a little spat. I'd like some time apart from him, so please don't let him on the bus if he approaches. Tell him I'll talk to him tomorrow."

Might as well get them used to this. Once I break things off with Jarvis, we'll be having this conversation often and in more severe terms.

Their surprised looks don't surprise *me*, but I'm glad I said it when a weight immediately lifts. I hadn't even realized how much his presence drags down my spirit. Funny how Val does the opposite.

"Of course, Ms. Scott," Travis says, his brow furrowed.

"We got you," J-Dawg assures me with an emphatic nod.

"Thank you. Really. I so appreciate you all and everything you do."

"It's an honor, Ms. Scott," Travis says.

"Ugh. Why can't you call me Larinda? I've been asking for years."

A slight smile pulls at the corner of the hard man's mouth. "Won't happen, Ms. Scott. Have a nice night."

I give him my best mean face which just makes the smile grow further.

"One day I will break you," I huff, and now J-Dawg is grinning as well. Great… Maybe there's a course on being mean I can take.

"You're welcome to try, Ms. Scott," Travis says through a chuckle.

I return a playful grunt as they punch in the code to open the door.

Bubbles erupt in my stomach when I hear Val's voice from inside the bus. My fingers tingle with the desire to touch him. I miss the hard warmth of his body, the sweet fire of his kisses. I miss feeling the opposite of how I've felt all day.

His gaze lands on me the second I appear, but it's Nash who comes forward first.

"Hey! How'd it go tonight?" he asks, moving in for a hug.

I throw my arms around him and squeeze.

"It went fine," I say, my voice muffled against his shoulder. "Still not sure about the transition into 'Moonlight Musings.' It's too abrupt, in my opinion."

I brought up this issue multiple times in rehearsals but they insisted the transition would work once we ironed out the timing. Four shows in and nothing has been ironed.

"Maybe see if they can adjust the tracks and lights to a hard stop to shave off a second or two," Val says, his gaze locking on me.

My insides swirl around, my pulse racing. What is he thinking right now?

"It's counterintuitive," he continues, "but killing the energy completely instead of trying to bring it down might work better. Not ideal, but would probably be the easiest change to pull off on the fly."

I swallow hard, nodding through the knot in my stomach.

"I'll look into it. Thanks," I say quietly.

He nods back and averts his gaze.

My heart pounds as I study him. The way he's braced against the wall has my body straining to press into him. It's become my default position, so not being close feels wrong. My fingers ball into a fist at my side.

"Hey, so we have to talk to you," Nash says.

I force my attention to Nash, still burning beneath Val's intense stare. Did he read the letter? Or is this just the tension from everything else that's happened lately?

My stomach ached the entire time Jarvis forced him to watch us together. I never hated my ex. I've never hated anyone, but in that moment, the true ugliness of that man was on full display. The fact that he would bully someone he knew couldn't fight back, almost made me call it off right then and there.

But Val *did* fight back. Somehow my brilliant, fearless boy managed to turn that entire situation around and steal it from Jarvis. Based on my ex's sulking for the rest of the day, Val is going to pay dearly for that, but it was worth it to see Jarvis groveling for once. He was furious when he looked at his photos and saw the countless images of that same pole. I could barely hold in my laugh and was bursting with love for Val at that moment.

And now he won't even look at me.

What if he read the letter and is even more wary of me?

"You might want to sit down," Nash says.

My stomach drops at the strange suggestion, and I cast a quick glance at Val.

"It will be okay," Val says gently. "We just want to fill you in on something we've learned."

That wasn't the tone of someone who hates me, at least.

With shaky legs, I lower myself on the couch beside Nash. Val is still leaning against the wall on my other side.

"There's no point in sugarcoating this," Nash says. "We don't have time for that anyway. Val found this in Jarvis' dressing room." He hands me a tablet showing a photo of a piece of paper. I recognize Jarvis' handwriting, but the rest doesn't make sense.

"*Get her to dump me. Better if she cheats*? What does this mean?"

"We think it means this engagement is part of some bigger plan," Val says. "We don't know what it is yet, but we do know you breaking it off is a big phase of it. He *wants* you to break up with him, Larinda. He may have proposed for this very purpose."

My world spins for a second. The lights, the air, time itself—it's all hazy as those words settle around me. He *wants* me to break up with him? He forced this proposal I didn't want just so he could hurt me with it? What kind of monster would do something like that?!

The kind that cares about no one but himself. The kind that would bully subordinates because he can. The kind that would... wait.

I stiffen and twist back to Val.

"The green room," I say, meeting his gaze. "That's why you said all that stuff. You were trying to prevent me from calling off the engagement because of this threat."

He looks down, and my heart breaks at the pain on his face.

"Val," I breathe out.

"Of course I didn't want to lose you," he says. "Hurting you fucking gutted me. I just didn't know what else to do."

Oh my gosh.

I jump to my feet and pull him against me. His arms fold around me, and I burrow close, determined never to let go again.

"And I feel the same way," he says softly against my hair. "You don't have to wait for anything."

Relief and joy explode inside me. He read it! He read the letter and accepted it. Emotion lodges in my throat as I hug him tighter.

I love you. So, so much.

And I don't even have to say it because I already did. There's a lot more to tell him, but maybe not with an audience.

Nash and Paige don't seem as horrified as I expect when I glance at them, however. Paige is tucked against Nash in a similarly protective embrace and their smiles give me hope that our fairy tale could have a happy ending somehow.

"So what's next?" I ask, turning in Val's arms so my back is to his front. He starts to pull away, and I grab his wrists to lock them across my chest. His soft laugh at my possessive move sends all kinds of warm fizzles through me.

He'll be lucky if I ever let him go again.

"Next we find out the rest of his evil plan," Nash says.

"Any ideas on how to do that?" Paige asks.

"I do," Val says, and I tilt my head back to him. He kisses my forehead, which sorta makes me melt. "I'll work Chad. He brags about how involved he is in Jarvis' activities. He might know something."

"*Chad*?!" Paige and Nash say in unison.

"Bet he was thrilled to see you," Val says to Nash in a dry tone.

"Chad isn't exactly a fan of mine," Nash replies. "You should do your best to underplay your friendship with me."

"He said you're a terrible spy."

"He's right," Paige quips. "Love you," she sings at his wry look.

Nash rolls his eyes.

"And in the meantime, I guess I'm staying engaged?" I say.

Val deflates behind me, and I lace my fingers with his in reassurance.

"I don't like the idea of him touching you," he mumbles.

"I don't either, which is why if he tries, he's getting an elbow instead," I say matter-of-factly. "You, on the other hand…"

I turn to face him again, and my blood goes hot as we slide together. It's like my body's been starved of contact with him for years, not hours. I don't know how you can miss something you barely had, but here we are.

"What *about* me?" he returns with a sly smile.

My teeth sink into my lip as I cast a quick glance at the others. Sigh.

I face him again and frame his head with my hands.

"You're bunking with me tonight," I whisper, pulling him in for a soft kiss.

I just love the taste of his grin.

17—INTERSTATE 55

LARINDA

Nope. I won't be spending an incredible night of steamy bliss with my boyfriend, because instead of having the love of my life on my bus and in my bed during the drive to Indianapolis, I have Sage and Coriander.

They haven't fought this hard since they both wanted the same hair color.

"You know I'm right!" Sage barks as she stomps into the room where Val and I are on the bed trying to work.

"Sagelicious is so much better than Corialicious!" she whines.

"And you can't both be… licious?" I ask.

She gasps and shrinks back like I hit her. "We can't have the same handle! I'd think you of all people would understand that."

I should probably be offended at that remark, but I'm not entirely sure what I was attacked for. Also, I will take this to my grave, but Sage is right. Sagelicious sounds way better than Corialicious.

Val's amusement is all over his face as he balances the laptop on his stomach, one arm tucked behind his head. I'm sure he too was disappointed that our epic night was crashed by a fight I still don't fully understand, but he also tolerates "ridiculous" better than anyone I know.

"Don't you both already have accounts?" I ask.

"Yes, but we're starting a blog."

"A blog," I say skeptically.

"Yep."

"About what?"

"Touring, silly! Being a famous musician!"

"Okay, but you're not. You're just… never mind. If you're writing a—"

"Videos. It's a video blog."

"Oh. So a vlog."

"Yes, but it won't be *just* videos. We'll also do clothing or makeup or something."

"You're starting an entire brand?"

Val shifts on the bed. Yep, he's definitely stifling a laugh. I'd glare at him but then I'd have to look at him, which would make *me* laugh (and mad that I'm not kissing him right now).

"Or makeup. Maybe lighting."

"Lighting?"

"Name one celebrity lighting brand."

She places a hand on her hip and waits with a smug expression.

"She's got a point," Val says without looking away from the screen. "What's more ubiquitous than lights?"

"Exactly!" Sage agrees, even though there's no way she knows what ubiquitous means.

Now I *do* glare at him, and crap. I was right. I have to swallow a snort at the glint in his eyes when they flicker to me. How is he able to look so adorable and hot just lying there pretending to work? His studio headphones are draped around his neck which is how I know he's not.

"Okay. Sounds like you've really thought this through," I say. "So if you're filming a vlog or… selling lights… why do you each need a separate social media account? Wouldn't you have one account for the entire… whatever this is?"

She opens her mouth to argue. Then closes it. Then squints at the ceiling.

"So you're saying, we use Sagelicious for all of it and not even have one for each of us? Huh. Interesting."

"Well, that's not—"

"Cor!" she shouts, jumping off the bed. Before I can stop her, she's out of my room and halfway to the main lounge. "Larinda had a great idea. We use Sagelicious for everything. We don't even need more than one account."

"Why not Corialicious for everything?"

"Are you freaking kidding me? That will look *ridic* on a tote bag! Seriously, Cor."

While the fight resumes, I shut the door. Then lock it.

"I'm so sorry," I groan. "I just don't feel right about passing them off to someone else when they get like this. That's not fair to Bruce and the rest of the crew."

"It's fine," he says with a smile. "I love how big your heart is."

"Yeah?" I say in a coy tone as I climb toward him on the bed. "What else do you love about me?"

His grin is so stinkin' special. And kissable. I lean in for a small taste. Then a bigger one. Then… sigh. Why fight it?

Soon I'm removing the laptop, his hat, headphones, and anything else preventing me from crowding him into the sheets and stealing the kiss I've been craving all night. The heat of his body burns between my thighs where we connect, and I sink down to enjoy enticing friction. He inhales sharply at the pressure, his eyes closing with a groan.

"This is a bad idea," he mumbles, casting a look at the door where my two companions can still be heard arguing about… something that probably isn't lighting science.

"So bad," I say, leaning down for another deep, probing kiss.

Gosh, it feels good to have him again. I stretch over him, guiding our movements with my grip on his hair.

"No one can know about us," he murmurs through our kiss.

"Correct," I say, yanking his head back to suck on his neck. "I won't leave a mark," I tease against his skin.

His soft laugh erases any chance he has of convincing me to stop.

"Thanks."

In one swift move, he flips us around and applies slow, hard pressure between my legs. I'm burning as I pull his head down for another kiss, practically whimpering when he drags his hips against me, over and over. My right leg tucks behind his to force him even closer. Agonizingly close.

"Maybe just a little?" I plead.

"A little what?" he says against my skin as he runs his lips over my collarbone.

"A little sex."

"A little sex?" he says through a laugh. "What's a little sex?"

"Gah! I don't know. Just… this is killing me."

"We can stop."

"No! I want more, not less."

His grin as he shakes his head is not helping. I tug him back to taste that too. My fingers tangle in his hair again as we kiss, our bodies grinding and exploring the other. Fire rips beneath my skin. Everything is burning and throbbing. This is absolute torture.

"Val…" I moan as he runs his hand along my side beneath my shirt. His fingertips taunt me with each brush just at the edge of where I want them.

"Yeah?"

"Touch me," I whisper. I cover his hand and mold it to my breast.

Chills rake over my skin as he slips his fingers beneath the soft lace and begins a gentle massage. I arch into his touch, moaning at the sparks firing from each graze of my nipple. He pinches it gently, sending me writhing into the sheets.

"This okay?" he asks, kissing along my jaw.

"I've been waiting months for this."

I feel his smile against my skin and trail my fingertips over the back of his neck.

"What have *you* been waiting for?" I ask.

He looks up with a devastating grin. "You really want to know?"

"Actually, I want to guess. This?" I graze my hand down his back and push beneath the hem of his sweatpants. He sucks in a breath when I sink my fingertips into the dense muscle waiting for me.

"Or maybe this?"

His eyes grow hot when I slide my hand over his hip to the front. We might have slipped back into *my* fantasy when I run my palm over the hardening bulge in his boxer briefs. Gosh, he feels good. And yes, I imagine this. All. The. Time.

I grip his hair with my other hand to resume our kiss, loving his immediate surrender. How the heck am I so lucky?

A thump at the door has us tensing in surprise.

Or not...

Val starts to roll off me, and I yank him back in place.

"Don't you dare," I whisper. "What?" I shout.

"Larinda? You in there?"

We exchange a look, and he stifles a laugh.

"Um. Yep," I call back.

"Okay. We have a question about the cappuccino machine."

My boyfriend's silent laughter as he drops his forehead to my shoulder somehow manages to pull an exasperated smile from me as well.

"Yeah? What is it?"

"Can we show you? It's pretty complicated."

The entire process is two steps, one of which is pushing a button.

"Can we do it later?" I ask.

"Of course! No problem. We'll wait here."

Grr…

"It's fine," Val says, kissing my cheek.

I sigh and take his hand after he lifts off me.

"Tomorrow night. I promise," I say, squeezing his fingers.

We lean in for another quick kiss…

That becomes more…

That becomes more…

That becomes… ugh. I force myself to let go.

"I'm dying to play with that bassline, anyway," he says, reaching for the laptop.

I glare at the door. Funny, because I'm dying to play with something very different.

18—INDIANAPOLIS (CONVENIENCE STORE)

VAL

I can't decide if spending the night with Larinda and not touching her is worse than not spending the night at all. I do know that there's no version of spending the night with Coriander and Sage that I want to repeat.

Either way, it's been a constant battle with myself not to think about Larinda every second since. How it felt to crowd her on the bed, to touch her, to feel her hands on me, to *finally* get intimate with her beyond—

"Hey! Earth to Mr. Andrews! I asked a critical question that requires an urgent response," Chad hisses at me. "This or that?"

I tune back in to the present to find my companion holding up identical bags of breath mints.

"They're the same."

"No. Look."

He turns them around. They're still the same.

"That one," I say, pointing at the one on the left.

"Really? Hmm…" He tilts his head as he studies them. "I don't know. The ink on the serving size text might be a tad darker on this one. You don't have to squint as hard to see it."

"Um, sure. So that one."

"But this bag is less creased." He gives me a grave look. "We can't screw this up, Val."

"Buying a bag of mints?"

I don't even know *how* you'd screw that up.

"They're for Jarvis. He trusted me with this assignment. Do you know what happens if I do this right?"

"You get to buy him more mints?"

"Exactly." He puts both bags back. "Maybe this one?"

Still the same mint.

"Okay, well, while you work on that, I'm gonna grab some stuff."

I'm not sure he heard me, which is for the best as I wander away.

I try to appear aimless on my way through the aisles, but my hidden sights are clearly set on the reproductive health section toward the back of the store. For a second, I worry Chad might follow me to get supplies for himself, then decide his mint situation should take a while to sort out. Plus… I mean… Let's be honest…

I peek back and see the top of his blond head still motionless as it decides between eleven of the same thing. I should be good.

I have no idea if I'll need condoms anytime soon, but I have every intention of being prepared should the opportunity arise. In some ways, I'm glad Larinda's entourage was there to crash the party last night because I wasn't exactly stocked for the occasion. Forgive me for not assuming I'd be having clandestine forbidden sex with my longtime celebrity crush on her bus while I was packing for the tour.

After grabbing what I need, I pick up a few other things, then check on my friend again. He's now making his way toward the register with an armload of what must be *all* the mints. Well, that's one solution.

"Go ahead," I say, waving him in front of me.

"Of course not! You were here first. I insist."

"Really, it's fine. You've got your hands full."

He gives me a hard look. "That's not how the code works, Mr. Andrews."

The code. Right. Good to know *The Code* has provisions for convenience store checkout scenarios.

There's now another person behind Chad, another on the way, and a very irritated associate behind the register.

"Dude, just go," the guy says, motioning for my items.

Crap.

I drop everything on the counter and try to hide the condoms from Chad's view as much as possible. I'd rather my grandma watch me buy these than the genius behind the Mer-Kin.

My fingers tap nervously on my thigh as I sneak glances at his eyes to judge his attention. Maybe he saw them? No. I'm just paranoid.

"You okay, buddy?" the employee asks me.

"What? Yeah."

When he casts a warning look at the security camera to his right, I clench my fist and force myself to calm.

"That's forty-six ninety-three," he says.

I manage a tight smile as I tap my credit card on the reader and take the bag he hands me.

"Need the receipt?"

"Nah, it's fine."

"You should take the receipt," Chad says. "This is tax deductible."

Is it? As if I'd list "condoms" under itemized deductions even if it was.

"I'm good," I say, stepping away before this gets worse.

The clerk still watches me with a wary expression as he rings up Chad's purchases. You know you've screwed up when you've raised more red flags than the guy clearing your shelves of the same wintergreen mint.

Chad pays, gets his precious receipt, and follows me into the sunshine. We're two steps down the sidewalk when his phone rings.

"Oh shit! It's my pre-girlfriend. You mind?" He shoves his bags at me. "Careful with those. They're for Jarvis."

That fact makes me want to wrinkle *all* the bags and smear every serving size number so he has no idea how many mints make up 20 calories, but it's Chad who would pay the price, so I suppress the urge.

I should get a medal.

"Hey, Cashew Bug," Chad says, grinning at the screen. "How's the artisanal nut business?"

I think he's joking until a female voice says, "Good, actually. I'm already out of the special edition pine nuts. Who knew there'd be a parfait convention down the street this week?"

"Parfaits! No way! Yogurt? Please tell me it's yogurt."

"I don't know. Probably. I'll find out. How's the tour going?"

"Great. I've only fallen out of the bunk twice."

"Ouch. Are you okay?"

"Of course. I had that martial arts class last year. Remember I told you about it?"

"Right, yeah. You earned your white belt."

"Yep! And I still remember how to roll."

"Ooh. Maybe you can add a roll to your stripper routine."

She's not laughing. Why isn't she laughing? He can't actually be an exotic dancer, right? Then again, it would almost be weirder if he wasn't at this point.

"Yes! Excellent idea. I'll ask Nate for suggestions. Did I tell you Nate waived my tuition for stripper school as long as I fill out all the questionnaires and agree not to wear the mesh biker shorts again? I have to bring my own snacks too."

I'm so lost. Also, these bags are heavy, so how long is this going to take?

"Hey, can we at least walk while you talk?" I whisper.

"Oh, shit! I almost forgot. Brooke, this is my tour bestie, Val. Val, this is Brooke. She sells nuts."

"Hey," I say, twisting a smile. I can't see her with the sun glare, but she sounds nice. The nuts part I got.

"Hi! So nice to finally meet you. Chad talks about you constantly."

"He does?"

"Oh yes. He can't give many details because of your *mission* or whatever, but he says you have really cool tattoos."

"Oh. Um. Thanks."

"He really does," Chad agrees. "I'll get some photos for you."

Nope.

"Hey, babe, I'd love to talk more but we're actually on an important mission right *now*. You're not going to believe this, but Jarvis asked me to get his mints today! *Me*!"

"No way! That's so cool. Does that mean you'll get to see him in person?"

"I see him all the time, babe. We practically live together."

Not even a little true.

"Oh my gosh. I can't believe my pre-boyfriend is famous. Let me know if he ever wants nuts. I can totally hook him up."

"I'm only your *pre*-boyfriend for another two months, right, honeybee?"

His triumphant grin doesn't seem to match any of this conversation.

"We'll see," Brooke says. I can't see her face, but her tone didn't sound as triumphant. "It was great talking to you, though. I'm loving all the updates."

"I'll call you soon! Miss you."

"Aww, that's sweet. Bye!"

"Bye, miss you, bye!"

He hangs up and shoves his phone in his pocket. "Whew. Thanks for not blowing my cover."

"No problem."

I don't even understand his covers enough to blow them.

"You're becoming quite the spy," he says.

"Thanks. So, uh, what exactly is a pre-boyfriend?"

"It's like a boyfriend, but you're not actually together."

"So... a friend."

"No, no. There's romantic intent, just not contractually. You're still in the waiting period."

"The waiting period?"

"Eight months." He shakes his head with a chuckle. "Wait, sorry. Eight months from the inauguration."

He motions for the bags, and I hand them over.

"You have a partner or pre-partner?" he asks.

I force away the sudden rush of my pulse. "No, not really."

"Ding, ding! Good answer." He leans close. "I saw those condoms, you sly dog. Are you one of those dude dudes who has a girl in each city? Or wait… Is it Sage and Coriander?! That could get messy. Unless you're dating both? That's it, isn't it!"

"Huh? No! None of the above. Can we just walk?"

"Sure, yeah. You wanna go downtown to look for some of that city-sponsored art? Most cities have that now. Like the ginormous eggs and shit?"

"Yeah, um, we should probably get back. Plus, all our stuff."

I hold up the bags I'm still carrying.

"Right! Of course. I need to get these to Jarvis, anyway. I'm hoping one day he lets me buy *his* condoms. That would be the day, right?"

I cast him a look, but as usual, he's dead serious.

"Sure…?"

"Mallory did it last time, but if I ace these mints, I'm sure I could get the next run. He goes through them quick enough." He winks and resumes walking with the vigor of a man certain he will get the chance to buy condoms for another man in the near future.

My stomach drops as I follow.

Why does Jarvis need condoms if he's supposedly engaged to a woman he's not sleeping with?

* * *

Larinda: I'm finally alone. Can you come to my suite? 612.

Me: We're on our way back to the hotel. I'll drop my stuff at my room and be up as soon as I can.

Larinda: Ugh. How long?

Me: Maybe 30 minutes?

Larinda: Grr fine. Hurry. This gorgeous bed is being wasted.

My heart pounds as I reread the text conversation Larinda and I had on the way back from the store. It's been almost an hour, and the delay has been killing me. At least it's a good kind of pain for once.

I bite back a smile as I follow Chad off the elevator. Maybe things are finally starting to go my way. It's an off day which means we get real rooms with real beds. And that win was *before* this invitation from Larinda. There's a million things she could do with her free time, and the fact that she wants to spend it with me is… well, the reason my heart is about to punch through my chest.

"Want to get a late lunch?" Chad asks as we part ways in the hall. "I could go for a grilled cheese sandwich, how about you? Did you know Indianapolis is known for their grilled cheese?"

Is it?

"Probably not today, man. We'll catch up later, though, okay?"

"Sigh. Fine."

Interesting. That might be the first time I heard someone verbally sigh.

I toss him a quick smile before sliding my key card into the slot and pushing the door open. I should probably take a quick shower before…

"Oh good, you're back. I was going to call you but wanted to discuss this in person."

Bruce is here. Why is our tour manager here? Wait, why is any of this shit here?

"Um, okay. What exactly *is* 'this'?"

I scan my room which has transformed into a horror movie set overrun with Jarvises. At least a dozen of those weird cutouts are positioned in various outfits and poses. It's like the creepiest cocktail party of all time.

"I'm so sorry to do this to you, but we kind of need your room," Bruce says. "Jarvis is concerned about the cutouts being stacked on the truck all the time and wants to give them a chance to breathe. They were stressing him out with all the negative energy."

I stare at him. No way that means what it sounded like.

"So, if you could just hand over your key when you leave, that'd be great," he says when I don't speak.

"I'm sorry, you're bumping me so a cardboard sign can meditate?"

"Well, fourteen, actually. Fourteen signs."

Strangely, the number of signs doesn't make it better.

"I… *Seriously?* You're serious. This isn't a joke?"

He looks apologetic, like maybe he too sees why I might be upset at losing my room to a cardboard-Jarvis mental health retreat.

"Look, I'm really sorry, man. Jarvis insisted, and the hotel didn't have any other rooms available, but I'm working on finding you a new bed now. Oh! Hey, Chad just responded. One sec."

Chad?!

"Good news! He says you can share his room. He's in four-thirty-seven, just down the hall. Even says he already has an extra key… and toothpaste if you need it."

He slaps my arm on his way to the door.

I'm still numb as it clatters behind him. This is clearly another targeted attack from Jarvis, but what am I supposed to do? What *can* I do?

Anger courses through me as I throw my suitcase beside the cutout reclined on my bed. Thankfully, I didn't do much unpacking since Chad wanted to run out for supplies right after we dropped our belongings in our rooms. Could this be the reason for his invitation? I went along to work him for info on Jarvis. Was he instructed to distract me for their own plot? How many spy networks are we dealing with on this tour? I can't trust anyone at this point.

Once I have my bag packed, I slam the door behind me and trudge down the hall to Room 437.

I've barely finished knocking when it swings open. A baggy light blue polo shirt flies at me and crushes me in an enthusiastic embrace. At least it's not cardboard.

"We're gonna be roomies!" Chad says, rubbing my back a few times before letting go.

"Guess so," I mumble. "Thanks for letting me crash."

"You kidding? I've been hoping for this since the day we met! Want to help, roomie?"

He motions toward a giant grid of tiny white mint circles on the bed.

Wait. *The* bed. There's only one bed. I'm supposed to share a bed with him too?! If he tries to snuggle, I'm sleeping in the hall.

He doesn't wait for an answer before returning to his task.

"That's the keep bag and the reject bag," he says waving toward two open mint bags on the floor.

"I'm sorry?"

"See how this one is slightly crooked?" He plucks a mint from the sea of wrappers on the comforter.

"I mean, it's a circle, so not really?"

"Look closely."

He shoves it toward me, and I squint at it.

Still don't see it.

"The L is chipped."

I blink at the mint. Then at him.

"Reject bag."

He tosses it in the overflowing bag to his right. There are maybe six in the other one.

"It takes some practice, but I have faith in you," he says. "You look like a guy who knows how to sort things."

"Yeah, um, thanks. Hey, you clearly have a good flow going here. I don't want to mess that up. Larinda and I have to work anyway. Maybe later?"

He gives me a cautioning look. "Well, there probably won't be anything left to do later. I have to get these to Jarvis by oh-eleven-hundred-zero hours."

Since that was two hours ago (and not remotely correct), I'm confident he doesn't know how military time works.

"I totally understand and will live with the disappointment. Good luck."

I twist a quick smile, while transferring some belongings to my overnight bag. I'll just freshen up at Larinda's place. I have a feeling Chad will take his role as host way too seriously for my comfort and I don't need him holding the towel for me when I get out of the shower.

"Okay, well, text me when you're finished," he says. "Maybe we can take a walk or hit the pool. I saw a tree I want to check out before it gets dark. I didn't even know they *had* trees in Indianapolis!" he laughs.

"Sounds good. I'll let you know, but don't wait for me. I'd hate for you to miss the… tree."

He returns to his mint sorting, and I sneak out before he can stop me again.

19—INDIANAPOLIS (LARINDA'S SUITE)

LARINDA

Go figure right after I messaged Val to come over for some much-needed cuddle—er, *working*—time, Nash and Paige showed up to say hello. Since they're staying at a different hotel, I felt bad sending them away. Hopefully, Val doesn't mind an impromptu double date?

His smile when I open the door makes me regret not sending them away.

"Hey," he says.

"Hey."

Ugh. I see him every single day. Why does my stomach still buzz like a sixth grader at a middle school dance when those green eyes land on me?

Before he can say anything, I tug him into the room and shut the door. His chest moves in a deep sigh as I snuggle against him, and I know exactly how he feels. I can't wait for the day when this can be our permanent position. No caution. No hiding.

"Thought you were alone," he says quietly.

He kisses my hair, while I twist my fingers in the back of his shirt.

"I was, until they showed up. I'm sorry. I don't think they're staying long."

At least, I hope not.

Something about Val's energy has my relief at seeing him fade.

"Hey, you okay?" I say, pulling back to search his face.

He crosses a distracted look toward the open door where we can hear Nash and Paige arguing (about sandwich toppings?) on the couch.

"Fine. Yeah," he lies. His weak smile confirms it, and I brush the X tattoo at his eye to bring him back to me. I never told him this, but it's always been my favorite. Now that I know a little more about the story, it's become yet another part of him to adore.

"You're fine? Sure. I'm supposed to believe that?"

"It's nothing. Just some mix-up with the rooms. We're sorting it out."

"What kind of mix-up? Did you let Bruce know?"

"He's the one who made the change. It's seriously nothing."

He extricates himself from my arms and adjusts the backpack slung over his shoulder. Looks like he brought more than his laptop this time. Guess he's planning on staying a while? No arguments from me.

"Hey, man. Nice of you to finally show up," Nash says as we move into the living room. Their argument must have ended—or at least suspended—since Paige is tucked against him with his arm draped over her shoulders like nothing happened. I swear bickering is their love language.

"Yeah, sorry. I spent most of the day helping Chad buy mints for Jarvis."

Nash lifts a brow, and Val shrugs. I haven't spent a ton of time with Chad, but nothing about that sentence surprises me for some reason.

"Oh, by the way, what's up with you and Mom and Dad?" Paige asks. "I got your text the other day, but we haven't had a chance to catch up. They messaged me this morning asking about you. It was weird."

Val's expression drops, along with my stomach. What's she talking about? Why hasn't he mentioned his parents are bothering him?

"Yeah, uh, I'm not sure, really," he says. "They contacted me a few days ago."

Paige straightens from the back of the couch, eyes fierce. "Are they going after you again? What else could they possibly want from you?!"

"They're not. I mean, I don't know."

He scrolls through his phone and hands it to his sister. Her expression goes from angry to surprised to perplexed in a matter of seconds.

"What's it say?" I ask.

Paige glances at her brother before squinting back at the screen.

"I'm not exactly sure, to be honest. Who talks like this?"

"Mr. and Mrs. Andrews trying to apologize, apparently," Val mutters.

"They're apologizing?" I ask.

"Sort of?" He shrugs. "They said they messed up and want to meet in Pittsburgh."

I stare at him, equal parts shocked and concerned. His expression is unreadable, except for the slight clench of his jaw. There's definitely more to this, but it's going to be impossible to get it out of him. He never complains about himself. Half the time I'm not sure he even realizes he's been wronged. It's like he expects people to treat him like garbage, something I fully understood after seeing how he's treated by the people who were supposed to teach him his worth.

My last memory of his parents was about a year ago when I accompanied Val, Nash, and Paige to a meeting where he handed over thirty thousand dollars they claim he owed them for a semester of college. Really it was extortion and an attempt to be shitty human beings. They nailed it.

Now, they want to hang out?

I take his hand and lace our fingers. He glances over with a weak smile as I squeeze.

"What did you say?" Paige asks, handing his phone back.

He shoves it in his pocket. "Nothing yet. Which is probably why they contacted you."

"I don't blame you," Paige says. "You have every right to ignore them. If you do decide to hear them out, though, I'm going with you, okay? You're not facing them alone. Promise me you won't confront them without me."

Val lowers his eyes, and Paige narrows hers.

"Promise me, little bro."

A slight smile flickers over his lips. "Sure. Yeah."

"That's not a promise."

"I promise."

"I'm going too," I say, tugging his hand.

He tosses me a smirk. "Not a chance."

I glare back. "Give me one good reason why I shouldn't."

"You'll be performing for eighteen thousand people that day."

Oh. Yeah. That's a good reason.

"Fine," I mumble. "But Paige is right. You can't face them alone, so take her with you or don't go."

"I already promised I would," he says in exasperation. "And I haven't even decided if I'm going. You all can stop babysitting me now."

He pulls his hand away and crosses to the minibar to survey the contents. I've never seen him drink, so I'm pretty sure this is just a distraction. For him or us?

I exchange a look with Paige and Nash, not sure what to do. Paige shakes her head in a sign to let it drop, and I pull in a deep breath. It's so hard to see him hurting. I feel so helpless. All I want to do is storm a castle somewhere, not sit around watching him pretend he's fine. I don't even care which castle, although it would be awesome if his parents were in it. Is this how Val feels watching my drama with Jarvis from the sidelines?

"You mind if I use your shower?" he asks, adjusting the bag.

Guess I was right about the booze distraction… and his extra belongings.

"Of course," I say.

He returns a weak smile and takes off toward the bedroom.

"What do we do?" I ask once we're alone.

"There's not much we can do until he decides what *he's* doing," Paige says.

"The kid is a lot tougher than he lets on," Nash says. "He'll be okay."

That much I know, but just because he can withstand a blow doesn't mean he should have to.

Another blow, I guess. He's already faced plenty from Jarvis. And his role in my career slide. And whatever happened just before he arrived.

Yet, despite all of this, he was willing to sacrifice even more to protect me.

I study the closed door to my room, my heart pinching in my chest. The worst part is he hasn't said a word about any of it. He's been bearing it all alone for heaven knows how long. How can it not be crushing him?

"He's amazing," I say quietly.

I feel Nash and Paige's surprise but I don't care. "Yeah, he's a pretty great human being," Paige says.

I nod, still staring at the door.

"You really love him," Paige says softly.

I glance at her while something lodges behind my ribs. "Yeah, I think I really do."

She pushes up from the couch and wraps me in a hug. After pulling back, she searches my eyes.

"He's had it rough his whole life. He deserves someone amazing, and I think that someone could be you, just… please don't hurt him."

Don't hurt him. Gosh, I'd rather poke out my own eyes, but what if I can't help it? What if all the forces working against us prove to be too much? What if…

"Larinda?"

"I can't promise he won't get hurt, but I can promise I will do everything I can to prevent it."

I hold my breath as Paige studies me.

After several seconds, she smiles.

"Good." She turns to Nash. "Okay, that's our cue. Let's go, rockstar. This woman needs to do some stuff with my brother that I have no interest in witnessing or thinking about."

I can't help but giggle as Nash makes a face.

"Do you always have to say stuff in the weirdest way possible?" he mumbles, following his girlfriend to the door.

* * *

The water is still running by the time I return to my bedroom after ushering the others from the suite. I've never showered *with* Val, but I've spent enough time traveling and working with him to know he's usually in and out.

Should I check on him?

He left the bathroom door open, so he can't be too concerned about privacy. I approach the opening and do my best to survey the activity as discreetly as possible.

Steam obscures most of the glass wall of the shower, but I can still see his defeated silhouette. Head down, shoulders slouched, he's not even moving as he stands beneath the spray.

Liar. He's not okay.

I move through the door, and he immediately straightens.

"Almost done," he shouts over the thunder of the water.

"Okay," I shout back. "No rush. Just checking on you. You've been in here a while."

"Yeah, sorry."

He turns off the water and yanks the towel slung over the shower door.

I force my gaze away as the steam starts to dissolve.

"I'll, uh, let you finish up."

"Larinda, hey, wait."

I turn back, my breath catching at my fantasy come to life. Messy dark hair hanging in his eyes, tattooed body glistening and wet... even the white towel around his waist seems designed precisely to show off the art it's barely covering. He's so beautiful, but it's the look in his eyes that takes my breath away.

"Thank you," he says quietly.

"For what?" I clear my throat when my voice comes out hoarse.

"For checking on me. For caring."

For caring.

Tears prick my eyes as I study him in the soft light. I wouldn't have to know anything about his past to know he's not used to that.

Do you have any idea how much I care about you?

"Of course," I force out. "You hungry? I can have food sent up."

His intense gaze sends shockwaves through my body. My own focus drops to his tattooed fingers holding the towel. I find his eyes again, desperate to read the storm raging in them.

"What do you really want to ask me?" he says quietly.

"What do you mean?"

"You know what I mean."

I trace his body slowly before returning to his eyes. "What's the whole story behind the X tattoo? The long version."

He flinches but doesn't look away. "You already know the basics."

"Maybe. But I don't think I know the important parts. How it affected you. What it truly means."

After another lengthy pause, he sighs and steps from the shower.

"You sure you want the whole story? It's not pretty."

"I not only want the whole story, I want all these stories."

He smiles when I run my fingers over more of the tattoos on his arm.

"We'll be here the entire night if I tell you all of them."

"I have all night."

He tilts his head, searching me. "Fine. But I want something in return."

"What's that?"

"All your stories."

I bite back a grin as my pulse picks up. "Deal."

* * *

I let him finish up in the bathroom, but do *not* let him get fully dressed. Not until we complete the private tour of his body. He didn't seem to mind my demand if his grin when I banned pants and shirts was any indication.

"So bossy," he says as I point to the bed.

"My room, my rules."

"Really…" he draws out with a sly smile.

"Really." I lean forward for a light kiss. Which becomes a heavier kiss. Which becomes my palm on his cheek, my fingers in his hair, my tongue in his mouth, and ah!

I straighten abruptly.

"Stop distracting me," I snap. "You're not getting out of this. Story time."

He laughs, then falls back to the pillow with a groan. "Fine. What do you want to know?"

"I already told you. Everything."

"Everything? I'm almost twenty-four. That's a lot of things."

"Great. So you better stop stalling and start talking. This one first." I brush the X with my thumb. "Long version, remember?"

His smile fades as his gaze drifts to the ceiling. "This was one of my more recent tattoos, but in some ways it was the first."

I take his hand, and his chest rises and falls in a deep breath.

"Tell me," I say gently.

He blinks at the ceiling, as if the story is playing out above him. "My parents had big plans for me from the day I was born," he begins in a distant tone. "They named me Perceval after my great-grandfather who started the family business."

"Which is?"

"Mobile home parks."

In a thousand guesses, I wouldn't have guessed that. "Huh. Okay."

"Exactly. Not really the passion I was wired for. I was never interested in their reality. It was a fight from day one. At the country club, I preferred hanging out with the employees than the other members. At my piano lessons I preferred playing around with my own melodies than the classical masterpieces I was supposed to be learning. At school I focused my efforts on art and music class instead of the 'important' subjects, as my parents called them. We fought constantly. I guess they kept hoping I'd grow out of it."

"Grow out of being you?"

He shrugs. "Apparently. My sister is probably the only reason we never killed each other. She stepped in more times than I can count when things got heated. There was this one time…" He shakes off a memory. "Anyway, she's the reason I even tried to follow their orders and go to Yorkshire for my business degree. She convinced me to earn the piece of paper, if only to buy myself some time and relief from their tyranny. Honestly, I think she was just tired of watching me get hurt and wanted a break for herself as well."

"I already know you went. One semester, right?"

"Yeah. It only took a month to learn it wasn't going to work. I was so miserable, even Paige agreed I had to change majors or drop out. I switched from general business to music business hoping that would help, but it didn't. I finished the semester, but told my parents at winter break I wasn't going back."

"I'm sure they didn't like that."

"They kicked me out of the house," he says with a dry laugh.

I wince as he stares at the ceiling again. "Anyway, Paige had her own place by then and let me move in. It was just supposed to be temporary but it's hard to gain any momentum when you have a force working so hard against you."

"Your parents?"

He nods. "For whatever reason in their twisted brains, they thought if they could keep me from achieving any success in what I wanted, I'd be forced back into what *they* wanted."

"That's horrible. I can't even wrap my brain around that."

My family has always been my rock and support system. What would it be like to have them trying to tear me down instead?

He pulls in a deep breath.

"No matter what I said or did, they wouldn't accept it. I had no idea how to get the point across that I would never follow their chosen path. Then, about two years ago during one of our many arguments, they said if I ever got a face tattoo, they'd cut me off completely. I went to my artist the second she could fit me in and asked for the smallest, simplest tattoo we could think of."

"Val…" I breathe out, tracing the small mark with my finger.

He shrugs and averts his gaze. "So that's the story. You wanted to know what it represents? Nothing. It's an X. Also, everything. It's my freedom. It's the most insignificant *and* significant one."

Wow. My stomach is in knots as I watch him struggle under the weight of the memories.

"I guess they followed through on their threat?"

He lets out a harsh laugh. "They sent some weird official notice informing me I was no longer their son a few days later. So yeah. I just wish it had also convinced them to leave me alone, but I wasn't so lucky. As you witnessed last year, that notice just changed the narrative from extortion to revenge."

I nestle close to him, resting my head on his chest. There's not a person on this planet who deserves that cruelty less than this one. My fingers drift over his skin in the silence, my heart so full of pain and love I don't know how to begin expressing it. I have so many things to say, but none seem like enough. His soul and mind run so deep. I'm not sure a lifetime would be enough to explore every piece of him.

A lifetime?

A strange feeling rushes through me at the thought. Do I really want a lifetime with him? I never thought I'd want that with anyone. All the guys I've dated in the past were barely tolerable for more than a few hours, let alone forever. It worked fine because our busy lives didn't allow for more than that anyway.

This one, though. This one inspires a surge of panic at the thought of *not* having him in my life.

"Well, that's one down," he says. "Your turn."

"You want one of my secrets?" I tilt my head up to him.

His lips turn in a weak smile. "I want all of them, but I'll take one."

I search his eyes for a second before pushing up to press a gentle kiss on the X tattoo.

"Okay. Here's one. Before I knew anything about the story behind it, the X was my favorite."

His eyes soften as they sift over my face.

"You're so special," I say, tracing my finger along his cheek. "I knew it before I even met you. I heard it in what you did with my music."

Emotion filters onto his face as something works its way through his head.

"I'm not the special one," he says. "You're the one who changed everything for me, and I'm not talking about a career. I'll never be able to convey how much your faith in me impacted my life. Up until then, I was starting to think maybe they were right. Maybe I was living a delusion. Maybe I wasn't any good at this and as worthless as they said. You didn't just give me a job, you gave me *me*."

I blink back tears as I nestle close, and he secures his arms around me. Silence engulfs us as we cuddle together, breathing in the scent of soap and clean linen while soaking up each other's warmth. His path was hard. So was mine. But would we be here together in this moment if it wasn't?

"Kind of funny, really," I say, breaking the long silence. "You've been saying no your whole life and know exactly who you are. You just don't have any faith in that person. I have all the confidence in the world, but have no idea who I am—and I'm too afraid to say no to find out."

"We make quite the pair, huh?" he says with a smile.

"Kind of perfect if you ask me," I say, leaning in for a kiss.

* * *

Val

"There is no way you wanted to be a stockbroker when you were little," I laugh out.

In my eagerness to lift the heavy mood, I forced another secret from Larinda. As much as I love the fact that *she* loves my tattoo, I'm not counting that revelation. I'm not sure I can count this one either, though, with the way my bullshit meter is spiking.

"It's true!" she cries, swatting my chest.

"Nope. Not a chance."

"Why is it so hard to believe? Because I'm some ditzy country girl?"

"Uh, no, because no five-year-old except the kids of stockbrokers want to be stockbrokers."

"Well, *I* did," she huffs. "Ask my parents."

"I'm going to." I reach for her phone on the nightstand, and she yanks me back. "Hey!"

"What are you doing?"

"I just told you."

"You're not actually going to message them from my phone!"

"Why not? You afraid they'll tell me five-year-old Larinda *didn't* actually want to ride the bull on Wall Street?"

"No. Because I did. But if you start that conversation, we'll be forced to talk to them for the rest of the night, and I have other plans."

"Really…" I draw out with a slow grin. "Tell me more about these plans."

She hits me again.

"Ow," I say through another laugh.

"No. Not until you earn it. You owe me more tattoo stories."

"Wait, that was it for *your* secret? I pour out my tragic life story and you tell me you wanted to trade stocks twenty years ago?"

She parks a hand on her hip. "What, my career aspirations aren't important?"

"Not when you were five."

"Fine. I'll give you a bonus secret, but only because I'm sick of listening to you whine."

"I accept that. Spill it."

She returns a defiant look. "How about this? I was so nervous the first time I sang a solo that I threw up on the stage."

"Oh shit," I say, eyes wide.

She lifts her brows. "Good enough?"

"Heck yeah. Tell me more."

"About throwing up? Ew."

"Not the process. Set the scene. Who, what, when, where… all the details."

She grunts and throws herself back on the pillow in an adorable pout.

"Hey, this entire thing was your idea."

Her glare is just as cute, and I can't help but sneak a quick kiss. She tugs me back to deepen it, and for a split second her deflection works. Then I remember she claims she had big dreams of shaking up Wall Street while drinking chocolate milk and coloring baby unicorns.

"Nope," I say, breaking away from the kiss. "I want to hear more about this epic stage collapse."

"Ugh. Fine! I was seven and it was Mrs. Cleggs' junior recital."

"And Mrs. Cleggs is…?"

"My first vocal coach. I started on violin, but I was terrible, so we tried singing instead. I was better at that. Or so we thought until the recital."

I bite back a snort at her warning look. "Sorry. Continue," I force out.

She rolls her eyes. "Anyway, the recital was at the community center and there were, like, fifty thousand people there."

I don't do much to hide my skepticism, and she grunts.

"Fine. It was probably more like fifty, but it seemed like fifty thousand to my seven-year-old brain. I was supposed to go first as the youngest, but I refused to go on stage. By the fourth person, she finally convinced me to go out, but I froze. I stood there for about a minute while she hovered just offstage whisper-shouting, *'From the diaphragm! From the diaphragm!'* over and over again."

The snort finally escapes. I can't help it. Poor Mrs. Cleggs. She got what she wanted, I guess, just not in the form she wanted.

Even Larinda is forcing back a grin. "The worst part is the bulk of it landed on Mr. Pickering who was playing the piano. He practically flew out of his seat and screamed *'FUCK!'* I don't know which was more appalling to Mrs. Cleggs, the action or the reaction, but she burst into tears and cancelled the rest of the recital."

"Oh my god." I'm laughing so hard I can barely breathe. "What did your parents do?"

"They took me out for ice cream to try to cheer me up. For the next four years Tia would ask me to throw up at all my recitals so we could get ice cream."

"No way. And did you?"

"No!" she cries, shoving me. "No. I practiced every day after that. Visualized the stage, sang in front of my family, then extended family, then church… more and more until I was an old pro by the next recital."

"Yeah, but did Mr. Pickering play for you again?"

She swings a pillow at me, and I swat it away, laughing.

"Yes, if you must know. In fact, he said I did a wonderful job compared to last year."

"I mean, 'not puking on him' would have raised the bar so…"

She hits me again.

This time I wrap her in my arms and hug her close. She squirms for just a second before erupting into giggles. I'd almost forgotten I was only in my underwear, but once she hooks her leg between mine, that fact becomes incredibly relevant. Her smile fades as she searches my eyes, the silence tense and heated. Her hand slides up my chest, triggering a rush of chills over my bare skin.

"My turn again. What about this one?" she asks, pressing a kiss to my right shoulder.

"It's in memory of my cousin who passed away when we were thirteen."

"You were close?"

"Very."

"I'm sorry. And this one?" She drags her lips down my side.

I pull in a steadying breath.

"Lyrics to my favorite Redburn song that inspired me to pursue music."

"And this?"

She tugs the band of my boxer briefs to expose the candle flame on my hip.

Shit, she's gonna kill me with this interrogation.

When her hand drifts up my thigh to join the fun, I groan and throw my arm over my face.

"This doesn't seem fair," I mumble through the growing heat.

"Want me to stop?"

"Hell no."

Her grin would make that impossible, and when she pulls the band down further, it's over. She's getting whatever she wants. Right now it appears to be the thing I've also been craving for over a year.

Her fingers tighten around me, then her lips in a coordinated dance that has me completely at her mercy. I grip the sheets as she works my body, fire ripping through every vein and artery. The room fades. Blood pounds. Intense pleasure rushes in wave after wave. Climbing, soaring, and—

"Hold on," I gasp out.

She looks surprised, maybe a little hurt, as she pulls back. "Really? You don't like it?"

"What? Of course I do. It's the opposite. I want this to last way longer and I want you there with me."

Her confusion makes my stomach drop. Shit. What did I say? All I want is for our first time to be as good for her as it is for me.

She stares at me, and my heart sinks further with each second of silence. When her eyes cloud, I kick myself.

"Hey," I say gently. "I'm so sorry. I just—"

"Will you shut up?" she mumbles, shoving me back down.

She climbs up until she's stretched over me, her face hovering just inches from mine.

I'm relieved, confused, and entirely turned on when she leans in for a long, deep kiss. She breaks it abruptly and straightens to pull off her top.

What exactly is happening right now?

The question fades quickly as I get lost in the art of her body. I've seen her in just her underwear and bra many times during costume and outfit changes. But it's different when the performance is for you. When it's not an accident but an invitation.

She's quiet as I run my palms along her sides. Goose bumps break out over her skin, and I can't tear my eyes away. She's straight-up mesmerizing. How is this happening? How can someone like me even be here with someone like her?

"You're so beautiful," I say quietly. "You're sunlight breaking through my clouds."

Tears well in her eyes, and I take a heavy breath. God, I'm such an idiot.

"Larinda, hey. I'm so sorry if I've done something—"

"I love you," she says, cutting me off. "I love you and I want to be with you. I don't care about the rules anymore. I can't even imagine being with anyone else. No one has ever made me feel cherished the way you do. No one has ever made a relationship about *me*."

Rare emotion pricks at my own eyes as I absorb her beautiful and heartbreaking confession. I don't understand how anyone who held her heart wouldn't appreciate the treasure in their hands.

"Larinda…" I shake my head. What do I even say to that? *I love you too* isn't nearly enough. *You're the best thing to ever happen to me* is true but too much of a cliché. *I'm so glad Chad made me help him buy mints so I could get condoms.* Also a no.

"I've lived in a shadow for as long as I can remember," I say, holding her gaze. "Of course this relationship is about you. You're my fucking *sun*."

Tears break from her eyes and trickle down her cheeks. It's no wonder I'm so mesmerized when I have a living rainbow hovering over me.

She moves in for another kiss that quickly escalates into more. My fingers tangle in her hair as I flip us around so I'm on top. Her hips instinctively lift to press against me, and suddenly, I really am grateful for Chad and his weird-ass spy missions.

"Please tell me you have a condom," she moans as we grind against each other.

I tug her head back to kiss down her neck, loving her impatient whimpers.

"I do," I chuckle through a string of kisses. She shivers at the tickle on her sensitive skin and slides her own hand into my hair. I love the slight burn of her desperate grip.

"Val, please. I'm tired of waiting." Her expression is too cute for words.

"Okay, just a sec."

I reach for my bag on the floor and pull it open. It only takes one look for my high to crash. Hard.

Oh no.

Pushing up, I swing my legs over the edge of the bed for a deeper search.

"What's wrong? Everything okay?" She settles behind me and rests her chin on my shoulder. "If you don't have one, it's fine. We can do other stuff."

"No, that's not the problem." Shit shit shit. "I mean, yes, but… *fuck!*"

I jump up and swipe my sweatpants from the floor.

"You're leaving?" she asks in alarm. "What's going on?"

"It's fine. I'll be right back. I have to find the bag."

"What bag?"

"The bag from the store."

She squints at me. "Okay? Look, I want to have sex with you too, but it's not a big deal if we have to wait a little longer."

I shake my head. "What I didn't tell you is that the 'mix-up' with my room was because *Jarvis* claimed it for his clone army. If the bag is still in that room, he might find it."

"So?"

I give her a look, and her eyes widen as understanding sets in.

"The condoms," she whispers. "And he'd know they were yours."

"Exactly. He already suspects something between us. I'll be right back."

I'm still tugging on my shirt as I make my way to the door.

This is bad.

This is worse than bad.

"Better if she cheats!!" plays on a constant loop in my head as I practically run to the elevator. Oh the irony that after sacrificing everything to keep her from falling victim to Jarvis' plot, I might be the reason he wins.

"How could you be so stupid?" I hiss at myself as I punch the fourth-floor button. "What is wrong with you?" My bare foot taps on the cold tile as I run a hand through my hair. When did these elevators get so slow?

Someone clears their throat, and I look up to see a couple back further against the opposite wall. Oh. Crap.

"Hi," I say with a tight smile.

"Hi," the woman replies, frowning with pity. "You okay, sweetie? Have you eaten today?"

"I'm sorry?"

"Here." She fishes through her purse.

The elevator stops at floor five, and before I can react, she shoves something at me as they step through the door.

"Take care of yourself," she says as it closes.

I look down to find a granola bar in my hand. Huh? What just happened?

It's then that I also notice I have no shoes, my pants are on backward, and my shirt isn't my shirt. It's Larinda's nightshirt that reads "Angel On Duty." The small tent in my sweatpants probably isn't doing much for my case either.

Shit. Oh well. That's the least of my problems.

I shove the snack in my pocket because I am kind of hungry, actually.

Once the elevator reaches my floor, I launch down the hall and pull the key from my other pocket. At least I remembered that. Shoving it in the slot, I hold my breath as I wait for the reader to click green.

It's red.

"What the hell?"

I must have done it wrong. I flip the card and insert it again. Still red. Other side. Also red.

"Shit, shit, shit."

I try it five more times but nothing works. What if they already changed the keys since they transferred the room?!

I run down the hall to Chad's room, praying I left the bag there and not in my original room.

He answers on the second knock, and for a fraction of a second I forget my nightmare.

What the…

"You like it? It's magical." He holds up his hands and spins amidst the resplendent purple glow outlining our room.

"Are those fairy lights?"

"LEDs. They're purple."

"I see that. Um…" Yeah, I got nothing. "You know we're only here for a night, right?"

"Exactly! Have to make it count. Actually, you're in luck. I just finished sorting *the goods* and was about to go deliver them to Jarvis. Want to come? Unfortunately, I can't give you credit, since you didn't help."

"I'm good, but thanks for the offer. Hey, did you happen to see my bag from the store lying around?"

I scan the room, which is markedly harder to scan now that it's purple.

"Yep. Right over there."

Thank heavens!

"Jarvis dropped it off a few minutes go."

Oh.

I force myself to calm through the sudden panic.

"I know what you're thinking," Chad continues. *"Why, Chad, how come you didn't give Jarvis his mints while he was here?"*

God, I wish that's what I'd been thinking.

"No explanation necessary," I say. "You do you."

I scoop the bag from the floor and rifle through it. My heart drops into my stomach when I notice the box is gone. Everything else is there, but no condoms.

Fuck fuck fuck.

"Well, the answer is, I forgot."

"Huh?" I say, looking up.

This is… What am I going to do?!

Think!!!

"I forgot to give him the mints," Chad says.

"What mints?"

"You know, *the* mints!"

I shake off my terror. "Oh, yeah, right. Okay. I have to run. Thanks for this."

I need to find the others and talk through this disaster. Maybe there's some way to spin it for damage control.

"I forgot because we got to talking about you, actually."

I freeze and turn around.

Chad's eager grin is even creepier in violet, it turns out.

"What about me?"

"Just gossipy stuff," he says with a chuckle.

"What *kind* of gossipy stuff?"

He shrugs. "Jarvis wanted to know if you were seeing anyone. Probably wants to invite you and a plus-one to the party tonight."

Probably not. Wait, what party? Never mind. Not important right now.

"What did you tell him?" I ask, heart pounding.

"The truth."

Oh god.

"That I didn't know but thought it might be Sage and/or Coriander. Sorry for blowing your secret. Sacrifice one for the many, though, right? It's part of the code."

Air rushes back into my lungs. I've never been so happy for his unintelligible code.

For maybe the first time ever, Chad's terrible spy skills might have saved Larinda and her career. I can let the world think I'm into Sage and/or Coriander if it means hiding the truth.

"Yeah, um, it's fine," I say. "Thanks."

"No problem. Relationships, man, am I right?"

So right.

* * *

After changing into real clothes, I barely make it into the hall before a phone is shoved in my face.

"And here he is!" Sage chirps. "You all ready to meet Val?"

I have no clue who she's talking to since Coriander is the only other person present and I'm pretty sure she knows me at this point.

"Say hi to our crew!" Coriander says, coming up on my other side.

"Uh, hi," I say to the phone screen. Wait, are they filming?

"In case you're just joining us, we're live with Val Andrews, Larinda's talented—and *sexy*—producer!" Sage says.

Wait, they're *live*?!

"Isn't he just the cutest?" Coriander adds.

I force an awkward smile, doing my best to scan past them for an out. How did they know where I was staying? Wait, why are they even here?

"So cute. And single!" Sage says.

"For now," Coriander adds with a giggle.

Huh?

"You mind if we ask you a few questions for our Cagelicious Crew?" Sage asks.

"Your what?"

"Our followers," Sage hisses, flipping the phone so I can see the screen.

And yep, that's me... looking like they caught me right after learning my condoms were stolen by my rival who's trying to destroy my secret girlfriend.

"First question," Coriander says in a grave tone. This must be her journalist persona. "What is your music?"

I blink at the screen as they wait.

"What is my music?"

They nod.

"I don't…"

"Ah! I think we stumped him, girls!"

I think they're right.

"Okay, next question. If you could only pick one, which would it be?"

She turns the screen back to me.

All I see is a baffled version of myself. What exactly am I picking? I'm gonna go out on a limb and guess they've never interviewed anyone before. Have they ever asked someone a question?

"The third one," I say dryly.

"Ooh, *scandalous*. I like it."

"Thanks?"

"Do you have any questions for us?"

The way they think questions work? No.

"Not really. It was great meeting you all," I say with a tight smile.

"You too," they say. "Kisses!"

They faux applaud for the camera.

Is anyone even watching this? Didn't they just decide there would *be* a "this" yesterday? I'm amazed they even got past the grueling name phase.

"We'll see you later, sweetie!" Sage calls as I start toward the elevators.

I lift a hand in acknowledgement without turning around.

"So lucky," Coriander says to someone. "Can't wait."

Are they talking to me? About me? I'm so confused.

"I don't know. Let's ask him. Hey, Val," Sage shouts.

I turn back to see the phone pointed at me again.

"If you could only be one candy, which would it be?"

"Mints."

They squeal and turn the phone back to them. "Oh my glory. Did *not* see that coming!" Sage cries.

"Me neither!" Coriander agrees.

"You heard it here first on… *Cagelicious*," they say in unison.

I do my best to ignore them as I continue my journey back to Larinda.

I've barely finished knocking when a hand grabs my arm and yanks me into the room. Larinda closes the door and leans against it with a deep breath.

"Careful. Sage and Coriander are streaming," she whispers. "Don't say anything about the condoms."

Um. About that…

"We should be safe. They're on my floor now," I say.

"Oh no. Did they track you down too?"

"I think so?"

She looks irritated as she stomps toward the couch and throws herself down. "I get that they want to be vloggers, or sell light fixtures or whatever, but they can't use *my* life and *my* career for content! I can't believe they just showed up at my room expecting me to be on their show! And now they're going after you too?"

That was a "show"?

"I totally agree with you. This whole thing is a huge invasion and violation."

"I know! I thought they were my friends, but I feel so used right now."

"Probably because they *are* using you."

"Gah! I want them to stop. My life is *my* life, not theirs. I'm so tired of them following me around and acting so entitled."

"So tell them to stop."

She furrows her brow and stares at me. I squint back.

"What do you mean?" she asks.

"I mean, tell them this isn't working for you anymore and they need to move on."

Her eyes widen. She opens her mouth to speak. Then closes it again.

Has it really never occurred to her to set boundaries?

"You know all of this is in your control, right?"

Her anxious gaze flickers toward the foyer as if her contingent could show up at any second. And they could. That's the problem.

"They might hate me," she says quietly.

"They might."

I lower myself beside her and pull her against me.

"But isn't that better than being held hostage in every aspect of your existence? What do they contribute to your life and well-being?"

She shakes her head, and I tighten my hold.

"I'm… not sure."

"Relationships are supposed to go two ways," I say softly, kissing her hair. "You don't have to decide anything now, just think about it. It's okay to set boundaries. No one has a right to your life but you."

She threads her fingers with mine and grips hard as she thinks.

Is this getting through? I really hope so. I'm tired of watching everyone take advantage of her. I hate that she's so shocked by my deference. She deserves to be worshipped, not used.

"Speaking of boundaries," she says. "Is everything good with the condom situation?"

"Well…"

"Val?"

"Not exactly."

"You couldn't find the bag?"

"No, I found the bag."

"But…?"

"The condoms weren't in it."

She bites her lip as we exchange a long look. "That's not good."

"No."

"Do you think Jarvis suspects they were for me?"

"No. I think he suspects they were for Sage and Coriander."

I expect hysterical laughter. Her pensive squint is mildly alarming.

"Larinda? That's ridiculous, right?"

"Of course. Or… well… maybe not."

"Maybe *not?*"

This conversation just keeps getting worse.

She tilts her head back to me, and I take a deep breath at her concerned expression. "It might explain some things, that's all. I had something to tell you about tonight. It didn't make sense at first, but maybe it does."

"What about tonight?"

"Um, Jarvis is insisting on going out."

I release a breath. "Okay. I mean, we knew stuff like this was going to happen."

"Yeah, but he's insisting on inviting you too."

"Me? Why would he want me along?"

"I don't know, but given all of these developments, it can't be good, right?"

"That's a pretty safe bet."

"Which is why you can't go."

I huff a laugh. "I'm not leaving you alone with him, especially if he's up to something."

"But what if it's to hurt you somehow?"

"It probably is."

Her brows pinch, and I plant a kiss to soothe them.

"Whatever he has planned is just the latest ploy in his scheme. He probably doesn't know we're onto him, so we have the advantage of going in prepared."

She settles back, drawing my hand to her lips. "It's not right," she whispers.

"No. None of this is."

"What are we going to do?"

"About what?"

"About everything?"

I sigh and study the far wall. "I don't know, but we're doing it together."

20—INDIANAPOLIS (CLUB D LUX)

LARINDA

It takes exactly four seconds to realize this is a double date.

Sort of.

I'm not sure what it's called when one pretend couple is on a date with a nonexistent throuple. Val is sandwiched between Coriander and Sage on the couch perpendicular to Jarvis and me in our private VIP section of Club D Lux. Interestingly, my fake fiancé has seemed more interested in the other "couple" than me since leaving the hotel. I'm fine with that, except for the piece of my heart that's reaching for Val.

In addition to looking uncharacteristically dapper in a black button-up shirt he should definitely wear more often, he's also been the perfect gentleman since we climbed into the limo. If I didn't know better, I'd think he's actually been enjoying the company of his surprise dates, including the present conversation about the difference between snails and slugs and why it's a travesty that more people either are or are *not* talking about it.

"How do we know slugs don't have shells, though?" Sage asks.

"Because look at them!" Coriander argues.

"Just because you can't see it doesn't mean it's not there. You know, like rain. Maybe it's teeny tiny. Or invisible. Hummingbirds have wings even though you can't see them."

Val's brow furrows as he works out how to mediate a debate he can't follow.

"Would you care for another mint?" Chad asks, bending low to offer us a handful of individually wrapped mints. Did I mention Chad is also in attendance as Jarvis' "valet"? I honestly can't tell whose idea it was or who's benefiting the most from the odd arrangement, but he's been hovering beside him all night, dutifully waiting to serve his... I'm not sure. Employer? Friend? Idol? I'm not entirely clear on their relationship at this point.

Jarvis waves him away, and Chad straightens again to wait for something.

"Gotta say. I never saw this coming," Jarvis says to me.

"What?"

"That." He motions toward the other couch where the argument has escalated into... charades? I can't tell which of them is the slug and which is the snail, but that fact is probably proving someone's point.

"They look good together, don't you think?" Jarvis asks.

"Slugs and snails would rule the world if they overcame their differences and joined forces."

He rolls his eyes. "You know that's not what I mean. I'm talking about Valerie and your girls. Think he can handle two at once?"

I swallow the lump in my throat. "I'm not sure they're together."

"No? Pretty sure they are." He snaps his fingers, and Chad leans down. "Tell her what you told me earlier today."

Chad nods eagerly. "There's a reptile in New Zealand that has three eyes. It starts with a T, but it's not a tortoise. It's... crap. A taurus? No. Tua-loo—"

"Not that," Jarvis grunts. "About them." He flicks his fingers toward the others.

"Oh! Yes. We think they're having sex."

Jarvis' rapt attention has me on edge. We know he suspects Val has feelings for me. Does he suspect mine as well? I need to be very careful how I navigate this obvious trap.

"So what if they are?" I say in a bored tone. "They're adults. It's not like it's the first time in history people have hooked up on a tour."

Jarvis runs his gaze over me, and I do my best to ignore his intense stare.

"True, but won't that get messy when things go bad?"

I shrug. "Who says they will? And how is that my problem anyway?"

"You'd have to choose between your producer and your lifelong friends."

"Not necessarily, and besides, what exactly do you want me to do? Forbid them from seeing each other?"

"Whoa. No need to get defensive, sugar doll," he says, holding up his hands.

"Don't call me that."

His gaze narrows on me, and I glare right back. After a short standoff, he sighs and pushes to his feet. "Let's not tussle. Let's do the hustle instead."

He holds out his hand to me, and I cross my arms. "Let's not."

"Larinda, come on."

"I don't want to dance. I'm tired."

His gaze goes cold as he crosses another look to Val. Crap. I should dance with him just to keep our cover, but the thought of being close to him right now sends a shiver through me. I'm counting the seconds until this whole thing is over and I can swap this frog for that prince.

"Fine," he pouts. "You. Let's do a lap," he barks at Coriander and Sage.

They rocket to their feet with excited grins.

"Can we film it?" Sage asks.

"Sure. Whatever," Jarvis mumbles, already halfway to the exit.

"Wait!" Coriander says, pulling out her phone. She turns the screen toward her and gives the peace sign. "Cagelicious to the dance floor!"

"We promised you all the things, Crew-bugs!" Sage says, poking her head into the frame. "Here's another thing!"

They're still babbling to their "fans" as they follow Jarvis out of view. His security (and Chad) accompany him, while Travis and J-Dawg stay with me and wall off access to us. They also provide a nice privacy screen.

Val and I stare at each other from our adjacent couches for almost a full minute, neither of us sure what to do. We can't do what we want. We won't do what we don't want. So we sit and enjoy a moment of getting lost in each other's eyes for a silent conversation.

"I want to be touching you," Val's look says.

"I want that too," mine replies.

"This is torture. I can't wait until it's over."

"I know. We'll figure it out."

"I love you."

"I love you too."

"Are you okay?"

"Yeah, you?"

"Yeah."

We exchange a smile, and I check the entrance again before stretching out my leg to brush his. He adjusts to settle even closer, and I can't stop my foot from running up and down his leg. He closes his eyes, visibly frustrated as my strappy heel does what my hand and mouth want to be doing.

His gaze crosses to Travis and J-Dawg's backs before he leans forward and runs his palm over my foot and up my ankle. A shiver runs through me as his fingers graze the smooth skin of my calf. Sometimes it's not a good idea to touch someone you've been desperate to touch all night. This is probably one of those times.

I need so much more than this and glance at Travis and J-Dawg again.

Maybe if we…

They must sense our attention and throw a glance in our direction. I stiffen and pull away from Val, forcing a tight smile.

Travis frowns as his gaze passes between the two of us.

Oh no. Crap crap crap!

There's no way he didn't see that.

I shift even further from Val's couch, but I don't miss the look my body-guards exchange. They know! They must. It's literally their job to know every-thing. Heck, they're supposed to know more than I do.

Val's worried gaze lands on me. He must be concerned about the same thing.

What is wrong with you?! I yell at myself. *How could you be so careless?*

They wouldn't say anything, would they? I mean, they're on my team, right? *My* allies.

Travis leans toward J-Dawg and whispers something. J-Dawg nods, then straightens back to attention as Travis approaches.

"You don't look well, Ms. Scott," Travis says. "Maybe we should get you to a quieter, more secure location?"

I swallow the panic and force a smile. "No. I'm fine."

He widens his eyes in a silent message and tilts his head toward the rear of the VIP area. "No, really. We're worried about you."

What's going on?

I'm even more confused when Val jumps up. "Thanks, man. You're right. She could definitely use some air."

I give him a sharp look, and he returns a silent request to play along.

Hold on…

J-Dawg peeks back at me with an almost imperceptible smile. Travis has one too when I look closely. I narrow my eyes at them. Wait a second…

"Oh. Uh, yeah. That would be great," I say as Travis takes my arm. Val flanks my other side, and J-Dawg leads us through the VIP area toward the private rooms. He whispers something to the host, whose eyes go wide as she nods with concern.

Soon we're following her past several closed doors to an empty room at the end of the hall.

"Here we go. It's yours for as long as you need it, Ms. Scott. May I get you anything? Some water? An almond plate?"

"Water would be great," J-Dawg says. "Thanks, Ashley. We owe you."

"Don't be ridiculous. It's my pleasure. We're so glad you're here," she says to me. "I'm sorry you're not feeling well."

"I'm sure it's nothing," I say. "Just tired."

"I can't even imagine the stress of touring. Well, I'll have water sent right away and let us know if there's anything else we can get you."

"Hey, Ash," J-Dawg says. "Can you do us a favor and not let anyone know she's here?"

"Of course! Why would you even think you need to ask?"

He leans close. "No, I mean, *anyone*. Ms. Scott needs some breathing room. If *anyone* is looking for her, just tell him you're not sure where she is and he should message us."

Her expression floods with understanding. "Oh. Yes, absolutely. Not a word… to *anyone*."

"Thanks, Ash. You're the best."

She beams back at him, and I have so many questions. I've heard of rockstars having flings in various cities, but bodyguards? It makes sense, I guess.

"You mind looking after her?" Travis asks Val once we're alone.

"Not at all. I'm happy to."

Travis nods and exchanges a long look with Val before turning back to me. "We'll be right outside, Ms. Scott. You tell us if you need anything."

"I will. Thanks, Travis."

"Always," he says with a wink, then closes the door behind him.

After a few seconds, Val and I burst into laughter.

"Did that just happen?" I say, still chuckling.

"What? Getting kidnapped by your own bodyguards for a clandestine booty call?"

I snort a laugh and fall into his arms. Honestly, I'm just relieved to be free of the others and back where I belong. Travis and J-Dawg are getting a huge raise for being the best security detail in the world. How long have they known about Val and me? Probably longer than we did.

"As much as I appreciate this, it probably wasn't a great idea," Val mumbles against my hair.

My arms tighten around him as I breathe in the woodsy spices I love.

"I know," I say with a sigh.

"Jarvis is going to be pissed when he comes back and finds us gone."

"Probably."

"What if he suspects—"

I pull his head down and kiss away the rest of his fears. They're all legitimate and all ones I share, but we're here now, so let's be here.

I frame his face and draw him in deeper as he backs us toward the couch. We drop to the cushions, and I'm already squirming for more when he stretches over me.

"You look incredible tonight," he says through our kiss. "It's been so hard not to touch you."

His palm slides up my inner thigh, past the hem of my sapphire minidress. Tingles run over my skin, spreading higher and deeper with each inch he touches. My hips instinctively squirm for more contact.

"So do you," I breathe out, gasping when his palm molds over my center.

This is what I've been craving all night. He tastes incredible as my lips devour and my hands explore. My hips shove against his hand in slow, hard demands that he obeys with increasing pressure.

I moan as each pass sends another surge of electricity through me. Over and over, harder and harder, and just when I'm about to beg, he slips his fingers beneath the lace.

I burn at the rush and widen my legs for him. My tight dress rides up, giving him full access as his fingers rub and play.

"Val," I gasp out.

"Yeah?"

"Never stop touching me."

His soft laugh is everything. "You got it," he murmurs against my lips.

He's a liar, though, because suddenly he's gone. So is his touch, and I'm about to protest when the wet heat of his tongue takes over.

Oh!

I arch back as the streaks of fire burning through me become scorching waves. Soon I'm drowning in sensation, the room fading around me as I climb higher and higher. It feels so good. Everything, *right* there. Just… a… little…

Explosive stars shatter me into oblivion. I can't breathe as surge after surge of intense pleasure make it impossible to move. Aftershocks quiver through me for several seconds, my body buzzing even as my stiff limbs relax into trembling mush.

"Holy bananas," I mumble.

Val laughs and crawls up to hover over me again. "That okay?"

I tug his head down for a soft, tender kiss.

"Can I tell you a secret?" I say, pulling back.

"What's that?"

I run my thumb over his cheek, searching his pretty eyes.

"In a cage match I'd put my money on the slug, not the snail."

His eyes widen for a second before he chokes out a laugh and drops his forehead to my shoulder.

21—INDIANAPOLIS (ROOM 437)

VAL

"Okay, what?!" I snap at Chad as I pull on my jeans.

"*Nooothiiiing,*" he draws out.

"There's obviously something."

Know how I know that? Because he's been acting weird since he returned from the club last night. He was weird while I got ready for bed. He was weird while I was trying to maintain a safe distance on the king mattress to sleep. He was weird while taking down his fairy lights at 5:30 this morning, and now he's being weird while following me around as I get ready.

"Chad. Seriously, dude, just tell me what's up."

He releases a sigh. "Fine. But you have to promise not to do anything rash like start a survivalist cult or mass produce genetically modified tomatoes that mess with people's immune systems."

Right... um...

"Pretty sure I can restrain myself from... that."

He looks skeptical but leans forward anyway. "Okay. It affects you."

"I figured as much. What is *it*?"

On the outside I'm calm and mildly irritated. Inside, my heart is pounding.

What happened with Larinda at Club D Lux was amazing and very irresponsible. We both agreed it was too risky and we should keep our distance over the next few days, just in case. The last thing we need is any evidence to support suspicions that may have been aroused. We even left the club at different times in different vehicles to provide a cover.

Despite our efforts, I can't shake the image of Jarvis' dirty looks for the rest of the night. I couldn't tell if they were new dirty looks or my brain adding new evidence to the same ones. Either way, I have no idea where his head is which scares the crap out of me.

Maybe I'm about to find out?

"It's… ah! This is so hard. I don't want to hurt you, bestie." He cringes. "Shit! I meant, *tour* bestie. Marcos is already my *bestie* bestie. I'm so sorry. Please don't be upset. If I could have two besties, you'd be the other one, I swear. It's in the code, though."

Of course it is.

"It's fine. So what's the news about me?"

"Oh! Right. It's about your amours."

"My *amours*?"

He chews on a thumbnail and nods. "I overheard something…"

"… which was?"

He glances around nervously again. "Cheating," he whispers.

Oh no.

I force a calm expression through a burst of panic. "Cheating? What about cheating?"

He groans and covers his eyes. "It's so bad. Ugh! Fine… I overheard your girlfriends gushing about a threesome with an A-lister. And since you're clearly not an A-lister, it clearly wasn't you."

Ouch to that last part.

He peeks through an opening in his fingers, and I do my best to look dismayed not relieved.

"I see," I say with a hard expression while my insides sip cocktails on a palm-lined beach. Thank god it's not about Larinda and me.

"I'm so sorry, my friend. Bring it in." Before I can react, I'm being yanked toward a cologne-drenched chest for a suffocating Chad-hug.

After a few seconds, I extricate myself and offer an awkward smile. "Thanks," I say. "Do you know who they were talking about?"

That's something a jealous boyfriend would ask, right? Plus, that info could be helpful down the line.

"No. I wish. I'll keep an ear out, though. A man should know who his girlfriends are sleeping with, am I right?"

"Right."

"Oh! Maybe it's Phil!"

"Who?"

"Phil—I forget his last name—but he played the park ranger on that show about forest fires?"

I squint at him. Not sure what show he's talking about but pretty sure "Phil" with no last name isn't an A-lister.

Although I'm happy to hear my non-girlfriends are cheating on me, I'm nervous about my lack of progress on discerning more of Jarvis' plan. We've been so distracted by our own scandal, we're behind on spying on the others. Maybe Chad will have a lead I can use.

"Well, if you find out, let me know," I say. "So, what's on your schedule for today? Any more mint runs?"

"Hmm… well, it's a show day, so Jarvis will be busy with show stuff but… oh! He did say we're making an exception to go belt shopping!"

"Belt shopping?"

"Yep. He never goes out on a show day, as you know, but his favorite belt boutique is in Indianapolis."

Interesting. He's breaking his golden rule for a belt? And why not get the belt yesterday which *wasn't* a show day? This development screams of potential subterfuge.

"Cool. And what store is that?"

"Hmm… something with ponies?"

Ponies. Well, there can't be too many of those in the greater Indianapolis area. "And, uh, around what time do you think you'll be going?"

"The car leaves promptly at ten fifty-seven. I'm pretty excited. I've never been to an exclusive belt boutique. He already said I can be the person who holds the ones he doesn't want until the store people take them to put them back."

"Wow. Good for you, man."

He beams as he imagines holding belts, and I offer a quick smile to hide the returning nerves.

Jarvis doesn't break his traditions lightly. Something's going down at the pony belt store. Guess I'm going "belt shopping" today as well.

I pull out my phone to text Nash and research pony-themed belt retailers.

22—INDIANAPOLIS (THE BELTED STAG)

VAL

From the outside, The Belted Stag is not as impressive as one would think for a must-see celebrity attraction. I guess it *does* deliver on the promise of "belt store." I also haven't seen a single reference to ponies in the half hour Nash and I have been staking out the place from the café across the street. We have no guarantee this is the right location, but it won points for having an animal reference and pretentious logo.

More impressive is the fact that the business is closed to the public and contains an entire camera crew. In a bout of irony, we've been taking photos and filming *them* for the last few minutes. You know… just in case.

"Guess that explains why Jarvis was willing to break his *no leaving the venue on a show day* rule," I say.

"What could they possibly be filming in a belt store?" Nash asks.

"Commercial, maybe? He might have a sponsorship deal with them."

"Can't. He's exclusive with Sandeke Telecom. Trust me, the Lord Commander His Majesty Denver Sandeke made sure his prize pet was locked down hard with legalese."

"Then maybe he's planning to jump ship."

"Yeah, probably. I heard the belt industry is really driving today's futures. What even is telecom?"

"Okay, fine. Then, I have a better question. What's *she* doing here?"

Nash follows my attention to the business-suit-clad woman exiting a vehicle stopped in front of the store.

"Oh shit! That's Rena Rivera from Lakebend Records. Why the hell would she be in Indianapolis?"

"At Jarvis' belt store with a camera crew? Great question."

"You got her on video?"

"Yep."

We exchange a look that doesn't do much to soothe the tension in my stomach. None of this can be good. Chad seemed to legitimately think they were "going belt shopping," which means he didn't know the full plan either. (To be fair, if I had a high-stakes evil plot, Sandeke Telecom's *Administrative Talent Liaison vis a vis Something* would be the last person I'd tell as well.)

"We really need to get in there and find out what's up," Nash says. "*You* can't go in, for obvious reasons, but maybe I can give it a shot? Technically, I worked on Jarvis' Sandeke pitch for five minutes. He might not hate me as much. Doubt he even knows I was involved."

"He knows you're close with Larinda, the focal point of whatever this betrayal is. That's enough to get you booted."

"Yeah, good point. Shit, what do we do?"

"Maybe it's time to activate my in with my touring bestie." I grab my phone and pull up the text stream with Chad.

"Who's your touring bestie?" Nash asks. "Wait, *what* is a touring bestie?"

"Chad, and I have no idea."

"Chad's in on this?"

"I don't think he knows he is, but yeah."

Nash huffs a laugh. "Sounds about right. Oh hey, look. The guest of honor has arrived."

We watch through the window as a large, souped-up SUV double-parks in front of the store. No less than six people climb out, two of which are Chad and Jarvis.

I see why Chad hasn't responded to my text when he marches behind Jarvis with the laser focus of a man who takes unwanted-belt-holding seriously. Let's hope he likes to brag about his clutching privileges just as much.

"Can I get you anything else? Would you like a refill?" our server asks, drawing our attention from the events outside.

Her question comes with a smile that's not quite flirty but a tad above friendly. Maybe she'd be interested in helping us?

"A refill would be great. Thanks, Kim," I say. "Hey, do you happen to know what's going on across the street? We thought we just saw Jarvis McKinnley."

"No way. He's here?!"

She leans forward to look through the glass like he might still be standing on the sidewalk.

"Pretty sure it was him," Nash adds, following my lead. "I heard he's really into… belts."

"Totally! He's in town for a show tonight. A few of my friends are going, although, if I'd been able to afford tickets, it would have been to see Larinda not him." She leans close. "Between you and me, his music is okay but he sort of seems like a jerk."

Yep, she just earned herself a hefty tip.

"Sorry, that was mean," she says with a wince. "I'm sure he's not what he seems."

He is.

"Anyway, I'll ask the owner and see if she knows anything about what's going on."

And there's an even bigger tip.

"That would be great. Thanks," Nash says.

We continue scouting the street after she leaves, the gravity of our situation sinking in as evidence mounts that this conspiracy runs even deeper than we thought. If Rena is here, that means Lakebend is involved. Since Lakebend is Larinda's label as well, why isn't she being included in whatever this is? And why all the secrecy?

It only takes a few minutes for Kim to return with wide, excited eyes.

"This is top secret," she whispers. "Sam said they're shooting a music video. One of our employees is even an extra in it! So freaking cool!"

Nash and I exchange a look before forcing a smile.

"Wow," he says in a somewhat believable impressed voice.

"I know, right? Sam also said the big order we're filling now is for them! I wonder which drink is Jarvis'."

Probably whichever one is needlessly complex and obnoxious. Is there an order for a *large non-fat chai Frappuccino in a medium-sized cup at exactly 178 degrees with freshly squeezed oat milk, 113 granules of sugar, 1.23 pumps of caramel, 2 ounces of organic triple-whipped cream, a pinch of tarragon (if you have it, if not Saigon cinnamon), and an emptied tea bag that once had Meyer lemon tea* on the list?

"Okay, well, I need to check on my other tables. I'll let you know if I hear anything else."

"Great. Thanks," Nash says as she takes off.

"A music video?" I hiss once we're alone. "Why would they be filming a music video hours before a concert? There's already enough chaos to deal with. What's the rush?"

"And why would a top-tier label exec need to be here for it? They have entire departments for this shit."

Right, yeah. Good point.

"Could it be related to the engagement? Some publicity stunt?" Nash suggests.

"Without Larinda? She doesn't know anything about this. I'm sure she would have mentioned it if she did."

A chill runs through me as I peer into the store for some phantom clue about what's going on. Something isn't right. I feel it in my gut and suspect whatever it is might be related to the notebook threat I found.

"I have to get over there and find out what they're up to," I say.

Nash shakes his head. "Dude, I get your concern. Believe me, I feel it too, but there's no way for you to do that. They have the place completely sealed off." He waves toward the window where we can see some of Jarvis' security blocking the entrance to the store. Behind them is a circus of flashing lights and movement that definitely seems excessive for belt browsing.

"There must be a rear door," I say. "We could sneak behind the store—"

"And what? Even if you get inside, then what?"

"I don't know, I'll figure it out, but I can't sit here and do nothing!"

"Well, you can't just march over there and say 'Hey, how's the evil belt scheme going?' either. I've been abducted and interrogated by imitation mobsters, and trust me, it's not fun." He scrunches his nose in thought. "Actually, it was kind of fun, but the point is, yours probably won't be."

"Yeah, I've already had my own run-in with security," I mumble.

He's right—about all of it—but I also know this gnawing sensation isn't going away.

"So what are we supposed to do?" I ask, adjusting my hair beneath my ball cap. My knee thumps the underside of the table.

"Okay, look," Nash says after a pause. "Try Chad again. Maybe he's got something."

"There's no chance of distracting him when he's in Jarvis mode. He takes his servant role very seriously… too seriously, really."

Nash grunts and leans back in his chair, his fingers now tapping the table as well. If there was a mainstream market for "anxiety beat" music, we'd be hitting charts.

I scan the café in search of any magical solution, but several seconds later, all I've got is recruiting the elderly couple two tables over to run interference while we try to sneak past the guards.

Then I spot the small display of Kitty's Kafé merch. They're even selling the hats and t-shirts worn by the employees. The idea forming in my head is 100% not a good one, but what fun is a spy caper without a disguise?

"Hey, I have an idea," I say, signaling Kim.

Nash's concerned expression is justified but I don't have time (or interest) in letting him talk me out of this.

"Need something?" Kim asks as she approaches.

"Yes, please. The check and also…" I point at the merch display. "How much for those hats and shirts?"

* * *

I was right. Nash hated my idea. He really hated the fact that with Kim's help, we were able to make it happen.

"This is beyond stupid and never going to work," he hisses at me as we approach the back entrance of The Belted Stag with drink carriers in hand. We're also wearing the Kitty's Kafé uniforms (ish) we purchased.

But the best part? My new favorite server asked her very busy manager to let her deliver The Belted Stag order while we tagged along to carry it. We then convinced Kim that the most polite way to do so would be through a back entrance so as not to interrupt any activity—for example, music-video filming —that might be occurring inside the store.

I'll admit "the plan" isn't exactly ironclad. It doesn't even extend past this part.

"You wait here just in case," I say to Nash.

"In case of what?"

"I don't know. In case I'm neutralized. We need a witness to report back to basecamp about what happened."

He gives me a look that shows me just how much that didn't increase his excitement about any of this.

"And *basecamp* is…?"

"Whatever you want it to be, I guess."

"I see. And how long do I wait before *reporting back to basecamp*?" His tone is not one that I appreciate at the moment.

"I don't know. Five minutes? Ten? A half hour?"

In the movies, they always know how long their partners should wait before leaving them behind and blowing shit up. When they say to proceed *if they're not out in fifteen minutes*, was that based on a carefully constructed practice run? Were they going off their vast experience of blowing up bad guys' hideouts? Personally, I'm reluctant to rest my fate in the hands of a guestimate, but Nash already thinks this is a terrible idea.

"Twenty minutes," I say confidently. "If I'm not back in twenty, assume I've been compromised and… Larinda. Yes. Larinda is 'basecamp.' Tell her."

"Tell her what? That you left this world trying to deliver coffee to a belt store?"

I scrunch my nose. "Maybe not that. But be sure to tell her I love her. Oh! And that 'Third Last Kiss' still needs work on the bassline before engineering."

"Sure. Or you could just text her that stuff."

"Where's you sense of spy adventure? It's way more dramatic coming from someone else."

"My spy days are over, dude. Well, they were supposed to be." His eye roll is yet another clue that he's not fully on board.

I ignore his skepticism and focus back on Kim who takes the carriers from Nash, while also doing an excellent job of pretending she didn't hear any of that weird conversation.

"There's definitely a back room we can hide in, right?" I ask her.

She nods at me. "No one will see you. Well, unless they go in the back room."

"Do people go in there a lot?"

"How should I know? I don't work here."

Hmm. I decide not to relay this potential hiccup to Nash, who's now leaning against the side of the building looking slightly irritated and very bored.

I give him a thumbs up when he glances over.

"*Basecamp*," I mouth.

"Whatever," he mumbles.

Good enough.

He does at least open the door for us, but the second Kim and I slip inside, it becomes clear our attempts at silent sneaking were unnecessary. Music blasts throughout the building. The song is clearly a Jarvis McKinnley track, but not one I recognize.

Kim looks back and motions toward the opening ahead, which must lead to the main area of the store and the origin of the music.

"Hide somewhere," she says at my ear. "I'll deliver these."

"You can't carry them all."

"I'll make two trips."

I don't argue, mostly because I just realized Nash was right. This plan is stupid.

"You know what? Maybe we should just—"

"And every tear I cry, each promise held true

Makes a fool outta me, and a liar outta you

While you're breakin' hearts, I'll break in these boots

Walkin' away, walkin' away from you."

No.

Effing.

Way.

I freeze in horror as I absorb more of the terrible lyrics hiding an even more terrible truth. This can't be what it sounds like. It *can't*, but then, wouldn't that explain every puzzling clue we've discovered so far?

After several excruciating seconds, I drop the carriers on the table and march back outside to Nash.

"It's a fucking breakup song!"

"Excuse me?"

"The music video!" I wave toward the door. "They're filming a video for a new breakup song!"

"Huh? Why would they…" His eyes go wide. "Oh shit."

"Yeah! Exactly." I slap my hand against the door. "That must be why he wants Larinda to dump him!"

"And why it's 'better if she cheats.'"

"But why would Rena be here unless…"

My blood goes cold.

Nash must arrive at the same conclusion when his expression sinks.

"Those bastards," he whispers.

"Larinda has been at odds with Lakebend since the day she told them she wanted to work with me instead of the big-name producer they lined up for her. They must have had enough and are finally choosing sides. I bet they're going to drop her by blowing up the infamous on-again-off-again melodrama with Jarvis once and for all."

"And making her the villain of the story," Nash spits out. "They'll brand her as the cheater, so their guy's the saint with a poor little broken heart. Then they release a sappy breakup song that goes viral, and bam. Instant smash hit. Jarvis will be more popular than ever while Larinda is left in the dirt."

"Even worse, if the song is finished, they must have been planning this for a while."

"Long before the joke engagement."

We're silent as the horrible plot ferments into reality. *The Curdler* strikes again!

I *knew* something was up. From the beginning, this entire tour, the engagement, the meet and greet, that strange photoshoot in Jarvis' dressing room—all of it has been... wait.

Oh no.

What was that strange photoshoot in Jarvis' dressing room?!

"Shit..." I say.

"What? There's more?"

"Maybe. Back in Dallas Lakebend made me do this odd photoshoot with Jarvis and his cutouts in his dressing room. Remember I told you about that?"

Nash clearly remembers and clearly has similar concerns.

"Did they ask for you specifically?"

I nod. "Chad even spouted off this whole corporate rationale for why it had to be me... *fuck!*"

I kick the door before leaning against it. Eyes closed, fists clenched, I scour my brain for any clues that could explain what that was about and how they're planning to use it against us.

"You need to go back in there," Nash says.

"What?" I straighten in surprise.

"Take your phone and record as much of the song as you can. If they're shooting a video, they'll be replaying it over and over. We need a copy so we can pick it apart and look for other clues."

Crap. Yeah. We need all the evidence we can get.

"Be careful," he says as I reach for the handle. "If we're right, they're going to be more than pissed if they catch you spying."

I nod back, and we exchange a long, commiserating look. Maybe I finally understand Chad's "Blood Brothers" code. Nothing brings people together like belt drama.

Inside, the song is still blasting and the back room is still empty. I pull out my phone as I duck against the wall, just beside the opening to the main floor of the store. The song sounds like it's about halfway through based on the amount of instrumentation and backing vocals.

Also, it's awful. No surprise there. It would make me want to rip my ears off even if it wasn't about Larinda cheating on him and breaking his heart...

and boots, apparently. I suppose we have bigger questions to ponder, but a huge part of my brain really wants to know why they decided a belt store would be the ideal location for a song about boots.

Now that I'm paying attention, I hear speaking voices as well. A director calls out instructions, although they're too muffled and drowned out by Jarvis singing about his uncomfortable shoes to interpret them.

I'm feeling good about our (new) plan, until a figure appears in the doorway. I jump back in alarm, but breathe easier when I see it's Kim. She gives me a curious look before taking my arm and pulling me further from the doorway.

"I'm finished delivering the drinks. We should go."

"Yep, I'm right behind you," I lie.

There's no way I'm leaving until I have this whole damn song on my phone.

She continues to the exit, thankfully not looking back to check on me. I'm confident that once she's outside, Nash will run enough interference to give me the time I need. Unfortunately, I only get a few more seconds of recording time before someone screams to stop the music.

"I said seven-eighths oat milk and two-eighths soy! This is clearly six-eighths oat milk and one-eighth soy!" that same voice roars.

One guess who it is. Hint: it's the person who also can't math.

"We're so sorry, Mr. McKinnley," another person says.

"Exceedingly sorry, sir!" And *that's* Chad. "I'll go personally to get this fixed."

"You better," Jarvis snaps. "Well, don't just stand there! And where's my belt? Not that one, the one for verse two! How many times do I have to explain that each one is a different emblem of speech?!"

Probably a lot since that makes no sense.

"Would you like—"

"No, dammit! Just play the song!"

"Right away, Mr. McKinnley. Should we take it from scene—"

"No! No cameras! Just the song. I need to re-center myself and find my inner lake after this disaster. Someone liquify me!"

The music resumes its melodic lying, this time from the beginning. I check my phone to make sure it's recording and hold it as close to the doorway as possible.

There's no obvious sound or movement for over a minute. Everyone must be remaining deathly still as Jarvis recovers from the trauma of an incorrect milk ratio. In addition, my brain is now devoting way too many neurons to figuring out if seven-eighths plus two-eighths is *that* different from six-eighths plus one-eighth. If you have seven-eighths, take one away, add three to make nine-eighths, that's really… I don't know, but it definitely tastes exactly the same.

"What the frick?!" a voice shrieks directly beside me.

Uh-oh. I was so distracted by seventh-grade fractions I didn't sense anyone approach.

I force an easy smile through the pounding in my ears. Are my hands shaking too? Hopefully not. I shove them (and my phone) in my pockets.

"Hey, I, uh, heard you needed a new beverage?" I say to the fuming country music star.

Jarvis looks ready to implode, and I straighten to my full height for the coming confrontation. I really hope Nash includes some colorful commentary about my bravery and commitment to the betterment of humanity in my eulogy.

"What the hell are you doing here?"

"Just stopped in to see if I could help. Did I hear something about an oat milk emergency?"

"How did you know we were here? Turn that damn music off!" he shouts into the other room.

The song screeches to a halt, and Jarvis directs his fury back at me.

"It was obvious," I say, forcing myself to calm. "Filming a music video is a pretty big deal."

"Yeah, but no one is supposed to know! It's a secret."

"Really? Why?"

"Because!"

I wait several seconds for the rest.

Okay. Guess that was it.

"Well, while I can't argue that unshakable logic, I don't get why you're so upset. I just wanted to help."

"Well, I don't need your friggin' help! How have you not gotten it by now, *Valerie?* Nobody needs you. Nobody even *wants* you. You're a fraud and an embarrassment. You. Don't. Belong. Here."

I flinch, but manage to disguise how much that hurt.

"I see. So… I guess… good luck with the belt video?"

"Where do you think you're going?!" he growls as I start for the door.

"You literally just told me you don't want me here."

"I don't!"

"Right. So I'm going somewhere that isn't here."

"Like hell you are."

I'm so confused.

I squint at him, hoping there will suddenly be captions floating across his forehead that'll translate his brain for the rest of us.

Belts equal emblems.

Math equals *eh*.

"You think I'm letting you out of here to go blab my secret to the universe?"

"And what secret is that, exactly?"

It's then that I notice our audience. Rena in particular looks very unhappy about my presence and this turn of events.

Chad looks… I can't tell, actually. His fixed grin says he's thrilled to see me. His popping eyeballs say he's not. His hands are too wrapped up in unwanted belts to interpret.

"Who told you we'd be here?" Rena asks, stepping forward.

Not gonna lie, her angry face is a tad more formidable than the previous one that was unraveled by milk.

"No one told me," I say.

"It was me! I told him! I'm so sorry!" Chad blurts out.

I give him a hard look.

"No you didn't," I say, widening my eyes at him. Because he really didn't.

He reminded me that Jarvis liked belts and would look for a pony store. If anything, his information was more of a misdirection than a hint.

"It's his eyes! When he looks at you, you just… I don't know. *Look* at him," Chad explains with a groan. "They're all green and shit and the lashes!"

Oh great. Twelve people are now looking at me and none of us knows why.

I blink, hoping that's also some magical power.

It's not.

"Okay. Enough. I'll take care of this," Rena says to Jarvis and another woman who is probably the director. "We don't have much time before Jarvis needs to be back at the venue."

Fists clenched, eyes narrowed in rage, Jarvis steps like he's going to come at me, then recoils like someone held him back. Since no one did, it just looks like he walked into an invisible wall.

His gaze is hostile as it fires more daggers in my direction, but he doesn't move until his assistant, Mallory, takes his arm and directs him around. At that point, he moves so easily he was clearly waiting for someone to do exactly that. Seriously, does he commission a script-writing team to spell out his day every morning? Hey, maybe *they* would know how many minutes Nash should have waited before reporting to basecamp.

Any hint of amusement fades when Rena's icy stare lands on me.

"Let's go."

She points at the door behind me, and I turn with a deep breath.

Yeah, this is gonna be bad.

23—PITTSBURGH (LARINDA'S BUS)

LARINDA

None of it makes sense and nobody will tell me anything.

I had to perform last night having no idea where Val was or why I hadn't heard from him. Nash told me on the phone not to worry and they'd explain it all soon, but even he wasn't going to be able to visit me for a while. He also reminded me not to break up with Jarvis for any reason, and if anything, make a public spectacle of how much I fake-love him.

That seemed impossible, so mostly I've done my best to avoid "my fiancé." Paige is the only one allowed near me, apparently, but even she's a vault of silence except for the little she's authorized to say.

"So they're here?" I ask, crossing my arms.

"In Pittsburgh, yes. But not on site."

"So Val isn't on the crew bus?"

She shakes her head.

"But he's in the city… somewhere?"

She nods.

This is so frustrating.

"Why can't you tell me what's going on?"

"Because they're still trying to *figure out* what's going on."

"And why won't Val call me?"

"He can't."

"Why not?"

"It's complicated, but he loves you. No matter what happens, don't question that for a second. All of this is for you."

"It's hard to believe that when he won't even talk to me."

Pain shadows her face as she studies me from the neighboring couch. I want to believe her. Maybe I do, I'm just so tired of people keeping me in the dark, even if it's "for my own protection."

My interrogation of Bruce and Steve didn't go much better. Worse actually. If they knew the truth, they kept it hidden as well. Bruce said Val had been recruited by Lakebend for a "special project"—no way that's true—and Steve said he never even saw Val after everyone checked out of the hotel. His bunk had already been cleared out when they returned to the bus. That part might be true but is equally unhelpful.

"Paige, please. I'm really scared."

"He's okay. I promise."

"Not just for him. What am I supposed to do without him? Inviting him on this tour wasn't just because I love him and want him with me. I can't do our music without him."

Her sympathetic expression doesn't help and neither does the defiant look she offers next.

"Well, first of all, you don't *need* him. It's your music too. What you create together requires both of you, and once it's out there, it also belongs to both of you."

"Maybe but…"

"Not maybe. I saw it last night in Indianapolis. You own the stage when you're out there, Larinda. You own the entire audience of thousands and thousands of people. Not a person in that room believed that wasn't your music."

Wow. Does she truly think that?

Paige and I have interacted plenty of times since I started working with her brother, but we've never been close. We've certainly never had a heart-to-heart. She doesn't come across as the encouraging type, but maybe I was wrong. Someone would've had to drag Val out of his mental and spiritual swamps before I came along to do it.

"Things are different on stage," I say, leaning against the backrest and staring at the ceiling like Val and I always do. "I know who I am and what I'm about up there. I live and breathe the music. The lights, the haze, the energy… the high of the moment. Things make sense when I'm performing."

"And it's incredible. So be that person off the stage as well."

"Right," I huff out.

She doesn't respond, and I roll my head to the side to meet her earnest expression.

"Why not?"

"You say it like it's so simple."

"Maybe it is."

I focus back on the ceiling.

Just be that person?

Just be the confident, accomplished, talented woman I pretend to be when I'm performing?

"It's easy when you can play a role," I say.

"*Are* you playing a role?"

Her question slams into me.

Yes, of course. On stage I'm the confident country star who knows who she is and what she wants. It's my job, part of the show, it's…

What? What's really happening when I'm the professional version of myself?

Paige shifts in the seat beside me, and I look over to find her leaning forward.

"So it's all fake? Not one part of the Larinda Scott we see on stage is real?"

"It's *all* real," I say defensively. "It's just a different side of me."

Whoa.

By her slight smile, I've just proved her point—and shattered my own.

Professional Larinda Scott isn't an act. I'm not pretending to be fearless and confident—I *feel* it in the moment. I strut around believing I can do anything and don't have to take crap from anyone. I've always loved who I am when I'm performing and interacting with fans. It's one of the things that's driven me to the height of my success. But it slips away when I step out of the spotlight and fall under the control of others and their expectations. That's when I shrink into this meek girl who follows orders and doesn't know who she is.

But what if I have it all backward? What if I can't figure out who I am because I already know? What if my "act" isn't the act, but it's the rest of me that's off? I don't need to discover who I am, just accept what's been right in front of me all along.

"Do you know what Val told me after he met you in person for the first time?" Paige asks softly.

"The day he and Nash came to my studio to review what he'd done with my songs?"

She nods.

My fingers tighten around an imaginary tattooed hand that should be in mine.

"What?" I ask quietly.

"He said, the world has it wrong about you. He didn't know why you perpetuated the narrative that you're some ditzy starlet, but he saw beneath the façade right from day one. And I can tell you with certainty that the woman he met in the studio is the woman we see on stage. I'm also pretty sure he fell in love with you the second he learned the truth."

I swallow hard and stare at my fist squeezed around a phantom hand.

If she's trying to make it better that Val's not here right now, she's doing a terrible job.

It's also time to step up and be the woman I want to be, AKA the woman I already am.

24—PITTSBURGH (J-DAWG'S BUDDY'S HOUSE)

LARINDA

"Where are we?" I ask as Travis pulls up in front of a small townhome.

"My buddy's house," J-Dawg says from beside me.

Should I be concerned I've been kidnapped by my own security detail hours before a show? Probably. But I trust these two more than my own family at times. (Not that my family would ever hurt me on purpose, but their decision-making can be suspect at times.)

"Your buddy is a big fan?" I ask skeptically.

He shoots me a smirk. "The biggest."

"Sure. Seriously, guys. What's going on?"

"You'll see," Travis says. "They asked us not to say anything until you were here and we agree it's better that way. Go check it out and make sure we're good," he directs to J-Dawg.

"You got it, boss," J-Dawg says as he climbs out of the SUV.

My knee bounces enough to shake the entire vehicle as we wait for the all clear, but I don't even bother pumping Travis for information. If my pleas, pouting, and threats haven't worked thus far, nothing will.

"You can trust us," Travis says. "I promise, it'll be worth it."

My glare must need work because all it does is draw a smile from my bodyguard. Come to think of it, my "threats" could probably use some training as well. It's not my fault being mean is so hard.

Thankfully, it doesn't take long for J-Dawg to return from the house with the green light. (Not only am I inpatient for answers, I was three seconds away from offering Travis a packet of almonds which would've severely wrecked my "mean" cred.)

After securing my hair under a ball cap and slipping on oversized sunglasses, I follow J-Dawg toward the house. Travis brings up the rear, and I sense their urgency to get me out of sight as quickly as possible. They were also more insistent than usual that I disguise myself. J-Dawg doesn't even knock before pushing through the door and leading me inside.

The second I see him, my heart bursts.

"Val…" I breathe out.

A door closes behind me. Other people say stuff. Time probably continues. I even think I spot Nash leaning against the wall, but none of it matters as stunning green eyes rest on me.

His lips tip up in a smile I've been craving, and I rush toward him.

He laughs softly as he squeezes me against him, and I cling hard to absorb as much as I can.

"I've missed you," he says quietly.

"I've missed you too. Where have you been? Why can't you talk to me?"

"It's…" His voice fades, and I feel the heat of his breath on my hair as he kisses me.

Whatever. All questions for later. Right now, I just want to get lost in the familiar scent of spicy forests and feel the soothing warmth of his body.

I rest my cheek against his shoulder as his arms tighten around me.

"We'll give you some time," Travis says.

"Thanks again, man," Val replies, his voice rumbling against me. "I owe you."

"No problem. You did *us* the favor. She was about to slip our protection and go hunting for you. This is way easier on us."

I smile and pull back just enough to send Travis a grateful smile.

He returns it and follows everyone but Nash through the open doorway to the neighboring room.

"What about me?" my friend says, crossing his arms. "You didn't miss me? Where's my hug?"

I shoot him a mock glare. "Of course I'm glad to see you. And I'll hug you in a minute. I'm still working on this one."

He chuckles and moves to an armchair in front of the TV.

Val leads me to the neighboring couch and pulls me down beside him. He slides his arm around me, and I nestle into his side. I'm aware of Nash's amused look as I draw Val's other hand to my lips, but so what? With everything going on, who knows when I'll get to see my boyfriend again, let alone be close to him? What if this is it?

"I'm so sorry for all of this," Val says. "It's not what we wanted, but we didn't know what to do."

"Can you tell me what's going on now?"

"Yeah," he says through an exhale. "And we know you don't have much time until you have to go back, so we'll make this as efficient as possible."

"Thank you. I'm listening."

His chest rises and falls in a deep breath. "I, uh, got kicked off the tour."

"What?!" I shriek, bolting up.

He shrinks with a sheepish smile. "Yeah, so, that's why I haven't been around."

"Heck no! Absolutely not. Is this Jarvis' doing? It is, isn't it?"

I yank my phone from my pocket, but Val tugs me back to the couch.

"And *that's* why we didn't want to tell you until we could do it in person and talk through it," Nash says, waving over me.

"Talk through it?! What's there to talk through?" I snap.

"Hey, don't kill the messenger," Nash says. "This is your boyfriend's show."

"Thanks, dude," Val mutters.

After way too many seconds, *my boyfriend* shifts in his seat to face me.

"I saw something I wasn't supposed to see yesterday. We'll explain it all in just a second, but the immediate issue is that yes, it's Jarvis' doing, but he has the full support of Rena and Lakebend Records. In fact, Rena is the one who kicked me off and threatened me in every way possible to keep me from communicating with you. If they find out we've been in contact, things will go very badly."

My limbs don't seem to know what to do as I absorb this information. They want to punch one person, hug another, climb something (anything), kick more things, run a marathon… well, half marathon. Or just watch a marathon. I don't know, the point is, *what?!*

Val takes my hands and mercifully gives them something to do.

"What kinds of things? How did they threaten you?"

He shakes his head. "Lots of ways, but we don't have time for that. What matters is that you know the truth about what's going on, especially since it's going to be a lot harder for us to help you now."

"Wait, did they ban you as well?" I ask Nash.

"Oh yeah. They confiscated my all-access pass so hard."

"Okay, but… hang on."

Val tugs my hands to draw my attention back to him. "We'll be fine. What we need to tell you is *why* we got kicked off. We were right about everything, Larinda. Jarvis has been plotting against you since the beginning. Actually, based on what we discovered yesterday, this goes back *before* the beginning."

His expression is dark and tortured when it lands on me, and I brace myself for battle.

"At least we know what they're up to," I say. "Let's hear it."

Val and Nash exchange a look before his gaze settles on me. "Okay, well, remember that notebook I found in Jarvis' dressing room?"

The next half hour involves a deluge of information. Most of it is painful and hard to stomach. It would be easy to get knocked down, so I call on the newly accepted version of myself to stay calm and practical. There will be plenty of time for grieving and freakouts later. For now, it helps to sort the information into two main categories: learn and confirm.

Learn: there's been a breakup song about my engagement in existence longer than the engagement itself.

Confirm: Jarvis is a jerk-hole.

Learn: Lakebend Records is in on the betrayal and probably planning to drop me.

Confirm: Jarvis is obsessed with belts.

Learn: Val is willing to do anything (including wear a costume) for me.

Confirm: Jarvis is a jerk-hole. (Same confirmation from a different piece of evidence.)

Learn: Lakebend Records is also a jerk-hole.

Confirm: Val is amazing and Nash is a great friend.

I'm not sure what to say as the ugly story draws to a close. On the one hand, my heart is bursting that Val and Nash risked so much for me. On the other, everything else.

Val draws me against him as I stare at the far wall, everything they said swirling around in a painful, confusing vortex. I've been betrayed plenty in my life, including by the man at the center of the current one. But this...

"I'm so sorry," Val whispers. "It was nearly impossible not to punch him in the face right then."

"I really wish you had," I mumble.

His gentle laugh is too much and releases a few of the tears that have been threatening for a while now. His arms tighten around me as I bury my face in his shoulder.

"We're going to fix this," he says.

"How?"

His silence is the only answer I need. Exactly. How do you fight one of the top artists and labels in the industry when they team up against you?

"And now we can't even be together? When will I see you again?" I ask.

"I don't know."

"Wait." I pull back and search his face. "Pittsburgh. We're in Pittsburgh."

"Yes."

"That thing with your parents! Are you doing it?"

He lowers his gaze, and my stomach tightens.

"You are," I say quietly.

"I have to." His eyes lift to me again. "They're not going to stop until I hear them out."

"Val…"

"Paige is going with me."

"I tried to go too, but he won't let me," Nash says.

"Yeah, because they hate you too. This is about *de*escalating a situation."

I fan my palm over Val's cheek to draw his attention back to me. "Are you sure about this? You've already been through so much over the last few days."

He shrugs with a weak smile. "Exactly. What's one more punch in the gut, right?"

I give him a hard look. "Yeah, well, I'm tired of watching you get punched in the gut."

"I've been dealing with this shit my whole life. I'll be fine."

Will he? He always says that and I always know he's not, but there's no point wasting time arguing.

I slide my arms around him instead. "I love you, Val Andrews. No matter what happens, know that in my head, I'll be holding you like this all the time. Don't ever forget it, okay?"

"Only like this?" he teases. "I mean, we can do a little more than this in your head, no?"

"Oh, trust me, we've done *way* more than this. In fact, remember that time you—"

"*Annnd* I'm out," Nash says, jumping up from the chair.

Val and I snicker as he takes off to join the others in the kitchen.

Val's gaze turns serious once we're alone. "Look, I know this is bad and the odds are stacked against us, but we're going to find a way. I'm not sure what that is yet, but I'm not giving up."

I trace my fingers along his jaw as his words sink in. I trust him. At least, I trust his *will* to solve this dilemma. But what if it's bigger than us? I've never been a believer in "willpower." I've seen what this big ugly world can do when it turns its wrath against you. You can fight all you want, but at the end of the day, all you really control are your thoughts, feelings, and actions. I'm not sure that will be enough to solve this one, and right now I have a very ugly obstacle in my direct path.

"I don't know how much longer I can pretend with Jarvis," I say, searching Val's eyes. It can't be easy for him to see me with another man, especially one as awful as this one. "I can't even stand to look at him, let alone be engaged to him."

"I hate it too," Val says before his frown tips up in the slightest smile. "But I guess it helps that he doesn't want to be engaged to you either."

I bite back a snort at the absurdity of that statement. Gosh, it captures the essence of this mess so perfectly.

"Do we have anything else important to discuss?" I ask in a sly tone.

"A lot, actually."

I lean close and brush my lips over his. "More important than kissing me?"

His grin breaks. "Nothing could ever be more important than that."

"Yeah? Prove it."

25—PITTSBURGH (THE IVY LEAF)

VAL

There was a lot more on my list to tell Larinda at our secret rendezvous, but once the kissing started, I forgot all about spy games. It just felt so good to be with her again, to absorb her smile and suck up her light. It wasn't until Nash and I were making our way back to the hotel that I remembered I was supposed to mention how Jarvis sampled some of *my* work for his awful song —production I had done as a favor to Larinda during their final (very brief) "on" phase about ten months ago.

Since, technically, working with Jarvis would be a breach of contract, I don't want credit anyway, but just the fact that he'd use my samples for this specific song has me on edge. It's disconcerting to say the least, so we've added that to the list of likely threats to watch for.

I also forgot to mention that one of the more explicit threats (this one courtesy of Rena) was having me kicked off Larinda's album if I tried to contact her before the end of the tour. That one would have held more weight if we didn't suspect Larinda was going to be kicked off her own album soon. Most of the other warnings issued by Rena and Lakebend's lawyers were similarly weak, but a few had my heart racing a little faster and dread pooling in my stomach. Since we don't have a counterplan yet, we have no choice but to lie low and give in to their demands while we regroup.

I feel a little better about the situation now that I've had a chance to see her, though, even if our time was way too short and way too supervised. I don't like that she's essentially on her own in that viper den, but Nash promised to bring Steve into the loop, so at least she'd have one ally behind enemy lines. Her meddling PA was never my favorite person, but he loves Larinda, and most of his offenses stem from too much loyalty, not too little.

For now, I have my own battle looming.

"You don't have to do this," Paige says after the rideshare drops us at the fancy restaurant my parents booked.

"I do, and you know it."

She squeezes my arm, but I avoid what I'm sure is a pitying expression. I don't need comfort right now. I need to stay strong and emotionless, to lock away the years of pain and rejection. No one can see the true depth of the wounds that have punctured my soul, despite my best efforts to cover them.

Nobody needs you. Nobody even wants you.

I take a deep breath and force down the familiar chant that's been echoed so many times throughout my life. Jarvis thought he was being so original, but he was just the latest voice telling me what I already know.

"Let's do this," I say. "Hopefully, this is one of those places that has fifty-dollar crackers with a dab of mush on it. I'll be ordering all of those."

Paige smirks as she pulls open the outer door to the restaurant. "Same. *'Make that two mush-crackers, please.'*"

I toss her a smile and hold the inside door for her. "Do you think I'm over-dressed, though?" I ask.

She does a dramatic once-over of my "nice" jeans and only button-up shirt.

"I think you're good," she says dryly.

Unlike me, she looks the part in a sparkly green cocktail dress she insisted on wearing because "this might be her only chance." Really, I'm betting she and Nash have plans after this, and she knows she'll win every one of their arguments while wearing that dress. For my sister, that's probably better than sex, although I'm guessing there will be some of that too.

Ew.

"Do you have a reservation?" the host asks.

"Should be under Andrews," I say.

The host scans a screen, then my outfit, then makes a brow adjustment that comments on my outfit.

"For four? Two members of your party have already arrived. This way, please."

As we weave through the restaurant, I can't help but notice I'm not just the only person in jeans. I also appear to be the only person not in clothing one would wear to a debutante ball. (Or so I assume. I have no idea what people wear to debutante balls, but I'm pretty sure it's not this.)

"Here we are," the host says, leading us into a private room. "Please enjoy your evening. Your server will be with you shortly."

He closes the glass doors on his way out, leaving us alone with my par—Burt and Rhonda Andrews. Guess I can't really call them my parents anymore, can I?

"Perceval," Rhonda, formerly my mother, says in a breathless voice. That alone is weird. Weirder still is her urgent push from the table and dash toward me. She pulls me into her arms and squeezes as I stiffen. Paige and I exchange a confused look over her shoulder.

"So good of you to come!" she says, stepping back.

She frames my face and gazes at me with an adoring expression that would be awkward even if we got along. This moment might work in movies, but I can say with certainty that it does not work in private rooms of The Ivy Leaf restaurant in downtown Pittsburgh.

I withdraw from her touch as awkwardly as she initiated it and take the seat across from Burt, AKA my former father.

"And Paige, what a surprise," Rhonda says dryly.

"Really? You clearly made a reservation for four," she quips.

Rhonda and Burt frown before directing their attention to me.

"We thought you'd be bringing Larinda," Burt says.

Huh?

"Why would you think that?" I ask. "Besides, she's halfway through her set right now."

"Oh! Why didn't you say so in your response?" Rhonda says with exaggerated regret. "We could have scheduled this for tomorrow so she could join us."

"We roll out after the show. We're only here for a day."

And why are they being so strange about this? Since when did they care about Larinda's schedule?

"But hey, *I'm* here, so let's get this over with. What did you want to discuss?"

"Oh, honey! Why would you assume such a thing?" Rhonda says. "We told you. We missed you and wanted to mend our relationship."

"Cut the crap. I know that's not why I'm here. What do you want?"

"Sweetheart, how can you even think we'd want anything other than a reconciliation with our beloved son?" She even presses a hand to her heart like she's just learned she lost the family homestead to a rail tycoon two hundred years ago.

"And you can stop talking like a Civil War soldier letter. It's not making any of this more believable."

Her frown is a step in the right direction. *That* I believe.

"Your mother and I just want to make things right," Burt says.

"My mother? And who would that be? You made it very clear you don't consider yourselves my parents."

Those frowns—borderline scowls—I definitely believe.

"Yes, and we regret that."

"Really…" I say, not even trying to hide my skepticism.

"Really!" Rhonda replies. "We shouldn't have done such a dreadful thing. We know that now."

"And which *dreadful thing* are you referring to? There are so many."

"Oh, Perceval, please don't be like this. We love you and accept your many interesting life choices. Including your charming face tattoo!"

I don't even have a facial expression for that one.

"Yeah? Okay, well, it's way too late for that. Just tell me what you really want so we can move this along."

"We told you. We just—"

"No! I'm so sick of this. I didn't have to hear you out, but I came anyway, so what is it? Why am I here?"

"Nothing! Just—"

"Tell me!"

"Sweetie, really, I don't—"

"Cut the bullshit! I'm not going to—"

"We want to adopt you back!"

The table goes deathly still.

No one moves as those strange words echo around us. I think I heard them wrong, but the other stunned expressions indicate they heard them too.

A server must have been waiting for the worst possible moment to enter the room and approaches our table.

"Good evening. I'm Joan. Can I get you started with—"

"A bottle of red and a bottle of white, most expensive you have," Burt snaps. "And give us ten minutes."

The woman stiffens before recovering with a tight smile. "Of course, sir."

Paige and I shoot her an apologetic look as she turns away.

Yeah, sure. They're just regular saints now.

"You want to adopt me back? What does that even mean?" I say, my stomach in knots despite my attempt at indifference.

"We want you to be our son again," Burt explains.

I stare at them in numb silence. How do you even react to something like that?

Paige snorts a laugh

I suppose that's one option.

"Are you freaking serious?" she cries. "You've treated him like shit our entire lives, legally disowned him, and extorted thousands of dollars from him. Why would you suddenly want him back? And even more important, why would *he* want that?"

They give her a hard look, and I brace for an explosion. We've rehearsed this script so many times:

Mom and Dad come down hard on me.

Paige defends me.

Mom and Dad come down hard on her just to make me feel even worse about the whole thing.

But it doesn't happen this time. Instead, Burt takes a shaky breath and schools his expression into something eerily close to "calm." Wow, could they actually be serious?

"We understand," he says in a cool tone. "We made a mistake—several, maybe. That's why we're reaching out and extending this olive branch."

"Is that what this is?" I ask, leaning back and crossing my arms. "You buy me dinner and I forgive twenty-three years of being tormented."

"Tormented is a bit of a—"

"Understatement," Paige snaps. "He's being generous. How about abused? Betrayed, terrorized… take your pick."

Their eyes go dark as they rest on my sister, but again they don't react the way I expect. Could they really have changed?

My head is a mess, my heart even worse.

Nothing they're saying makes sense. This entire situation is ludicrous. So why is a piece of me still clinging to a shred of hope that it's real? After everything they've put me through, how can I still be a little boy that just wants his mommy and daddy?

"This isn't about you, Paige," Burt says with a hard look. "We're here for him. So what do you say, Perceval? Will you accept our apology and give us another chance?"

I swallow hard, my chest tightening with each breath. My nails dig into my palms as my fists clench beneath the table. I don't know what to do. I don't even know what to think.

The others are waiting with intense expressions but it's all becoming a blur. The room is shrinking, the floor swirling and wavering beneath me. There's no air in here. Just spinning and flickering and—

"Excuse me," I mumble, pushing up from the table.

I don't even know where I'm going, just that I can't be here.

I need… I don't know! I just have to leave.

After escaping the suffocating room, I stumble toward the sign for the restrooms. Thankfully, it's empty when I smash through the door and brace myself against the sink counter.

Several splashes of cold water help soothe the internal chaos, although it takes several more to bring much-needed air back into my lungs.

I stare at the face in the mirror for a long time. Drops of water cling to my lashes, and one slides over the small X beside my eye. I reach up and smear it across that volatile brand.

I shouldn't even be listening to them, let alone considering their offer. It can't be real, it *can't,* and yet…

God, I've been alone for so long. Sometimes it seemed like Paige was the only person on the planet who gave a shit about me, who believed in me. Then Nash came along, and for the first time, it seemed like maybe this hard, lonely path had been worth the pain.

And he led me to Larinda.

I would do anything for her. I'm doing it now. Risking everything for the person who risked everything for me, and maybe this is something I owe her. Family is so important to her. I watched with a mix of joy and envy the other day as she and her family filled that room with a touch of chaos and a ton of love. It was a glimpse of what family *could* be. I have no doubt she'll pull me into hers when the time comes, but what do I have to offer in return?

Can I forgive Rhonda and Burt for how they've treated me? For all the damage they've done and pieces of me they broke? I don't know, but I'm not sure I can look Larinda in the eye knowing I had a chance to fix things and threw it away out of pride and resentment. Is that the kind of man I am? The kind I *want* to be?

I'm not sure what's led to this sudden change of heart, but if there's any chance it's real, maybe I need to consider it. What if there's a possibility that I could have this burden lifted and a huge cloud removed from my life? We don't have to be the smiling stock-photo family in a new picture frame, but it would be nice to not feel a cramp in my chest every time a thought or memory surfaces.

You don't have to love them. You don't even have to forgive them, but wouldn't it be better to have a civil relationship than a hostile one?

At the very least, they'd leave me alone and let me live in peace instead of actively trying to derail my life. What can it hurt to hear them out?

With a deep breath, I dry my face and move toward the exit.

I can do this.

I *have* to do this.

I'll never have the future I want if the past continues to drag me down.

"Okay, I'm listening. What are you proposing?" I test the words out loud.

It sounds doable. It sounds necessary.

My phone buzzes, and I pull it out to see a text from Nash. Shit. I don't have time for this right now. I'm about to shove it back in my pocket when I see the words:

I figured it out!

Crap.

I force myself to read the whole text.

Nash: Jarvis used your samples because he and Lakebend want to bury you for breach of contract! The random photoshoot in his dressing room seals the deal. They can say you were working together on tour. Once that gets out, you won't only get kicked off Larinda's team, no one will work with you. Your career as a producer is done.

My career is done? Might be extreme, but it's certainly not going to help my reputation to be the guy who betrayed his first artist.

Fuck, fuck, fuck.

Now what?

It's not like I can defend myself and tell the world I didn't consent to a sample no one knows he used on a track no one knows exists. And even if I did, it's my word against his. You don't have to know a single thing about words to know who's winning that debate. Not to mention, he has a mountain of evidence supporting his version of the story, and I have… the fact that he's a dick.

Yeah. No lawyer is taking those odds.

But none of it matters when Paige grabs my arm the second I exit the restroom.

"Ow!" I say, trying to pull away.

By the pinch on my bicep and furious expression on her face, she's had a very different internal dialogue about the state of affairs over these last few minutes.

"We're leaving," she hisses.

"What? But—"

"No! We're not going back to the table."

She yanks me down the hall, and I tug my arm from her grip.

"Look, I get that they don't deserve it, but maybe we should—"

"I said, no! We're leaving!"

I lock myself in place and narrow my gaze. "How do you get to make that call? *I'm* the one in the crosshairs."

"Just… can you please trust me? Not here. We need to go."

"No. I think we should hear them out."

"There's nothing to hear! Let's. Go!"

She grabs me again, and I tear my arm away with a hard look.

"I'm not a little kid anymore. I can take care of myself."

I move down the hall, forcing her to follow.

"I get that but you can't trust them."

"You think I don't know that?" I snap before entering the main dining room. "I'm not naïve."

"But this is—"

"I know we're never going to be a sunny, happy family. There's more at stake than just me, though."

"Okay, but—"

"It's my choice!" I hiss, pulling open the door to our room.

Burt and Rhonda rise when we enter, but they don't look like the apologetic, hopeful parents I left. They look…

Oh god. Oh no. No, no, no.

"Dad's trying to sell the company and wants to leverage your connection with Larinda," Paige spits behind me.

I go cold.

My gaze locks on our parents, my heart cracking in my chest.

"Val…" Rhonda says. "Please just—"

"Is that true?" I force out, my voice barely audible. Their gazes lower as the room shrinks further.

"Answer me!" I say a little louder. "Is it true this whole thing is about using me to get to Larinda?"

Burt shakes his head, his demeanor clearly in business mode. "It's not what it sounds like. If you just listen to our proposal…"

I don't hear the rest. Sound stops completely as I stagger out of the room.

"Val, wait!" Paige calls behind me.

I don't. I fucking *can't* as I weave through the restaurant toward the exit.

This is…

I can't…

I drag my sleeve across my eyes as I push outside into the cool evening air.

"Val!"

I flinch when a hand grabs my arm and spins me around. Paige's expression is tortured as she grips my sleeve. "I'm so sorry. I figured it out and confronted them after you left. That's why I tried to stop you… god, Val. I'm so sorry."

I shake my head, tears choking my lungs.

I still can't believe it. It can't be. It just can't. They said… They were… oh god.

Even they wouldn't be so cruel. But I just saw it. I…

What is wrong with me?! How fucked up do you have to be that your own parents don't want you?

"Hey… look at me," she says softly. When she searches my eyes, tears well in her own. "I hate them," she hisses, pulling me in for a hug. "I hate them so much."

I'm still numb as reality crushes me into a pulp right there on a city sidewalk. There *are* worse things than losing hope. There's trusting in it. There's believing in something better only to have it violently ripped away.

They were going to use me? After everything they've put me through, they were going to squeeze one last manipulation out of the little trust I had left?

And I almost let them. I did, I almost let it happen!

"I'm so sorry," Paige whispers.

I can't breathe as her arms tighten around me.

"Val, please talk to me."

Tears leak from my eyes when I squeeze them shut.

"What's so wrong with me, Paige? Why is loving me so hard? What am I doing wrong?"

She pulls back with a fierce expression. "Nothing! There is *nothing* wrong with you. It's them. You know that."

I shake my head, liquid obscuring my vision.

How am I supposed to believe that when all the evidence points at something else? Even my own sister gets punished for choosing me.

Nobody needs you. Nobody even wants you.

I wipe my sleeve across my eyes as I back away.

"Val…"

"No. I have to go."

"Will you—"

I yank my arm from her grasp. "Just… Don't follow me, okay? I want to be alone."

"Val, wait! Please!"

I ignore her as I charge down the sidewalk.

Nobody needs you. Nobody even wants you.

Not even your own parents.

The air outside is no less toxic. I still can't breathe as I stumble along the sidewalk. Years of pent-up tears fall harder with each step. They sear down my cheeks and burn the collar of my stupid button-up shirt. I don't even try to stop them. What's the point? No one's here to notice them.

Because nobody needs you. Nobody even wants you.

I undo the buttons as I walk, ripping the shirt off my shoulders and slamming it into a waste bin I pass. Several bystanders stare at me, but I don't give a shit. I'd shove more stuff in the garbage if I had anything else.

It's a chilly May evening as I continue on in just my undershirt and jeans, but it feels right. All that's missing is a good old-fashioned mugging or hit-and-run to round out the evening from hell. Would anyone care if I never returned to the hotel tonight? No one would even notice. Paige and Nash have their own room on a different floor. Larinda won't even be in the city for much longer.

I'm completely alone.

My phone is buzzing in my pocket, and I pull it out just to shut it off. I don't need more lies from anyone. Not Paige telling me it's everyone else who's the problem or Rhonda and Burt trying to con their own son into a fucking namedrop. I especially don't need Larinda pretending there's a chance in hell our impossible situation will work itself out. I don't doubt her feelings for me, but I doubt every other fantasy we've constructed about our forbidden fairy tale. That's not how things go for me. I give everything and lose it. I surrender my soul only to be crushed and stomped on over and over. And *still* I'm willing to trust and get trampled again.

I'm the guy who gives up everything in exchange for a broken heart no one wants.

It's a really bad fucking day when you realize the only person who's truly been honest with you is Jarvis McKinnley.

26—PITTSBURGH (SOME RANDOM STREET)

LARINDA

"You're already ten minutes late for bus call," Travis grumbles. "Please just let *us* search for him. We promise to keep you updated."

"Not a chance," I say from the back seat of our vehicle. "Keep driving."

J-Dawg has been suspiciously quiet while Travis and I argued since leaving the venue to search for Val. He must be the smarter of my two trusted bodyguards because he's figured out that there will be no talking me out of this. Once Paige told me what their parents did to my boyfriend, the war was on. Even Steve stepped up and agreed to cover for me with the tour folks as much as possible.

I've sent Val at least a dozen texts, but so far haven't received a response. My calls are going straight to voicemail. I'm scared, as are my knees that keep bouncing and my teeth that keep chewing on my thumbnail.

"Wait, is that him?!" I cry, pressing my face against the window.

"Where?" Travis asks in an exasperated tone. So what if this is the forty-third time I thought I spotted my missing producer on the crowded streets. Statistically speaking, it's still the same odds that it's him as all the other times. I think. I don't actually know much about statistics stuff.

"There! With the cowboy hat!"

"Have you ever seen him wear a cowboy hat?" Travis asks dryly.

"No, but he's smart. Maybe he's disguising himself so we *don't* think it's him."

The glow of the downtown city lights clearly illuminates the look they exchange.

Fine. I know I'm sounding a tad desperate, but it's because I am. Val has fought and overcome so much in his life—in these last few days, even. If this latest blow was enough to knock him down, it's worth being worried.

My phone dings, and my gaze darts to the screen. But it's Paige, not her brother. Maybe she and Nash are having more luck with their search?

Paige: Nothing yet. You?

Darn.

Me: Nothing. Unless you think he'd wear a cowboy hat as a disguise?

I squint at the guy through my tinted window. Maybe…? I suppose the person is too short, too round, and too nothing like Val to be Val.

Paige: Unlikely.

Darn.

"There!" I cry, lowering my phone. "At the café table!"

"Larinda, please. I know you're—"

"Shit, she's right," J-Dawg interrupts. "Pull over!"

My heart slams against my ribs as Travis hits the brakes and double-parks beside a red sedan.

"You stay here," J-Dawg says, then stops when he realizes I'm already climbing out of the car.

"Larinda!" he calls, but I ignore him as I slip between the line of vehicles to reach the curb.

I know I'm getting looks. Not sure if it's because I'm Larinda Scott or because I'm wearing a sequined bustier with sweatpants (which was as far as I got in my post-show wardrobe change when Nash and Paige called). Either way, none of it matters. All that matters is the guy at an empty café table, his fingers locked in his hair, staring blankly at the rusted metal surface.

"Val?" I say gently as I approach.

His head shoots up in a startled search, and when his broken gaze lands on me, I forget all about our audience. Who cares what they think? This is the only opinion I need right now.

"Larinda?" He pushes to his feet. "What are you—"

I cut him off as I pull him in for a hug. "Paige told me. I'm so sorry."

He's silent as I squeeze tighter.

"You shouldn't be here," he says quietly.

"Where else would I be?"

I feel his chest deflate in a heavy exhale. "I… It's nothing. I'm sorry for making you worry."

"Stop it. It's not nothing. It's horrible what they did, and it kills me that I wasn't there for you."

"There's nothing you could have done. It's my own fault for trusting them. I should have—"

"No," I hiss, forcing his gaze to mine. "Don't you ever apologize for having faith in something and trying to see the good in people. Your beautiful, genuine soul is one of the things I love most about you, and I hate them for stripping that away and using it against you. Their ugliness is on *them*, not you."

He lowers his eyes, and his silence sends a shiver down my spine. Something heavy is worming its way through his brain and it scares the crap out of me.

"Hey, what's going through that head of yours?" I ask, brushing his cheek.

His eyes flicker to me, but there's no truth in his weak smile.

"Nothing. Just... how did you find me?"

"We looked."

"You just drove around until you saw some loser at a table?"

"Yes, actually. And you're not a loser. You're my boyfriend and the love of my life."

When his brow furrows in confusion, I know I'm losing this battle.

"Val, please. I know you're not okay."

"I'm fine. Thanks for coming for me. You should get back, though."

His cryptic response does nothing to soothe the ache in my chest. I feel the slight tremble in his body, see the way his jaw clenches like he's fighting strong emotions. He doesn't want me to know the truth, but the truth is clawing to come out.

His parents lied to him.

Used him.

Humiliated him.

The very people who were supposed to protect him—

"They don't want me."

I wince and look up to see his gaze fixed on some distant object.

"Sometimes I'm not sure if anyone does. People say they do, but..."

"But what?"

"I'm always a secret."

His voice is barely audible as he blinks back more tears. "Why does loving me always have to be a secret? Why does it always come with a punishment?"

Oh god.

"Val," I whisper. "That's not true..."

My defense dissolves at his sharp look, because… he's right.

A cold chill moves through me as his words sink in. I don't want it to be true, but I've seen the punishment his sister gets for choosing him, how he downplays relationships to protect others.

Even with me, the one who claims to love him more than anyone, he's a dangerous secret. A risk I haven't been willing to take. Not really. I say I would, but like everyone else in his life, I've chosen my career over him. He asked me not to throw everything away for him because that's who he is, but the choice was there for me this entire time. At any moment, I could have chosen him. I could have said no. But I took the easy road. As always, I took the path of least resistance and did what was expected, even if it wasn't what I wanted. Even if it hurt someone I claimed to love.

His green eyes are full of the hurt of always being second. Of always being the "wrong" choice even though he deserves to be the *only* choice.

I've spent twenty-six years afraid to say no.

Twenty-six years afraid to be who I am and face the pain necessary to have the life I want.

Before he can stop me, I climb on the chair and wave my arms.

"Excuse me, everyone!" I shout. "May I have your attention, please!"

A crowd gathers, and I wait until I have the attention of at least two dozen strangers. Travis and J-Dawg look ready to tackle me and drag me away, so I better make this quick.

"Hello, everyone. I'm Larinda Scott and this is my producer, Val Andrews. I just want you to know that he's one of the most incredible people you will ever meet and I'm completely and hopelessly in love with him. He's my boyfriend, and I wake up every morning convinced I'm the luckiest person in the world that he's mine."

Val looks equal parts amazed and horrified as the audience breaks into an awkward applause. From this vantage point, I can also see the sour expressions of my bodyguards who have made space around my impromptu stage. Their faces are about to turn more sour.

"Thank you for your time," I say. "I would so appreciate it if you could please spread the word. Also, would anyone like an autograph or photo before I head back to my tour bus?"

"What are you doing?" Val hisses as he helps me down from the chair. "This is going to get back to Jarvis and Lakebend!"

"Yep." I take the pen and paper being shoved at me by a teenage girl.

"They're going to drop you!"

"Probably."

Next, I sign something I'm pretty sure is a takeout menu. Sushi. Yum.

"Can we get a picture?" the woman asks.

"Of course! You mind?" I ask Val, who returns a hard look.

But he's Val, so instead of being a jerk, he takes the stranger's phone and snaps a photo of me sandwiched between her and her companion.

"Thanks! It was so great meeting you! And congrats on your new boyfriend," she says.

I return a smile and address the next person.

By now, Travis and J-Dawg have transitioned into fan-publicity mode, subtly moving people along while also providing a barrier of protection. They really are the best. They're even doing a great job of looking appropriately intimidating, professional, and not mad at me.

"She shouldn't have said that. And now she's going to miss bus call," Val says to Travis, panic in his voice.

"She already did," Travis grunts.

"What?! Larinda!" Val tugs my arm, but before he can say more, I drop a kiss on his concerned frown.

"I'm choosing you," I say.

His eyes widen. "What?"

"I'm choosing you. Over everything else. You are my number one, Perceval Andrews. I should have done this from the beginning, and I'm sorry. But I'm doing it now. It's my life and my choice, and I'm choosing *you.*"

I fight back a smile as I return to signing autographs and imploding my career.

"Don't bother arguing with her," Travis says to Val. "This is her new thing."

My grin breaks as Val mumbles a bewildered response I can't fully make out.

I should be terrified right now. He's correct. There will be no coming back from this. For all intents and purposes, my career as Larinda Scott Country Music Superstar is over as I know it. Even worse, I've played right into Jarvis' evil narrative and gave him the ammunition he wanted to catapult his career to a level he doesn't deserve. I should be scared and mourning and running to my manager to start damage control, but that's not the thought blaring through my head. Something bigger just happened. Something so monumental and life-changing, it makes career sabotage seem petty.

I made a choice, and no matter the consequences, it was the right one because it was *mine.* I didn't just say no to being held hostage by other people's demands and expectations. I said *hell no,* and it feels amazing.

Whatever happens, I'm already lighter for shedding what I don't want, to chase something I do. By being afraid to stand up for myself, I've let a toxic reality govern my existence, and now that it's melting away, I feel liberated, not scared. If I get dropped by Lakebend, so what? It will free me to date Val without threats, fear, and repercussions. We can also do our music without having to fight the mold at every new idea and burst of creativity. And Jarvis? Fine. Maybe it's worth being branded a cheater to eject him from my life once and for all. *I* know the truth and so does everyone who matters.

Strong arms wrap around me from behind, and I lean into the security of my future. A future I want. A future I flippin' *chose.*

"If this is what you want, I will support you," Val says at my ear. "I will always support you no matter what."

Warmth floods through me as I settle against him.

"And I will always choose you no matter what."

He's quiet for a second, his cheek still resting against mine from behind. "You're amazing, you know that?"

"Yep."

His soft laugh is everything as it rumbles through me. "You ready to go back to the bus and blow shit up?" he asks.

"Bombs away," I say with a grin.

"Love, man," J-Dawg mumbles, shaking his head.

27—INTERSTATE 76 (LARINDA'S BUS)

LARINDA

Because I have the best personal assistant and security detail on the planet, Val and I make it back to my bus with very little drama. Everyone else has already departed for Hershey, but they were assured I was fine and would be following shortly once my "fashion emergency" had been resolved. (Steve also apologized for the weird lie but couldn't think of anything better to explain why I left the venue mid-dress.) Once everyone learns the truth tomorrow, the lie won't matter anyway.

For now, Val and I have one last night of freedom from drama and prying eyes. So what do you do with your final hours of bliss?

Rework the bridge of "Forever A Fantasy."

"What about this?" I say, strumming through a progression on my guitar.

Val is propped against the headboard of my bed, the laptop on his thighs. He removes his hat to adjust his hair before replacing it which means…

Ugh.

"Fine. What about this?" I say.

He reaches over and covers my hand to stop me.

"The other one was okay, it's just, that's basically the same progression as the verse, so if we're going to use it, we need to change up something else. Are you committed to those lyrics?"

"What's wrong with my lyrics?"

"Nothing if you want to call this verse three instead of a bridge."

I shoot a nasty look, and he grins as I shove his knee.

"Fine, genius. Then what are you thinking?"

I hold out the guitar, but he waves it away and pulls on the headphones instead. "One sec."

I watch with a little intrigue and a lot of awe as his fingers dance over the trackpad. I know my way around a DAW, but how he works so quickly and effortlessly always blows me away. It's like his brain operates in plugins and midi notes. (It's also incredibly hot, although I'd rather eat an entire tub of carrot-flavored almonds than admit that right now.)

After a few seconds of secretly drooling over my boyfriend, I return to picking through some chords on my guitar. I'm already counting the days until we can get into my studio and play around with this stuff for real. Two more shows and we'll have a week off to go home before jumping into the next phase of the tour.

After tomorrow, though, who knows what will happen. I'm sure video and news of our little display on the sidewalk are already spreading like wildfire. As soon as Rena, Jarvis, and the rest of the enemy wake up, they'll have all the evidence they need to destroy us. The song Val and I are working on now isn't even for the next album. It's a new one we started for our indie production when Lakebend drops me and their lawyers lock our other songs in an untouchable vault.

"Okay, here," Val says, ripping off the headphones and handing them to me. "Let me know what you think."

His expression sinks from confidence to doubt in a split second. That's what always happens when he hands his work over to be critiqued. It's the strangest thing, and it bothers me to no end. While he's wrapped up in creation, he operates with the grace and skill of the talented expert he is. As soon as he leaves that creative bubble, however, his determined stare becomes wide, anxious eyes.

He fidgets with the edge of the comforter as I take the headphones and slip them over my ears. After pivoting the laptop in my direction, I hit the spacebar to listen and…

Wow.

This is…

Incredible.

He's layered the main keys riff of the intro over the rhythm guitar of the chorus and added a stripped-back, syncopated beat to give it a hip-hop vibe. It's a delicious surprise no one will see coming and the type of hook people will throw on repeat. How did his brain even think to do that?!

He must have started on this idea before now. It's already too polished and thought out to have been thrown together, which means despite everything that's happened this past week, he's still had faith in our music.

As he should, because this is amazing.

"Val…" I whisper.

His tense frown tips up into a relieved smile.

"You like it?" The hint of shyness in his voice is both adorable and exasperating.

I take off the headphones, close the laptop, and shove both to the other side of the bed.

He deflates as his gaze lands on the banished laptop.

"You didn't like it," he sighs out.

"Can I tell you something, Perceval Andrews?"

He straightens in surprise when I crawl toward him.

"What's that?"

I straddle him and frame his face. "I am so in love with your brain."

The worried crease in his brow softens, and lips I dream about tip up into the most beautiful smile.

"Oh," he says. "So you *do* like it."

"No, I just said I *loved* it."

"No. You said you loved my brain. That could mean you—"

"Shut. Up," I say with a debate-ending kiss.

His snark becomes a groan as I draw him in with a gentle bite on his lower lip. Gripping his jaw, I deepen the kiss into the one I've been craving. He responds with matching desperation that has me writhing for more. Hot blood pulses throughout my body, pooling between my legs which are already straining to reach the growing hardness in his jeans. The need is hungry and insatiable, which is why I swear it hurts me more than him when I abruptly let go.

"Nope," I say, shifting out of reach. "You're gonna have to earn it."

His mouth hangs open as he stares at me in disbelief. "Are you serious?"

"Very."

"Earn it how?" The pleading in his voice draws a smile from me. I sense that brain I love spinning wildly. The burning tension in his muscles as I run my hand down his chest toward his zipper tells me I could ask for literally anything and get it. But there's one thing I want more than sex right now.

"Tell me something good about yourself."

He flinches. "What?"

"You heard me. Tell me something good about yourself."

"Larinda… What are you—"

I cut him off with a hard look while my palm grazes the front of his jeans.

He sucks in a breath, his eyes fluttering closed before fixing on me in confusion.

I remove my hand. "Like I said, you need to earn it. So let's hear it. Give me something."

"This is stupid."

"Maybe. You know what else is stupid? Passing on this"—I wave over myself with playful cockiness—"because you're too chicken to play a sex game."

His expression is too cute.

"Oh, this is a sex game? I'm sure people are crashing porn sites in search of smoking hot *positive affirmation* foreplay."

"Okay, fine," I say with a shrug. "I'm going to grab a drink before bed. You want anything?"

I make a dramatic move to climb off him, not even a little surprised when he grips my hips to stop me.

"Ugh! Whatever," he mumbles.

I settle back and lift a brow. "Great. So what is it? Tell me something good about yourself."

"I have a clean driving record."

I search his face for a second, then snort a laugh when his grin breaks. I mean, technically he followed the rules. Guess we have to start somewhere.

With great ceremony, I reach toward my foot and slowly remove a sock.

"Wait…" he says with suspicion. "Is that how this works? It's like some weird version of strip poker?"

"Yep." I drop the sock over the side of the bed. "You want to try again?"

His hungry gaze scours my body, and I innocently drag a finger down my shirt between my breasts. "Unless you want to stop now and drink that bottled water?"

His glare is too adorable to count as ornery.

"You're evil."

"Opportunistic. Clock is ticking, lover boy. Tell me something good about yourself."

He clenches his jaw, but I already see him caving. "I have green eyes."

I roll mine. "Nope."

"What? It's true."

"Yeah, and the game isn't 'tell me a random fact on your driver's license.' It's 'tell me something *good*.'"

"Green eyes can be good."

"They can be. Are yours?"

He blinks those showstopping eyes at me as he thinks. Part of me is amused. The other part is aching at how hard this is for him. And that part is the reason we're playing this "game." I'm not above using sex to force him to acknowledge how amazing he is.

"I guess?"

"Not good enough." I cross my arms, waiting.

"Fine. Yes. I have nice eyes."

"Better." I pull off another sock.

"Socks? Really?"

"As I explained, you need to earn it. Little confessions get little rewards. Big confessions get big rewards. So far you're fishing in the sock pool, my friend."

His lips tip up in the slightest smile, even as his fist clenches at his side. He hates this, but he loves me and has no idea what to do with that dilemma. Good. That's why we're here to bridge the gap.

"Next," I say.

"I'm… um… patient."

His gaze drops to his hand as he picks at invisible lint on his jeans, and my heart stirs in my chest.

"You are," I say softly.

He looks up again as I tug off my oversized tee. I warm beneath his admiring scan that drifts over my bare chest before lifting to my eyes. I know it's breaking the rules, but I can't stop myself from leaning forward and brushing a gentle kiss on his lips.

"Keep going," I whisper.

His Adam's apple moves as he swallows and averts his gaze again. A shadow passes over his face. Something heavy is clearly making its way through his brain.

Please, baby. Please see what I do.

"I'm… uh…" He studies the hem of his shirt. "Resilient."

Tears prick my eyes when he blinks back the pain behind that confession.

I pull off my sleep shorts.

"Keep going."

He shakes his head.

"Val. Keep. Going."

"I can't."

"You can."

His tortured gaze flickers back to me.

"I'm… not a failure like everyone thinks."

I choke back emotion as I pull him against me and bury my face in his neck. "Not even close, baby. Gosh, not even close."

He wraps his arms around me, clinging hard.

"I belong here."

Unable to speak, I just nod, hoping he can absorb every affirming cell of my agreement. He's so incredibly special. Nothing seems as important as making him believe that in this moment.

He drags his fingertips along my lower back, sending chills over my skin. It feels so good, and I grip his shirt to help him tug it over his head. Once his warm skin is pressed against mine, I feel home.

"I love you so much," I say. "I didn't even think people like you existed. I'm so glad I found you and I can't believe you're mine."

His hold tightens, and I press my lips against his throat. Up his neck. Over his jaw until they're back where they belong, joined with his.

He threads his fingers into my hair as he guides me back on the bed. His hips press deep and low, tempting me with a hard promise I want so badly.

"Did you ever get your condoms back from Jarvis?" I ask, shoving my palms over his backside to force the friction where I need it. Except it's not where I need it. Not even close.

"Yeah, because he was so excited about the prospect of me having sex with you," he says dryly.

"I thought you bought them for Sage and Coriander."

He lifts up to give me a look, and I bite back a grin. "Fine. Then I guess we're living dangerously."

His eyes go wide. "What?"

"I'm having sex with you tonight, so it's up to you how. Do you want me to see if Rory will stop?"

"Rory?"

"The man driving the bus."

I make a move to crawl out from under him. "Rory! We need to stop and make a condom—"

Val clamps his hand over my mouth, and I burst into giggles. The look on his face is now up there among my favorites.

"Larinda, come on. You're not serious."

"I am. Was your last test negative?"

He glances at the closed door like there might be condom police waiting to intervene. In his defense, he's been harassed enough on this tour to warrant concern.

"I mean, I haven't been tested in a while, but I also never really had unprotected sex. I haven't had *any* sex in over a year. Not since…"

He quiets with a cringe.

My heart beats a little faster. "Not since what?"

"Since I fell in love with you."

I'm speechless as his confession sinks in. "You've been in love with me for over a year?"

The corner of his mouth tips up in a smirk. "Keeping a secret."

"Huh?"

"Another thing I'm good at."

With a quick laugh, I pull him in for a kiss. "Well, I too have not had sex in over a year."

His brows pinch in surprise. "Really? Not even with Jarvis?"

I scrunch my nose. "Um… So about that… Can you keep a secret?"

"I just told you I can."

"Right, yeah." I bite my lip and peek up through a squint. "Jarvis and I never had sex."

Whew. That felt good to say.

Also, why is Val staring at me like I just told him I was quitting music to be a lumberjack? Does he not believe me? Is he upset I never mentioned it before?

Please don't be mad.

Several long seconds pass before his forehead collapses to my shoulder.

"Thank god!" he says on an exhale.

I can't help but grin at his obvious relief. (Mine too.)

"Good news, I take it?"

He lifts his head to meet my eyes. "The best news. Fuck, Larinda. I could never figure it out."

"Figure what out?"

"All of it! How does he even *have* sex? Wouldn't it mess up his hair? Do those ridiculous cutouts participate? Does he take Meyer lemon water breaks? And the belts! Does he have a special 'fucking' belt? Are there multiple depending on the position?"

I burst into laughter. He does too, and soon we're laughing so hard we can't breathe. My sides hurt as I pull him against me, holding him close as I fall in love over and over again. Gosh, he's amazing.

"No idea, but thankfully, I'll never have to find out."

"So wait. Even when you were together …?"

"Ew. I couldn't even stand being in the room with him for more than twenty minutes. Do you really think I could have slept with him? It was all for show. We both had others on the side."

His brows knit as he studies me. Uh-oh. Is he upset at that last confession?

But he doesn't seem angry or judgmental.

"Do you think he does now?" he asks.

"What do you mean?"

"If you both had others on the side, would he have some now, even while you're supposedly engaged?"

"Probably," I say with a shrug. "Honestly, I hadn't thought about it. I didn't care until he decided to play this whole 'blame me for being a cheater' game. Kind of ironic, no?"

Val doesn't look amused as something works itself through his head.

"What is it?" I ask.

"Nothing. It's nothing." I don't believe his tight smile for a second, but I also don't want to be talking about Jarvis' sex life right now. I'm way more interested in my own.

"So are you gonna ravage me or not?" I ask, tugging his face—and attention—back to me.

"Ravage?" he says with a smirk.

"I don't say the F-word and 'make love' isn't enough for what I want."

His eyes go hot at my confession. "Really... so you're saying you want me to *F-word* you?"

"So hard."

I pull his head down for another deep, hungry kiss. It's been too long and takes nothing for my body to catch fire again. Val always has that effect on me, but right now it feels like life or death.

I shove my hand in his hair, gripping hard as I provoke his kisses into the aggressive fury I'm craving. His hardness presses between my thighs, and my other hand slides between us to skim over his zipper. He groans into our kiss as I rub him over and over, first through his jeans, then tugging open the button and shoving them down for more access.

"You're sure about this," he gasps out as we work our bodies into a frenzy.

"So sure. Please F-word me.*"

His smile is both sweet and wicked as he drags his lips along the sensitive skin of my neck, over my collarbone, and down to my exposed breasts. When he circles a nipple with his tongue, I let out a small whimper. It feels so good, and I've waited so long. My hands are still in his hair, guiding him, while my body is screaming frantic demands. He draws the hard peak into his mouth, sucking until I'm squirming and arching into the wet heat. Just when I can't take it anymore, he moves to the other side and resumes the torture.

My skin is on fire. My blood pumps scorching pulses to the apex of my thighs where his hard length drags against my enflamed core over and over again. What part of "F-word me" is he not getting?!

"Val…" I whine.

"What?"

"I want you inside me."

"Yeah? Good, because I want that too."

"No, I mean now!"

He lifts his head from my stomach to expose a devilish grin that absolutely kills me.

"Really…" he says in a smug tone.

On any other man, I'd want to smack them. On this one…

"Now, rockstar!"

He chuckles and adjusts to align our bodies. "Okay, okay. Geez."

I don't even bother with pleasantries as I yank his head down for another dirty kiss while he works his way inside me. We should have a condom, I guess. Lube, a few more discussions and assurances, but honestly? I'm not scared. Every version of the future I want includes him. In sickness and in health. With babies or without. On a luxury tour bus or a tiny apartment in Manhattan. Anything and everything is on the table. The point is, I've never considered unprotected sex with another person, and now that's all I want with Val. No one was ever worth the risk, until this one who doesn't even understand he's worth everything.

"Blessed," he whispers as he pushes deep inside me.

"Blessed?"

I moan at the intoxicating sensation when he starts to move. Streaks of fire tear through me and ignite what feels like every cell in my body. I'm so full, so warm and complete. This is what it's supposed to be. This is the reward for finally making the right choices—*my* choices.

"Another thing I am," he says. "So incredibly blessed."

I tilt my head back to smile up at him. "*Ding, ding*. And there's the winning answer! Congrats, you won the game!"

"Yeah?"

"Yeah." I buck my hips for another electrifying surge. And another. He pushes harder, matching my rhythm until I'm completely lost in a euphoric haze. I'm climbing and floating and reaching, reaching…

"This okay? You're sure?" he says, his sexy voice hoarse from his own arousal.

So hot.

I twist my fingers in his hair and drag his mouth to mine.

"So sure. Now shut up and F-word me."

28—HERSHEY (LARINDA'S BUS)

VAL

In what universe do I get to wake up with Larinda Scott in my arms?

This one, apparently.

I still can't wrap my brain around the fact that this is happening. As if our incredible time together wasn't enough, this woman risked everything to choose me. *Me.* The guy who less than two years ago was begging his sister for money to buy ramen and then cooked it in her microwave at her kitchen table in her apartment.

Yep, Larinda freaking Scott may have thrown away her entire career to tell the world how much *that* guy means to her. Let me tell you, that is a very bewildering place to be mentally and emotionally. (Physically, I'm good. My body is not even remotely confused about what's happening right now as it presses against her naked form.)

I watch her sleep like a certifiable creeper, tracing every inch of her with my gaze… then my finger, because come on. I'm respectful, not a saint.

"Morning," she murmurs with a slow smile.

"Morning. Sorry for waking you."

"You didn't."

We both know I did and exchange another smile.

"Know what I dreamt about?" she says as she stretches in the most stunning and brutal tease of all time.

My blood pounds harder at the mesmerizing display, and now my body *really* thinks it knows what's up.

"What's that?"

Sex?

More sex?

So, so much sex?

"Tax evasion."

Oh.

"Well, more specifically, the fact that my accountant didn't tell me I had to declare income for the international collaboration with—"

I cut her off with a kiss, and she swats me away.

"Stop! I have to brush my teeth first!"

"No you don't. I don't care."

I lean in again, and she nudges me back. "Really? Because *you* clearly did! Your breath reeks of refreshing mint."

"Yeah, well, I was up forever ago and didn't know what to do. It's not like I could go out there and hang with Rory to discuss how the I-76 corridor was lookin' last night at two AM."

"Why not? He's awesome. He probably would have had tons of stories to tell. Also, does that mean you used my toothbrush and stuff?"

"We had unprotected sex. You're probably pregnant with my baby. You really care if I used your toothbrush?"

"Ew. And I'm not pregnant. My contraceptive game is on point. Also, would that be so bad?"

"What?"

"A baby."

I stare at her. I can't even tell if she's joking. "Are you…? Hang on…"

"I'm kidding! Calm down." She shoves my shoulder, and I breathe a sigh of relief. "Not for another year or two at least."

Huh? Wow. Yeah, I got nothing. I mean, a kid? I'd never once thought about having kids. I'd never dated a single person I would've wanted to consider having a family with. It's a ridiculous thought in general.

Well, it was. Because suddenly all I can think about is how much this dark, ugly world needs more radiant supernovas like Larinda Scott. Shit, now I'm picturing little Larinda starbursts running around brightening up the place.

You're so weird, dude.

Yeah. I also haven't had my coffee yet, so whatever.

"Anyway, you don't have to worry," I say. "I didn't use your toothbrush, just your toothpaste and mouthwash."

She tilts her head, her smile fading as she studies me. "Huh. Interesting."

"What?"

She shrugs. "You're just as beautiful this morning as last night. Maybe more so."

I bite the inside of my lip, having no idea how to take that. "Okay?"

"I have a proposition for you."

Uh-oh.

These non sequiturs are really throwing me off, and without coffee, she might as well be spelling out some weird code in spaghetti.

Two noodles… no idea. Five more noodles… still no idea.

"How about we head over to catering right now and face the firestorm together?"

My heart stops as I stare at her. I must have heard her wrong. Those spaghetti noodles aren't making sense.

"I'm sorry?"

"Everyone has to know we're together by now, right? Check your phone. It probably blew up this morning. So let's just get it over with and show them we don't care."

I shake my head. I've done everything I could *not* to check my phone this morning for that very reason.

"I'd rather not."

"Val, we have to face this. It's going to happen, so let's just do it."

I draw in a deep breath. I still can't see myself doing that in a million years, but I suppose I should hear her out. I was willing to do it for my former parents who I hate, so I guess I owe it to the woman I love.

"Fine. I'm listening. What's the proposition?"

She crosses her arms. "I just told you."

"*No*, you said, we go to breakfast to confront everyone."

"Yep."

She lifts her brows. I furrow mine.

"Right. So a proposition means I get something in return. I do something ludicrous and absolutely unfathomable for you, and in exchange I get…?" I pause, waiting for her to fill in the blank.

"You get to be by my side as we face the storm together."

I open my mouth to respond. Nothing comes out.

"So, I guess… yeah. That's the proposition," she says. "We freshen up and head over to catering to watch our lives blow up."

"Um, that's not a proposition, babe. That's a command."

"Oh. Well, then, I have a command for you."

She swings her legs over the bed and pushes to her feet. I'm about to keep arguing but she's hovering completely naked inches away from me. What were we talking about again? Tax evasion?

"Give me twenty minutes," she says, moving toward the bathroom.

I'd give that ass twenty years.

Forty.

Sixty.

A fucking baby if she wants it.

I groan and throw myself back on the pillow.

She's completely wrecked me. There's no other explanation, because as she's "freshening up," future babies aren't even the most ridiculous thought rumbling through my head.

I'm going to follow her to catering.

I'm going to follow her anywhere, because I belong with her. I belong *here*.

I'm important to her, and if she sees me as a risk worth taking, I have to fight like hell to start seeing what she does.

In what universe do I wake up with Larinda Scott in my arms?

This one. A universe where I'm Val Andrews. A damn good producer who's trying his best to be a damn good human being.

And maybe, just maybe, that's enough.

29—HERSHEY (CATERING)

VAL

Larinda slips her palm into mine as we approach the door to catering. Plenty of voices can be heard, so we know the room is packed. How is she so calm about this?

Despite my pledge *not* to check my phone, I did. As expected, it flooded with notifications, and that's when I shut it off again because I've committed to following Larinda's lead on this, and there was no way that was happening if I spent an hour being publicly and privately eviscerated.

I get it. I'm a fraud, a cheater, a gold digger, a horrible human being for breaking up the fairy-tale romance of the country music royal couple. I am the devil incarnate because I'm a poor nobody and not Jarvis McKinnley.

"I love you," she says, squeezing my hand.

"I love you too," I say, squeezing back.

"I choose you."

"I choose you too."

We exchange a quick smile, and I try to breathe through the violent pounding in my chest. I don't even know why I'm scared. *She's* the one who's poised to lose everything over this. I had nothing for my entire life. Going back to nothing is, well, nothing. But maybe that's the problem. It's not me I'm worried about. When you love someone, their pain is infinitely worse than yours. I don't know if I'll be able to survive watching her get crushed because of me.

But it's her life. Her career. Her choice. And I meant what I said. I will support her no matter what she decides.

We step through the door, and the room goes silent. Over a dozen sets of eyes land on us, then drop to our joined hands. I force myself to breathe through the thumping in my veins.

It doesn't matter. None of it does. Even if you end up back at your sister's kitchen table with nothing, so what? You still have this amazing person.

I do. And that's everything.

I grip her hand, and she grips back.

Steve is the first to push up from his table.

"Hey, good for you," he says, clapping my arm.

He moves to Larinda and kisses her cheek. "Love you, Larry. You're an effing warrior."

Hang on. What?

Bruce is next, and is that… a smile?

"Hang in there," he says, patting her arm. "We got you. We support you. Let us know if you need anything."

Larinda and I exchange a confused glance. Soon the room is buzzing, but this time with utterances of support for us and rants against… Jarvis?

What the hell is happening?

"It's criminal what he did," Mallory spits in disgust.

Mallory?!

I blink to clear my vision, certain I'm hallucinating. But no, that's definitely Jarvis' personal assistant standing in front of us with a look of sympathy.

"I'm so sorry for not saying something sooner," she says. "I wanted to, I just… Gosh, Larinda, I'm so sorry. And I'm so glad you found someone you deserve."

She turns her attention to me and offers a weak smile. "You're a good guy, Val. I'm sorry for how he's treated you as well."

Okay. I'm so lost right now.

Before I can ask, her gaze locks on something behind me, and my stomach sinks when I spot what she does.

The absolute last thing we need in this baffling moment is…

Chad.

He throws his arms around me and pulls tight.

"I'm so sorry, mi amigo," he says, rubbing my back. "So, so sorry. Cry it out if you have to. I'm here for ya."

"Uh, thanks?"

"Don't be strong! There's strength in tears!"

"Yeah, um, it's… fine."

Maybe? I have no idea what's happening.

He transfers his hug to Larinda.

"You too, our precious little hummingbird."

Her expression is great for showing me what mine must look like.

"He's a monster," Chad hisses. "A diabolical wildebeest, and I shall not rest until you are avenged. I should have trusted you from the beginning," he directs at me.

He moves back to me and cups my face. "The blood code, brother. The fucking blood code, and I failed you. But I swear on Mr. Reedweather himself, I won't sleep until I make things right. *Follow the condom trail.*"

And he winks.

And walks away.

And I guess… that's it?

Yep. He's gone.

Somewhere in this great big earth there's a hidden artifact that explains the relationship between winking, condoms, and octopuses but I'm not confident I'll uncover it in my lifetime. I guess that's something for our future mini Larindas to tackle.

"What's going on?" I mumble under my breath.

"No idea," Larinda whispers.

Her phone rings, and she goes pale.

"It's Rena. I should take this."

I swallow hard and force a nod. We already know what's coming and have agreed to face it. Might as well get it over with so we can start the recovery process.

She grabs my hand and leads me back into the hall.

Once we're out of sight, she answers the video call and angles the phone so we're both in the frame.

"Larinda, hi!" Rena says, as cheery as we've ever seen her. "And Val! What a pleasure."

What the hell? Is the bar already open at 6 AM in LA?

"Oh. Uh. Hi," Larinda says.

I take her other hand and lace our fingers.

"Just wanted to check in and see how you were. We heard the terrible news, of course. We're so sorry. Just know you have the full support of all of us here at Lakebend."

Hold up.

Larinda stiffens and sends me a confused look.

I shrug back.

Maybe we're still asleep on her bus. If an accountant walks by railing against the IRS for punitive tax evasion laws, it'll all make sense.

"I guess you just never know with people," Rena says. "We were as shocked as anyone, of course."

"You were?" Larinda asks.

"Oh yes. Who could have guessed Jarvis would do such a thing? He seemed like such a wonderful, devoted partner."

I manage to contain my snort.

Now I know this is a dream.

"He… I'm sorry. What are you talking about?" Larinda asks.

Rena's eyes grow three sizes as she quiets and looks ready to throw an assistant at us.

Instead, she clears her throat and shifts uncomfortably in front of her stash of tiny cactuses.

"The report, darling."

"The report?"

"It leaked last night. It's everywhere. No one knows who wrote it or why, but apparently there's been a mole on tour this whole time. Someone's been documenting everything, including the years-long affair Jarvis was having with Sage and Coriander."

Oh.

Shit.

Larinda recoils, and my heart breaks for her at that last revelation. I know she didn't love the guy, but still. To learn your pretend boyfriend was banging your most faithful… well, I still don't really understand what they did. To learn *they* have been banging your pretend boyfriend behind your back while he tried to frame you for banging your *real* boyfriend who you actually weren't banging until last night… that's a lot to take from a woman in a potted succulent forest thousands of miles away.

"Larinda," I say gently, tugging her hand.

She glances over at me… and bursts into laughter.

"Oh my gosh. Are you serious?" she cries.

Rena looks like she's not sure if she is as she blinks back. "Yes. Um. Well, yes. As you can imagine, we will be terminating our relationship with Jarvis. This kind of behavior goes against our core values here at—"

"Right, yeah," Larinda interrupts, waving her quiet. "Okay, well, thanks for the update. That's very helpful information. And you have no idea who this 'mole' is?"

"Not a clue. No one seems to know but the report is incredibly detailed and comprehensive. It must be someone intimately related to the tour, so I'd suggest you be careful who you trust."

Larinda nods, and… hang on.

No.

Freaking.

Way.

I think I know who the "mole" is. Somehow I manage to contain my raucous laughter as images of my "blood brother" meticulously removing fairy lights from our hotel room and sorting bags of mints on our bed flash through my mind.

Did he… Is the world's worst spy actually our unsung hero?

Wow. I don't even…

"Okay, well, I'm sure you have a lot to deal with," Rena says. "Just know that we—"

"Yeah, yeah. You support me. Whatever," Larinda says in the sassiest tone I've ever heard from her. It's actually… really hot. "Except you don't, though, do you? If *the report* hadn't gone public and ruined Jarvis' reputation, it would be *me* on the chopping block, wouldn't it?"

Rena shrinks back with a horrified expression. All that's missing is a dainty hand to her heart. She should give Rhonda a call for a demonstration on that.

"Larinda, I don't—"

"Save it, Rena. We *know,* and you know we know. You threatened Val with everything you had because he learned the truth. Well, guess what, the truth is still the truth, and you know what that means?"

Her expression tells us she's afraid she does know and she doesn't like it.

"It means you're down *two* country stars. You better go start damage control with Jarvis, because Larinda Scott is pulling on her own *new boots* and *walkin', walkin' away.*"

"What?! Larinda, please—"

"Don't even bother. Just do yourself a favor and make all our lives easier by quietly severing our relationship. We have all the evidence we need to expose Jarvis *and* Lakebend. The song, the video, the engagement plot—everything. Give me the rights to my unreleased songs, and let's try to move on with at least a modicum of dignity." She tosses her hair and narrows her eyes. "That's right, I said *modicum* because I'm effing smart and know so many words you never even dreamed I know in your efforts to stuff me in your ditzy pop-tart mold! Our lawyers will be in touch."

She hangs up.

Looks at me.

And that right there is the woman of my dreams, the love of my life, the queen badass of badasses, reminding the world, yet again, that it's way too small to contain us if we don't want to be contained.

"We're signing with Smart Play Records," she tells me.

She's already on her way back to catering when her words register in my brain.

"I'm sorry, what?" I say, pulling her around.

"I've been talking with them since I found out what Lakebend was planning. We're signing with them."

"Oh. Cool. And, um, who is that? I've never heard of them."

"Exactly. They're a startup. More importantly, they're thrilled to have me on board, and I'm thrilled they're giving me full control over my career and my music. Win. Win."

She pulls us to a stop just before the door, and her gaze softens as it rests on my face.

"One more thing."

"Yeah?"

"Check your phone."

Confused, I pull it out and stare at the blank screen.

"I meant to turn it on," she says in a dry tone.

"I know. It's just…"

"Do it, Val."

I suck in a deep breath and obey, bracing for the barrage of notifications. Yep, saw that coming. *So* many flashing banners, but before I can sort through the messages, Larinda tugs it from my hand.

She scrolls through them, snorts a laugh, and hands it back.

"I knew it," she says.

"Knew what?"

"That one. Look."

I glance down at the screen. An unknown number? What's she talking about?

Unknown: Val, this is Randall and Ruby Scott.

Oh. Well. Damn.

We just wanted to say thank you. We heard the news and are ecstatic (also relieved) to learn our precious girl chose you over that used tissue of a man, Jarvis. Take care of our daughter and welcome to the family, son. What's your favorite meat? We're grillin' as soon as you two get your rear ends back in Texas. Also, what's your shirt size? We need a sixth for the Scott Family team at this year's second annual Block of Blocks Block Party. The grand prize is a trip to the indoor waterpark at Candle Ridge Casino and Ruby already has her heart set on it. Oh, and don't tell Larinda I sent this. She doesn't like when we meddle.

I glance up, having no clue what to say as my girlfriend grins and crosses her arms.

"You… How did you know your dad messaged me?"

"Because I know my dad. They absolutely love you. I knew the second they learned the truth, they'd reach out to welcome you into the family."

"I… *what*? What do you mean they *love* me?"

She grunts and pulls out her phone. After scrolling for a second, she hands me a text stream of what looks like a group chat. An old one, based on the date.

Mom: It was so great seeing you for brunch, sweetie. We always love spending time with you. Please don't take this the wrong way but are you ABSOLUTELY sure about Jarvis? I mean, maybe just think about it a little more?

Dad: That idiot is a drop of melted wax.

Mom: Randall!

Dad: What? It's true. We all know it.

Mom: Yes, but if he's our daughter's beloved, then we will belove him.

Dad: I'm just having a hard time accepting our beautiful, intelligent daughter would choose an empty snap pea pod over that other boy.

Larinda: Which boy?

Dad: The one you brought with you today. Val.

Larinda: He's my producer.

Dad: So? That never stopped you before.

Larinda: Dad!

Mom: Randall! He WAS very cute though, Larinda. And so polite and sweet.

Dad: Tiara is going to marry him if you don't.

Larinda: Stop!

Dad: What? If neither of you do, I'm adopting him.

Mom: That's a good idea. What are the laws about adopting adults? Would that be weird for you, sweetie?

Larinda: I have to go now. Great seeing you. Talk soon.

Larinda is downright smug when I look up and return her phone. I shake my head, fighting like hell to block the smile that will betray how incredibly good it felt to read that.

"Told you," she says.

"Whatever," I mumble.

"They love you."

"They don't even know me."

"They want to, and when they do, they will."

She unlocks her screen again.

"What are you doing?" I ask.

There's no response as she types something into what looks like a text message.

"*Larinda*… what are you doing?"

I have my answer when my phone buzzes a second later.

I pull it up to see a message from Larinda—to a new group chat.

Larinda: Get him an XL, preferably a green shirt because that color looks amazing on him.

Within seconds there's a response.

Unknown: Perfect! Does he like chocolate mousse? Oh, he's here. Do you like chocolate mousse, honey?

I stare at Larinda.

"Mom asked you a question, *honey*. Do you like chocolate mousse?"

I swallow hard as I stare back at the strange message.

Um…

Larinda reaches over and squeezes my arm. "Make her day and say yes. She's been waiting twenty-six years to impress her daughter's boyfriend with her chocolate mousse. Trust me, none of the other guys I brought home would let a grain of sugar near their face."

I mean… I guess I could handle that much.

I love chocolate mousse, I type out. **Thank you, Mrs. Scott.**

Larinda's eyes are glistening when they rest on me. My own chest is heavy with a new kind of ache. Happy tears? Is that a thing?

Our phones buzz again, and we glance at the displays.

Unknown: Fantastic! Please come visit as soon as you can. We're dying to show you Larinda's 8th-grade yearbook photo and we need to pick out your Christmas stocking design so there's time to embroider it before

Christmas. Oh! And the chickens! We have to talk about the chickens. So much to do!

> **Unknown: Also, call us Randall and Ruby, son. We're family now.**

I swat at my eyes as I stare at words I never thought I'd see.

Yup.

Happy tears.

Who knew?

EPILOGUE (THE SCOTT BACKYARD)

LARINDA

"Shh! He's coming!" I hiss.

"Val is going to hate this," Nash mumbles. I fire a sharp look at him, and he shrugs. "He will. He told you not to make a big deal about his birthday."

"And I didn't."

"A surprise party, by definition, is a big deal."

"Who invited you anyway?"

Nash's lips tip up in a grin.

"Welcome to my world," Paige mutters.

Whatever. I'm not letting my broody friend ruin this moment. I learned two horrifying facts just over a month ago when the subject of Val's twenty-fourth birthday came up:

1. He didn't care and had no intention of celebrating it.
2. He'd never had a surprise party.

Neither were acceptable, so here we are. For his sake, I kept it small to just over a hundred close family and friends. Alright, so maybe that's a *tad* more than small, but once I started listing the people who really cared about him, well… Hey, I was able to narrow it down to one-fifty. And then only a hundred could actually make it, so there.

I can't stop a grin when I think about his adorable expression this morning when I surprised him with breakfast in bed and birthday sex. The breakfast in bed was a huge hit. The birthday sex needed some very aggressive coaxing, though, since he wasn't thrilled about the idea of—and I quote—"F-wording their daughter with your parents just down the hall."

They weren't even home since they had bowling league practice this morning (or so Val thought), and I finally managed to persuade him with an eloquent, carefully constructed verbal argument. It's possible the birthday lingerie I put on and mercilessly flaunted also played a role, but there's no way to be sure.

Then we got him out of the way by sending him with Dad to do father-son bonding stuff like "hunting." Since neither of them wanted to kill anything or fire a gun, I'm not exactly sure what that entailed. The only update has been a picture of Dad standing proudly beside a taxidermy buck in a sporting goods store. Val's accompanying text confirmed my suspicion:

Success! Just "bagged" my first ever 2-for-1 deal on swim trunks. We're about to go "fishing" for thermal socks next. Wish me luck!

And now they're on their way back. Time for the real fun. (Well, second real fun. Birthday sex is pretty fun, even when your boyfriend keeps pausing to whisper, "*Wait! Did you hear that? How long is bowling practice again?*")

"I'm so nervous!" Chad whisper-shouts beside me. His entire body is vibrating like he really might be. In his defense, I didn't invite him until yesterday out of concern for his ability to keep a secret. It was a risk even telling him at all, but I couldn't imagine celebrating Val's birthday without his "tour bestie." Chad booked the first flight he could get—and brought his girlfriend, who I'm not entirely sure knows she's his girlfriend.

Speaking of tour besties, the infamous joint tour is officially wrapped. All parties involved in the scandal agreed to complete the tour for the sake of the fans and sever official ties after the final show. Lakebend has been surprisingly amenable to my demands in exchange for my willingness to keep the mountain of evidence we have against them to ourselves. Not only could we prove all the awful things they were planning, we could have made their lives miserable for a very long time. They gave me my unreleased songs, waived any remaining provisions in my contract, and even sent a gift basket thanking me for being a valued artist and wishing me luck.

Jarvis isn't faring as well navigating his crushed reputation, however. In a head-scratching move, he still went ahead with releasing the "breakup song," but apparently singing about your heartbreak boots doesn't have the same effect when the world knows *you're* the reason you're stuck walking around in them. Guess he got his precious cheating scandal after all.

The best part? His song hasn't come close to Val's and my hit "Third Last

Kiss" which made several charts and even got a *Hot Rat Track* stamp from *The Tattletale Review.* (It's a good thing, trust me.) Our new label is thrilled, as is Jarvis' former assistant, Mallory, who I hired to replace Steve who decided *he* needed to replace Sage and Coriander. So now it's Steve following me around sipping iced coffee and telling me how great I look in everything. I don't mind. At least I like having him around and I know he cares about me. As for Sage and Coriander... I don't know, actually. I don't follow their vlog. I also haven't seen a single Cagelicious light fixture for sale, so I guess that dream died.

My phone lights up with a text from Dad letting me know they're pulling in.

Eek! It's happening!

Also, Nash is right. Val will hate this, but he'll forgive me because he forgives me everything. Then, once he reflects on it, he'll love it, and that's the moment I live for: when his cloud slips and frees a ray of the sunlight hidden inside him. It's been happening more and more over these past few months, and I'm dying for a glimpse of it today.

Everyone is deathly quiet at the scrape of the latch on the fence leading to the backyard. Will Val think it's weird Dad's taking him through the yard instead of the house? Probably, but oh well.

The gate swings open and...

"Happy birthday!"

"Surprise!"

"Val!"

"It's your birthday!"

"Hey yo!"

"Hi!"

"Woot!"

"Happy Labor Day!"

Crap. I guess I should have locked in a script for this part. Val's utter confusion kind of makes it work, though.

His wide eyes scan the crowd, the tote from shopping with my dad swinging loosely at his side.

I step forward, and his gaze snaps to me.

"Did you... what... I don't..."

My grin stretches my cheeks as I slide my arms around him.

"Surprise, baby," I say, squeezing tight. "Happy birthday."

"This is for me?"

I lean back and search his bewildered expression. "Of course it is."

His gaze lifts to survey the guests again, and I see the moment he recognizes each one.

"See how many people love you?" I say softly. "This is how many people *chose* you, Val Andrews."

He blinks away emotion as his focus flickers back to me. "I… thank you. I can't believe this."

"Well, believe it." I settle my cheek against his chest again. "And you're really in for a surprise when you see the mound of gifts people brought, even though I told them not to."

"This is amazing, but…"

My heart sinks. "But what?"

He gently tugs my hair to see my face again. "I already had plans today."

I give him a look, and he returns a sheepish smile.

"Well, you're going to have to cancel them."

He shakes his head. "Sorry. Can't. I promised your dad."

I step back. "What? You have to. All these people…"

He sighs and scoops the tote off the ground.

"Dad! You knew about this! Tell him," I demand, glaring at my father. That traitor just shrugs.

"Hey, I'm not getting in the middle of a lovers' quarrel."

"Guess we'll just have to do this in front of everyone else," Val says.

"Do what?"

He pulls out a small blue box and… oh my gosh!

Tears spring to my eyes as I gasp and cover my mouth. No way! Can't be! Oh my gosh oh my gosh oh my gosh.

His soft laugh confirms it, and when I see the beam on Dad's face as he places his hand on Val's shoulder, there's no point trying to stop the sob-fest.

Val clears his throat and searches my eyes.

"Larinda Scott, I planned to do this in private." His tone is quiet but firm. "There's so much I wanted to say to you, but I guess one of the things I love most about us is that we don't have to say things. It's always been that way with us."

I can't breathe as he opens the box to reveal the most gorgeous ring I've ever seen. Tiny gems fan from left to right, starting at an almost invisible size and stacking to a width of just over a centimeter by the end. It's delicate but complex, and completely stunning. The shape and way the gems sparkle in the light make them look like a comet… or shooting star… or…

A ray of sunlight.

More tears fall when I interpret the unconventional design. It's perfect. Of course it's perfect. It's Val.

"From the moment your radiant light burst into my shadows, I knew I would never find another woman like you. I would never love someone, cherish someone, or revere someone the way I would if you chose me, even though it seemed impossible. I still can't believe you did, but in front of all these witnesses, I want to make it clear I will always choose you too. Larinda Scott, please do me the honor of *not* being my wife."

I freeze and drop my hands. What did he just say? Did I hear him wrong? Did he *say* it wrong?

A murmur spreads over the crowd, confirming my fears that he said what I think he said. I don't understand. Why would he—

"Say no," Paige whispers, leaning in. When I glance over, her own cheeks are wet with tears. She's smiling too. "He wants you to say no."

What? Why?

My gaze snaps back to Val who's now grinning. What is going on?

Wait.

"Please do me the honor of not *being my wife."*

Say no.

Please not *be his wife.*

NO!

I burst out laughing, which sends another shockwave through the audience.

He knows how much I wish I had said no to my first proposal. How much I love saying no in general now. He's giving me the opposite of what I got (and hated) from Jarvis. He's giving me the first proposal ever where the person gets to say no to say yes.

Of course he would flip the most clichéd script of human behavior on its head.

"Not a chance!" I cry, throwing my arms around him. "I will not *not* be your wife."

He squeezes so tight, I start giggling again.

"Whew. Thank god," he says just for me.

"You're a dork, you know that? You gave me a heart attack for a second."

"Sorry. It worked better in my head. So that's a no?"

"It's a *hell* no."

We exchange a grin, and I melt into his soft kiss.

"I will always choose you," I whisper against his lips.

"I will always choose you too," he whispers back.

He tilts my head up for another kiss, and the audience finally bursts into applause and cheers.

"We really should explain what just happened," I say as I pull away to slip on the stunning engagement ring. I will never be taking this off. "Everyone is so confused."

Val threads our fingers and squeezes my palm. "Nah, it's all part of the code. They can read Chad's report tomorrow."

BONUS EPILOGUE

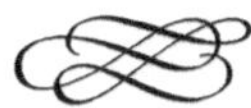

CHAD'S REPORT

Operation: Project Hummingbird
    Threat Level: Salmon
    Potential Hostile Operatives:

1. Larinda Scott (codename: Hummingbird)
2. Val Andrews (codename: Labor Day)
3. Jarvis McKinnley (codename: Autumn Blaze)
4. Sage and Coriander (codename: Cagelicious)
5. Steve

Friendly Operatives: (NONE) –Trust no one!!!!!

Mission:

Did you ever wonder what it would be like to live on a tour bus? I did. It was fun, and also more shocking than I could have imagined. They say follow the condom trail, but I never could have guessed where that dastardly path would lead. (OMG keep reading!!! You're not gonna believe what happens!)

DAY ONE (Oklahoma City):

. . .

Dear Mr. S-----e,

Today is the first day of today!! (Mr. R. III taught me that and it's changed my life.) It's also the first day of the tour. Can you believe it? I met Labor Day almost immediately after entering the bus and was able to grab the bunk across from him. His eyes are green. His hair is brown. He has at least five tattoos. (Probably 43 but that's just a guess and not actionable intel.) Also on the bus were other people. They are not important. On another bus is Hummingbird. On another bus is Autumn Blaze. They are important.

Here is a transcript of my initial contact with Autumn Blaze:

Me: Hello, Mr. (REDACTED)
    Autumn Blaze: Hey. Do I know you?
    Me: Yes! We've been working together for a couple of years. I represent Sandeke Telecom. I've managed several of your campaigns.
    Autumn Blaze: Oh. Do I need to sign something?
    Me: Nope! Just wanted to say howdy on behalf of Denver Sandeke and Sandeke Telecom.
    Autumn Blaze: Oh. Hey, can you hold this for a sec? Yo, liquify me! It's frickin' hot out here!

I then proceeded to hold his belt while he was liquified. This was my first exposure to Autumn Blaze's belts.

Also, I was wrong about Labor Day. He seems cool. I think I will hug him tomorrow.

DAY TWO (Dallas):

Dear Mr. S-----e,

I did not hug Labor Day. We did, however, get arrested together which was fun. He is very cool under pressure, so I would totally get arrested with him again. He was also treated abominably by Autumn Blaze. It was shocking considering Labor Day agreed to the cardboard photoshoot even though he looks weird on camera. (Not in person though. He's actually quite handsome.)

Of Note: I sold a King Chester Chestnut Mer-Nut Doll. Also a medium hoodie.

Also of note, I went on a "snack run" with Mallory to assist with procuring necessities for Autumn Blaze. I saw the box of condoms in the bag with his Meyer lemons. She denied it and said they're sterile gloves but I know the difference between a penis and a hand. I did not tell her this in case it was a trick.

P.S. Funny story. Autumn Blaze and Hummingbird got engaged last night. There was confetti.

DAY THREE (Little Rock):

Dear Mr. S-----e,

Something weird is happening. Nash showed up. Do you remember Nash? He plays the guitar and wears ugly shirts. That's not what's weird. It's the fact that he's here. He's friends with Larinda, but why would he come all the way to Little Rock? I have a friend in Bismarck and I don't show up to say hi when they're in Tallahassee or Albany.

Labor Day seems stressed. I think it's because Autumn Blaze is being very mean to him. He's being mean to everyone, including a parking attendant. Also, his future wife, Hummingbird. You should be nice to your future spouses. (You can show that part to Brooke.)

P.S. I know I'm supposed to be spying *for* Autumn Blaze, but something fishy (not the good kind) is afoot with him. Stay tuned.

. . .

DAY FOUR (Indianapolis):

Dear Mr. S-----e,

I was right. Octopi have beaks not noses. Also, Mallory sent me on a breath mint run for Autumn Blaze. I know, right?! But don't get too excited because I'm worried it was just to throw me off while she went on yet *another* condom run. I thought maybe Autumn Blaze really was using them as sterile gloves, you know, putting one on each finger, but I tried it and it doesn't work very well.

Labor Day bought condoms too, so I have to keep an eye on him as well. His hands are bigger than Autumn Blaze's, so maybe they'd work better as finger protectors. TBD.

P.S. We're going belt shopping tomorrow and I get to share a room with Labor Day! Do you like purple lights? I do. It's like sleeping in an eggplant. Wish me luck!

DAY FIVE (Still Indianapolis):

Dear Mr. S-----e,

I'm really worried. We were supposedly belt shopping, but I don't think anyone bought a belt. I do think something bad is happening. There was a sad song about Autumn Blaze breaking up with someone but the only person he's with is Hummingbird. Except he's never actually *with* her because they don't like each other. Who he *is* with a lot are Hummingbird's ladies in waiting, Cagelicious. Don't tell anyone, but I found three used condoms when he told me to take out his trash yesterday and they did NOT look like they were used for finger protection. He spent a lot of time with Cagelicious and no time with Hummingbird, so hmm… Also, why would there be a breakup song before a breakup?

Theory One: He's lying about something.

Theory Two: He's clairvoyant.

Theory Three: Adding vanilla to chocolate milk will make it regular milk again. (That's not related to the song, but I want to test it tomorrow at breakfast. Can you imagine if it works??)

Of note: Labor Day got in trouble when he showed up at the belt store wearing a Kitty's Kafé costume and now no one has seen him since. I hope he wasn't abducted by aliens. He's not very good at codes or the biggest fan of colored lights.

DAY SIX (Pittsburgh):

Dear Mr. S-----e,

More used condoms. On top of that, do you follow Cagelicious on social media? If so, you may have caught them eating a donut yesterday. It looked good but I forgot to ask where they got it. They also bragged about hooking up with an A-lister. I'm getting very concerned it might be Autumn Blaze. I know that sounds shocking, but they spend a lot of time together. I just learned that in Dallas they told Hummingbird and Steve they were going to a hot tub outlet, but based on the receipts when Mallory was filling out the expense report for Autumn Blaze, they were with him. (That information wasn't on the receipts, just the prices of things. Mallory told me the extra stuff. She also said, and please excuse the language in advance, QUOTE "He's a dirty cheater and has been fucking them for years." END QUOTE.) I asked Mallory if she wanted to hug it out and she said yes and then started crying, so I gave her some mints. Then she told me everything and said she was putting in her resignation. She also said she wished the world knew the truth about the kind of person Jarvis —I mean, *Autumn Blaze*—was and I said I had an idea.

P.S. Accidentally leaking this report tonight was my idea. Also, adding vanilla to chocolate milk just makes it weird-tasting milk.

Conclusion:

Autumn Blaze has been cheating on Hummingbird with her own friends for years, including right under her nose while on tour. He's also done everything he can to neutralize Labor Day, probably because Labor Day is nicer and better looking than he is. (Between you and me, I think Hummingbird and Labor Day would make a good couple. I'm going to buy them a keychain when we visit Duluth. Have you ever been? Probably. You've been everywhere. I'd love to pick your brain about the aquarium sometime. Is it true they have otters? Probably not real ones, though, right? Unless… never mind. I'm thinking of groundhogs.)

Thank you for reading this report. I hope you had a great week.

Love always,

Your Loyal Mer-Kin

P.S. I'm going to submit this report in six different fonts. Tell me which you like best.

P.P.S. I don't like music touring. Plus I miss Mr. R. III and don't believe Hummingbird poses a legitimate threat. Please assign me back to the office. I have some ideas. Thank you in advance.

P.P.P.S. Upon further examination, condoms *can* be used for finger guards. I stand corrected.

ABOUT THE AUTHOR

Thank you for taking this journey with me. I would love to hear from you! For updates, reveals, and more subscribe to my newsletter and join my fun, laid-back reader group on Facebook: Aly's Breakfast Club.

You can also follow Aly's original music wherever you stream music:
Spotify
Apple Music
Amazon Music

Find Aly here:
Facebook Reader Group – Aly's Breakfast Club
Newsletter
BookBub
Spotify
Apple Music
Facebook Page – Author Aly Stiles
Goodreads
Website
Instagram
YouTube
Blogger sign-up for notifications about future releases, ARC reviews, and cover reveals
Pinterest

Aly Stiles
PO Box 577
Trexlertown, PA 18087-0577

Find Smartypants Romance online:
Website: www.smartypantsromance.com
Facebook: https://www.facebook.com/smartypantsromance
Twitter: @smartypantsrom
Instagram: @smartypantsromance
Newsletter: https://smartypantsromance.com/newsletter/

ALSO BY ALY STILES

THE SAVE ME SERIES

RISING WEST (available on audiobook)

FALLING NORTH

BREAKING SOUTH

CRASHING EAST

GUARDING SHADOWS

CHASING RIPTIDES

THE WRECK ME SERIES

ASHTON MORGAN: Apartment 17B

CAMDEN WALKER: Apartment 8C

TRISTAN & ISABEL: Apartment 11F

THE HOLD ME SERIES

Available on audiobook.

NIGHT SHIFTS BLACK

TRACING HOLLAND

VIPER

LIMELIGHT

AN NSB WEDDING

SMARTYPANTS ROMANCE

STREET SMART

PLAY SMART

LOOK SMART

STAGE SMART

STANDALONES

YOUNG LOVE

ALSO BY SMARTYPANTS ROMANCE

Green Valley Chronicles
<u>The Love at First Sight Series</u>
Baking Me Crazy by Karla Sorensen (#1)
Batter of Wits by Karla Sorensen (#2)
Steal My Magnolia by Karla Sorensen (#3)
Worth the Wait by Karla Sorensen (#4)

<u>Fighting For Love Series</u>
Stud Muffin by Jiffy Kate (#1)
Beef Cake by Jiffy Kate (#2)
Eye Candy by Jiffy Kate (#3)
Knock Out by Jiffy Kate (#4)

<u>The Donner Bakery Series</u>
No Whisk, No Reward by Ellie Kay (#1)
Dough You Love Me? By Stacy Travis (#2)
Tough Cookie by Talia Hunter (#3)
Muffin But Trouble by Talia Hunter (#4)

<u>*Oh Brother! Series*</u>
Crime and Periodicals by Nora Everly (#1)
Carpentry and Cocktails by Nora Everly (#2)
Hotshot and Hospitality by Nora Everly (#3)
Architecture and Artistry by Nora Everly (#4)

<u>Small Town Silver Fox Series</u>
Love in Due Time by L.B. Dunbar (#1)
Love in Deed by L.B. Dunbar (#2)
Love in a Pickle by L.B. Dunbar (#3)

The Green Valley Library Series

Prose Before Bros by Cathy Yardley (#1)

Shelf Awareness by Katie Ashley (#2)

Dewey Belong Together by Ann Whynot (#3)

Checking You Out by Ann Whynot (#4)

Scorned Women's Society Series

My Bare Lady by Piper Sheldon (#1)

The Treble with Men by Piper Sheldon (#2)

The One That I Want by Piper Sheldon (#3)

Hopelessly Devoted by Piper Sheldon (#3.5)

It Takes a Woman by Piper Sheldon (#4)

Park Ranger Series

Happy Trail by Daisy Prescott (#1)

Stranger Ranger by Daisy Prescott (#2)

The Leffersbee Series

Been There Done That by Hope Ellis (#1)

Before and After You by Hope Ellis (#2)

The Higher Learning Series

Upsy Daisy by Chelsie Edwards (#1)

Green Valley Heroes Series

Forrest for the Trees by Kilby Blades (#1)

Parks and Provocation by Juliette Cross (#2)

Letter Late Than Never by Lauren Connolly (#3)

Peaches and Dreams by Juliette Cross (#4)

Young Buck by Kilby Blades (#5)

Package Makes Perfect by Lauren Connolly (#6)

The Teachers' Lounge Series

Passing Notes by Nora Everly (#1)

Band Together by Piper Sheldon (#2)

Story of Us Collection

My Story of Us: Zach by Chris Brinkley (#1)

My Story of Us: Thomas by Chris Brinkley (#2)

My Story of Us: Grayson by Chris Brinkley (#3)

Seduction in the City

Cipher Security Series

Code of Conduct by April White (#1)

Code of Honor by April White (#2)

Code of Matrimony by April White (#2.5)

Code of Ethics by April White (#3)

Cipher Office Series

Weight Expectations by M.E. Carter (#1)

Sticking to the Script by Stella Weaver (#2)

Cutie and the Beast by M.E. Carter (#3)

Weights of Wrath by M.E. Carter (#4)

Common Threads Series

Mad About Ewe by Susannah Nix (#1)

Give Love a Chai by Nanxi Wen (#2)

Key Change by Heidi Hutchinson (#3)

Not Since Ewe by Susannah Nix (#4)

Lost Track by Heidi Hutchinson (#5)

Ewe Complete Me by Susannah Nix (#6)

Meet Your Matcha by Nanxi Wen (#7)

All Mixed Up by Heidi Hutchinson (#8)

Bad Habit Book Club Series

Nun Too Soon by Lissa Sharpe (#1)

Educated Romance

<u>Work For It Series</u>

Street Smart by Aly Stiles (#1)

Heart Smart by Emma Lee Jayne (#2)

Book Smart by Amanda Pennington (#3)

Smart Mouth by Emma Lee Jayne (#4)

Play Smart by Aly Stiles (#5)

Look Smart by Aly Stiles (#6)

Smart Move by Amanda Pennington (#7)

Stage Smart by Aly Stiles (#8)

<u>Lessons Learned Series</u>

Under Pressure by Allie Winters (#1)

Not Fooling Anyone by Allie Winters (#2)

Can't Fight It by Allie Winters (#3)

The Vinyl Frontier by Lola West (#4)

Out of this World

<u>London Ladies Embroidery Series</u>

Neanderthal Seeks Duchess by Laney Hatcher (#1)

Well Acquainted by Laney Hatcher (#2)

Love Matched by Laney Hatcher (#3)

<u>Wolf Brothers Series</u>

Truth or Wolf by Anne Marsh (#1)